OPHELIA
AFTER ALL

OPHELIA
AFTER ALL

RACQUEL MARIE

MACMILLAN

First published in the US 2022 by Feiwel and Friends

First published in the UK 2022 by Macmillan Children's Books
an imprint of Pan Macmillan
The Smithson, 6 Briset Street, London EC1M 5NR
EU representative: Macmillan Publishers Ireland Ltd, 1st Floor,
The Liffey Trust Centre, 117–126 Sheriff Street Upper
Dublin 1, D01 YC43
Associated companies throughout the world
www.panmacmillan.com

ISBN 978-1-0350-1568-9

Pan Macmillan does not have any control over, or any responsibility for,
any author or third-party websites referred to in or on this book.

1 3 5 7 9 8 6 4 2

A CIP catalogue record for this book is available from the British Library.

Printed and bound by CPI Group (UK) Ltd, Croydon CR0 4YY
Book design by Aurora Parlagreco

To the queer & questioning kids,
I'm rooting for y'all.

And to Mom,
You were the miracle. Wherever you are now,
I hope it's good.

OPHELIA
AFTER ALL

ONE

The fabric of my lilac gown brushes my bare legs, sending shivers of delightful anticipation up my arms. The flowers cascading down my skirt are so wispy and delicate, they look sugar spun. Light flashes in and out of my eyes, timed to the rhythmic turn of the disco ball that casts the entire gymnasium in a haze of sparkling light. Warm hands curl around the small of my back at the exact moment the music swells. My heartbeat crescendos with the music as I tilt my chin up to finally see my dance partner, none other than—

I'm ripped from my daydreaming as Agatha violently chucks a textbook into her locker.

"Do you remember during freshman year when they *promised* us we wouldn't end up with a shitty graduation song?" She pulls her locker door in to look me in the eye. "We really have to send off our youth to *Don't Stop Believin'*? Just hold me back at this point."

"Is this outrage going to last for more or less time than

your annoyance about the prom theme?" I ask, recovering quickly as I swap out my chemistry binder for my US government notebook. Not for the first time, I'm glad Geraldo Inglaterra was so open to exchanging his locker—perfectly spaced between Linds's and Ags's at the front of the alphabet—with me for a few bouquets of my roses. I can't imagine all the chisme I'd miss out on if I was subject to my end-of-the-hall, *R*-last-name locker.

Lindsay's knees crack as she kneels to open her locker. "Don't get her started on that again."

"Sue me for wanting a classic prom theme," Ags shoots back.

"Technically *Under the Sea* is a classic theme," I say. "It's just classically shitty."

In every fantasy I've ever had of prom, not once did I imagine decor reminiscent of the scuba-diving expedition Mom and Dad took me on during our family vacation to Mexico two summers ago. Evidently, neither did Agatha.

Lindsay snorts. "I'm more concerned with this omnipresent *they* who knew what all our senior year selections would be when we were still puny freshmen who'd barely voted in our class representatives. We didn't even know how to open our lockers yet." She accidentally spins her combination too far and curses under her breath. "Okay, so maybe some of us are still working the locker thing out."

"Some of us are still puny too," I joke, nudging Lindsay with the toe of my sneaker. It earns me her stuck-out tongue.

"Whatever," Agatha says as we shut our lockers and head

down the hall. "After our reps made our class color that awful rusty orange, I should've known not to get my hopes up. If we had all just applied for senior council at the beginning of the year, *like I wanted*, this wouldn't be happening."

"Maybe I would've if the senior council president was still Vijay Khan from last year," I say, fanning my face while Agatha rolls her eyes. "Seriously, why couldn't he have just taken one for the team and been a super senior? He was easily the best president." Lindsay shoots me a look. "Okay, at the very least he was the most swoonworthy."

The stifling spring air hits me at the same time Lindsay's nudging shoulder does. I regret wearing my sunflower jeans, even if the floral patches make me smile, and envy Lindsay's breathable running shorts and tank top. At least I'm better off than Agatha in her turtleneck sweater dress, but it'll be a cold day in hell when Ags admits that comfort can trump fashion.

"Ignoring Ophelia's thirstiness," Lindsay starts, and this time I stick my tongue out at her, "need I remind you that senior council meets on Sunday mornings when I have church and Ophelia has her weird gardening rituals?"

Sammie and Wesley are already waiting for us at "our" picnic bench, mouths occupied with their food instead of with talking to each other. Wesley is picking at leafy greens while Sammie inhales a cafeteria veggie burger that looks barely edible, even under the mound of ketchup he's drowned it in.

"My gardening rituals are not weird," I protest, sitting beside Ags on one side while Lindsay squirms between

Sammie and Wesley on the other. She ruffles Sammie's mop of black curls and smiles at Wesley. Both boys look pleased by the attention.

Sammie swallows the last of his fries, speaking around the mush in his mouth despite missing the first half of the conversation. "You're right. It's totally normal for teenage girls to spend their weekends obsessively watering, pruning, and fertilizing their personal rose garden."

"I like that she didn't deny the 'thirstiness' part," Lindsay adds.

"I, for one, think it's sweet that O has a hobby she cares so much about," Ags says, patting me on the head. I swat her hand away. "I just wish it didn't get in the way of the thematic integrity of our senior year."

"No one said you couldn't join senior council on your own, Ags," I reply. Lindsay nods in agreement.

Ags rolls her eyes, her bedazzled lashes shimmering in the sunlight. I swear a light breeze fans my face as she blinks. "Like I want to deal with other people."

"Is she still worked up about the prom theme?" Sammie asks, making a face.

"Started off annoyed at our grad song, but we're circling around to prom again," I reply. Tomorrow, prom will officially be three weeks away, so her irritation was due to return.

Wesley, shockingly, speaks up, unshockingly keeping his eyes locked on his salad. "What's so wrong with *Under the Sea*?"

"It's a tragic cliché! It's like the school *wants* us to spike the punch bowl and lose our virginities in a limo," Ags huffs.

"Sounds good to me," Sammie says, chewed-up veggie burger threatening to fall out of his mouth as he speaks. "Plus, Linds can just wear a mermaid tail and call it a day." He tugs on a strand of her naturally vibrant red hair. She throws a carrot at him in retaliation, but he easily smacks it away, flinging it at Wesley's chest. I bite back a laugh as Wesley slowly brushes carrot water off his expensive-looking gray polo.

"I can glue seashells to everyone's corsages," I add.

"Don't make me protest prom, Rojas," Ags threatens, wielding her fork. I bite back a dinglehopper joke.

"You think I can wear swim trunks?" Sammie asks before lobbing the last of his burger into his mouth. "I think it'd be tastefully in theme."

"I think it's a surefire way to guarantee you'll be going stag," Linds teases. Sammie and Wesley both visibly stiffen. She clears her throat and bites another carrot.

I feign ignorance. "You *are* always complaining when men don't comply with the Met Gala theme," I say to Ags. Bless her, she doesn't double back to Lindsay's comment.

"Me? Complaining?" She gasps, lips twitching into a smile.

The conversation drifts off while I pick at my dried mango slices. I'm half listening to Wesley stumble through complimenting Lindsay on her hair when Agatha nudges her bare knee against mine.

"Check your phone."

I pull it out of my back pocket, no questions asked. I've got a new text from her.

wanna make a bet?

I raise my brows. We haven't made a bet in months. The last one was at Lindsay's eighteenth birthday party back in November, when I bet Ags three bucks that Wesley would be the first one to arrive and be immensely overdressed for the occasion. Agatha had faith he'd know not to show up to a house party in slacks and a tie, but she was horribly mistaken. Had Wesley ever tried to befriend me past casual smiles and obligatory greetings at lunch in the year since Lindsay pulled him into our group of friends, maybe I would've warned him to go with a graphic tee and jeans instead.

Suffice to say, I'd begun to worry we'd outgrown our betting. With Agatha trading in NorCal for SoCal when she leaves for fashion school in LA in the fall, part of me has taken every fragment of change in our relationship as a sign that she's going to forget all about me the second she's surrounded by avant-garde fashionistas whose wardrobes extend past floral print and canvas shoes. But maybe this means she isn't ready to let go either.

what are we betting? I reply.

five dollars says lindsay picks wesley before graduation

I give her a pointed look. "Really?"

She shushes me and motions to my phone, eyes flickering to our oblivious friends.

doesn't seem like our business, I reply

we've watched this shit show love triangle bullshit go on for months. i think it's our business now

She's got a point. I love a good love triangle as much as

the next romance fanatic, but if I have to suffer through one more movie night where Sammie and Wesley crowd Lindsay on one side of the room and ignore Agatha and me the entire night, I might spontaneously combust.

fine. but if she picks sammie you better pay up, I type back, and she smiles brightly, her matte magenta lipstick starting to crack.

"Shake on it?" she asks. It's then that I realize our other friends have gone silent.

"Are you two making a bet?" Sammie asks with narrowed eyes.

"We would never!" Agatha clutches her hand to her chest. "You know we gave up that immature practice *decades* ago, dear Samuel."

"You're so full of shit." He shakes his head at her, then turns to me. "You promised I could be in on the next bet."

"I didn't think there would be one," I admit, and shrug, slightly annoyed that the first time I successfully lied to Sammie in all our years of friendship came back to bite me in the butt.

"Hey, you've never promised me I could get in on a bet," Lindsay says to Agatha. Ironic, given how often she accuses us of being immature for betting chump change on meaningless things—like the time I bet Ags a quarter that more girls would wear purple to homecoming than red, or when Agatha bet me a dollar that she could go a whole day without cursing and lost before we even made it to third period.

"Sorry." Ags snorts. "I'll up the amount of empty

promises I throw your way."

"Come on, we want in." Sammie rubs his hands together.

Wesley musters up the courage to agree. "Yeah, me too."

I glance at Agatha, both of us trying to keep a straight face, though it's harder for me than for her. "I think you guys might want to sit this one out, trust me," I reply.

"Wait." Lindsay's face softens. "Is this about you two still trying to find prom dates? I told you I don't mind asking the guys on the track team if any of them would take you. It's really no big deal." She looks at me. "What about Trevor Yoon? You were practically drooling over him at my last meet."

"I was not!"

"You were," Sammie says. "It was gross. But doesn't Trevor have a girlfriend?"

Agatha shakes her head while chewing. "They broke up last week." She swallows. "He got into NYU and she's staying local, so they called it quits early. She was a *mess* in ceramics."

"She's going with Mark Vega now," I say, remembering the few weeks Mark and I spent as partners in freshman biology. He almost caught me doodling *Ophelia Vega* in the margins of my notebook more times than I'm willing to admit. "He asked her during English, I think?" I look to Ags for confirmation.

"Algebra," she corrects with a mouth full of spaghetti. "Big poster, bouquet of daisies, lots of glitter for Mr. Semenya to clean up."

Sammie scoffs. "How the hell do you guys even know this shit?"

Ags and I shrug in unison.

"Okay, so Trevor is on the market," Linds recaps, biting her lip before adding, "I hear Lucas is still looking for a date. You should talk to him."

"Snooze-cus?" Sammie laughs. "You practically threw O a party when he dumped her last year, and now you want them to go to prom together?" His laughter is cut short when Agatha shoots daggers his way.

Lucas is a sore subject for me. We dated for six months junior year, which feels like forever when you're sixteen and have never had even one of your dozens of crushes like you back, let alone kiss you.

I thought we'd at least make it to senior prom, followed by a tearful breakup–farewell at graduation, but two weeks before junior year ended, he dumped me with little to no warning after losing his championship soccer game. Agatha reassured me he was just pissed about the loss and would come around, but he avoided me until the end of the school year, and we haven't spoken a word to each other since.

I guess in retrospect, his only wanting to make out in my garden (surprisingly, not a euphemism) and sit in his basement playing video games he'd never give me a turn at should've been red flags. But, as many of us have been before, I was fooled by a blond soccer player with chocolate-brown eyes.

"I think I speak for both Ophelia and myself when I say we're good, Linds," Agatha replies, the tightness of her jaw betraying her calm tone. Lindsay's been offering to help find us dates for weeks now without once realizing that forcing one of her many suitors to take us to prom isn't exactly fairy godmother–level kindness. Yeah, it would be nice to not attend another—and my final—high school dance dateless, but a pity date isn't a much better alternative. I want the pretty poster, the bouquet of flowers, the silly social media post with a punny caption about saying yes to the prom-posal. I don't want some guy taking me just because I'm the next best thing to getting in Lindsay's pants.

"Well, if you change your mind . . ." Linds drifts off before snapping another carrot between her perfect teeth. I flinch at the noise and her words.

In three weeks, all of us will be dressed to the nines in my backyard, surrounded by the roses I poured my blood, sweat, and tears into, wondering how prom, the final peak of teenage experiences before adulthood, came so quickly. Either Sammie or Wesley will have his hands wrapped around Lindsay's waist, while Agatha and I will pose off to the side for our photography-loving parents.

But lately I'm a little haunted by the image I've always had of me dancing with a pretty boy in a tux. There was a time, when I was much younger, that I pictured Sammie next to me. Then it was Jackson from sixth-grade English, then Adam from Honors bio, then Ethan from the nursery on Main Street, then *both* Franklin and Nathan from PE (messy deal, crushing on twins), dozens of other boys—tall, short, kind, mean, sporty, nerdy, and so on and so forth. And finally: Lucas, the one I *really* thought would work out. He lingers there, even now.

Occasionally, as my mind wanders during class or while gardening, someone stands out against the collection of boys I've dared to want. Even considering Sammie and Lucas, this face has taken the strongest presence, especially as prom approaches.

But she shouldn't—doesn't—belong there.

❋ ❋ ❋

The air-conditioning in government feels heavenly on the back of my neck as I take my seat. The desk before mine is still empty, thankfully. I adjust the straps of my top and wipe at my undoubtedly shiny forehead, then busy my hands with twirling my pen.

I hear her before I see her, surprising given her usual shyness. But the tan work boots she wears every day, even days as hot as today, are heavy on the classroom tiles. Her tall figure casts a shadow in the doorway.

Talia Sanchez walks into class the way she always does, eyes trained on her bootlaces, thick, dark curls bouncing around her long, brown face. My pen slips from my sweaty fingers, tumbling to the ground. Before I can grab it, she's already bending down.

"Thanks," I say, throat dry. She smiles, tight-lipped, and takes her seat in front of me.

I pull out my notebook and flip it to a clean sheet, scratching down today's date so my fidgeting hands will have something to do other than, you know, fidget. When I finally find my voice again, it comes out shakier than I hoped. "Did you finish the mock DBQs?"

She turns around and tucks her hair behind her ear. "Almost," she says quietly. "Zaq and I are going to finish them after school. You?" She slides her notebook out of her bag, the one with the funky doodle of the White House I've always assumed Wesley drew for her. She and her best friend, Zaq, an artsy boy Agatha knows from our school's Black student union, are Wesley's other friends, i.e., the ones he actually makes an effort with. He spends lunch with them in the art studio on Tuesdays and Thursdays, sitting with us at the bench the rest of the week.

"I meant to work on some yesterday but had a gardening issue I had to deal with first. I forgot to ask my dad to buy fertilizer this week, so I had to steal bananas from Sammie's house to compensate. It took longer than expected to convince him to give them up though." Sammie made me promise he got first pick on corsage and boutonniere flowers. But joke's on him, I was going to give him first pick anyway. Next-door-neighbor privileges.

"I didn't know bananas were good for roses," she says. It's refreshing to talk about my roses with someone who hasn't known me for years. Strangers are always in awe of my knowledge, while my close friends only care about my garden when they need flowers for Mother's or Valentine's Day.

"Oh yeah, they're fantastic for them, but just the peels. They decompose really quickly and release phosphorus, nitrogen, and potassium into the soil, which the roses *love*," I explain, shedding the cracks in my voice. "Plus, my dad loves freezing the leftover bananas and using them to make plátanos maduros."

"Now I'm hungry," she laughs, starting to turn back around.

"I can show you updated garden photos!" I showed her the first of this season's blooms a few weeks back, but the Midas Touch bushes were her favorite and they've drastically blossomed since.

The final bell rings before I can get to my phone. Ms. Fell clears her throat and asks us to get ready for a pop quiz.

"You can text them to me later," Talia whispers, then turns away. My face warms, but I clear everything in my head that doesn't have to do with checks and balances.

Talia finishes her quiz after me, flashing me a small smile on her way back to her seat. It's impossible not to notice the way the harsh overhead lighting illuminates the golden ring hooked around her nose and highlights the lighter tones in her dark hair. As she sits, she pulls her thick curls into a bun with such ease, it almost looks like a magic trick. All that volume being condensed to defy gravity within seconds. When she drops her hands, the light catches on her glittery red fingertips.

When I formally met Talia at the start of senior year, I only knew four things about her:

1. She is friends with Wesley Cho and Zaquariah Field.
2. She is quiet.
3. Her nails are always painted a sparkly red color.
4. She once kissed a girl and liked it.

I never went out of my way to learn these things about her. But I've seen her around school enough that it was inevitable for me to recognize her face in a crowd and learn her name. Especially after Wesley started hanging out with both of us. I only noticed her nails because she and Lindsay had a math class together sophomore year. Lindsay thought it was weird that a girl who rarely wore makeup and whose closet seemed mostly comprised of flannels and khakis always had such pristine, glittery, in-your-face nails.

Our first real conversation happened in this class at the start of the year, after we were seated near each other alphabetically and coerced into an icebreaker about our summer break. It wasn't as awkward as it could have been, both in spite and because of the events the week prior, at Lindsay's end-of-summer party.

Half our senior class had been crammed into Lindsay's stuffy basement, chugging watered-down beer Lindsay scored using her new fake ID, a birthday present from her cousin. The cliché topics we all silently swore to leave untouched until school began started slipping into every conversation anyway. "Where are you applying?" "What majors are you considering?" "Are you taking a gap year?" "What did you get on the SAT? Or did you take the ACT?" I finally snapped the tenth time someone asked me what I planned to do with a degree in botany, practically shouting, "I don't know, maybe grow some plants?"

Agatha hauled me away before I could embarrass myself further, and shoved a Solo cup of Diet Coke into my hand.

She managed to pull Lindsay away from her third round of shots to play the ten-finger method of Never Have I Ever. Zaq dragged overdressed Wesley over, and Sammie joined soon after, because where there is Wesley and Lindsay, there is usually Sammie buzzing around them, trying to intervene. Slowly even the stragglers who I'd never seen at any of Lindsay's other parties were playing along.

The room shook with laughter at the expense of friends and echoed with whistling following every dropped finger, even if the admission wasn't particularly promiscuous. We all groaned when Evan Matthews said, "Never Have I Ever dyed my hair multiple colors at once," because his ex, Danica Peters, was sitting directly across from him with freshly dyed rainbow hair. Never Have I Ever could get extremely petty, and I was grateful Lucas wasn't there to tempt me.

My fingers stayed mostly raised due to what Lindsay likes to call my "lack of teenage experience." My only lowered fingers were from cop-out answers about crushing on someone in the room or having piercings. Lindsay and Sammie, on the other hand, were in the negative finger zone within the first few rounds.

Usually my raised fingers would've felt like a glaring sign above my head screaming "Look at me! I'm boring!" but something about the communal participation made me feel less on display. Like the collective vulnerability protected all of us from judgment. Maybe it was the feeling of senior year creeping up on me, the unspoken realization that it was the beginning of the end for our teenage years, but the laughter and cheers and ache in my cheeks from smiling so much made that night feel less like a subtle competition of slut shaming, blatant callouts, and discreetly raised or lowered fingers, and more like a celebration of whatever the past three years of high school had or hadn't been comprised of.

Most of my summer had been spent watering my roses with tears over Lucas. Even Agatha and Sammie dragging me to the local mall to scope out cute boys working at those clothing stores with shirtless guys on their bags couldn't cheer me up. But that night, surrounded by my drunken peers and best friends, I'd forgotten all about my heartbreak.

Agatha and Zaq got up to refresh their drinks, leaving an empty space between me and Talia. I'd been focused on ogling Lou Santos from across the circle, in all his basketball-playing, six-foot-five glory, but something about the way she stood out in the corner of my vision drew my attention away.

She turned and smiled politely when she caught me staring, raising her red Solo cup in friendly greeting. Even in the dim basement lighting I could see the way her nose ring and deep red lipstick sparkled like her nails. I'd never noticed how full her lips were before then. I opened my mouth to say something, anything, but a shrill voice interrupted my thoughts and drew Talia's attention away.

The voice belonged to Jackie Mitchell, one of those people you go to school with for ages but never actually get to know. The type whose birthday party you'd get a pity-invite to in middle school. That night, she wore a tight black tube top and a neon miniskirt that glowed in the dark room, accentuating her curves and leaving her collarbones on full display. I forced my eyes from her body, my face flushed from what was definitely jealousy over how good she looked, but I listened as she huskily said, "Never have I ever . . . kissed a girl . . . and *liked* it." She batted her lashes at Lou, and he grinned devilishly as she, against the rules of the game, dropped her finger with a wink.

Jackie's claim to fame was when, during our freshman year, she and her best friend snuck into some senior party and drunkenly made out in a pool together. Some of the boys recorded it and posted the video to Twitter, because "girl-on-girl action is *so hot*," making it the talk of the school for a week or so. I nearly broke Sammie's phone when I saw he retweeted it.

Most of the guys dropped a finger, and everyone moved on to the next confession, but I couldn't. The ease with which Jackie admitted she liked kissing a girl alongside the blatant use of that admission as flirtation with Lou made my stomach inexplicably clench. My tenseness must've shown, because when I looked up from my drink, Talia was staring.

She glanced at Jackie and rolled her eyes, then fiddled with her nose ring, dropping a finger discreetly in the process. Except she was looking straight at me as she did it.

I didn't react. I didn't know how to, given the hot, oddly pained feeling that the look she gave me left in my chest. More than that, I was overwhelmed by the confusing intensity of why I suddenly needed to know everything about her.

Before I could muster up the courage to scoot closer, Agatha and Zaq returned, passionately debating the difference between thrift stores and vintage stores, and I lost hold of what exactly I expected to get out of Talia in the first place.

We didn't interact for the rest of the night, the game dying out a few rounds later when Evan targeted Danica again and Sammie had to calm them both down before a fight broke out. Ags and I slept over once everyone went home, well into the night, and I watched in envy as Linds and Agatha comfortably shared a blanket on the other side of the couch. I wasn't envious of them cuddling together; I was envious that they could do it without feeling weird like I always did. I fell asleep to the sound of Lindsay mumbling about prom and Wesley, as I forgot all about Talia and her red lips, red nails, and red cup.

By the first day of school, a week later, the significance of Talia had completely vanished. But when she turned around in government to pass back the syllabus and said hello to me for the first time, it all came rushing back.

Every time she asked to borrow an eraser or reminded me of an upcoming test, I felt like I was sitting on that basement carpet all over again. I never brought up Linds's party, too uncomfortable with the memory of how our small interaction affected me. But no matter how hard I tried, my mind couldn't let go of the one thing I'd wanted to ask her most.

What did she see in my face that night, looking at Jackie and Lou across the room, that made her confess?

TWO

By the time we're back at our lockers after school, Agatha has a plan.

"I am *not* running for prom queen," Lindsay says, slamming her locker shut as she stands. "You know how I feel about Little Mermaid jokes. Why would I subject myself to that shit?"

"Because *you* know how *I* feel about this theme. A prom-campaign project could salvage the end of senior year." Agatha slams her locker even harder, like that'll solidify her point. "I'm getting bored."

Linds rolls her eyes far enough that her green irises vanish. She turns to me. "O, how would you feel if prom was *Hamlet* themed? Would you run for queen?"

"Of course I would. I'd finally have an excuse to re-create Ophelia's iconic mad scene. Prancing across a stage throwing flowers and singing off-key would be very on-brand for me." I mime pulling flowers from a basket, flicking my hand as if showering Lindsay with them. "Look, a fantasy of mine come true." She bats me away.

I get her annoyance, but if I endured an entire unit of studying *Hamlet* in English last fall without complaint, she can survive running for prom queen. If I had a dollar for every time Sammie told me to get myself to a nunnery, I'd have the type of financial security that would justify getting a BS in botany.

"I heard 'Ophelia's fantasy' and came running," Sammie says as he and Wesley approach from opposite ends of the hall. I mime barfing while he wraps an arm around Linds, leaving Wesley stiff as a board on his own.

"Agatha is trying to get Linds to run for prom queen," I say.

"We could get some real use out of that hair," Agatha says.

"We are not using my hair, nor my mortal enemy, Ariel of the Sea, to earn me a pointless plastic crown and a title that turns school dances into beauty pageants."

"Yeah, the title is what makes school dances about beauty," Sammie says.

Agatha raises her hands in surrender. "Fine. No go on the prom queen campaign." Linds huffs a sigh of relief before leaving, with Wesley close on her heels.

Once they're out of earshot, Agatha turns to Sammie and me with a mischievous glint in her dark brown eyes. "I'll get started on campaign slogan ideas, and we'll reconvene on Monday." She shimmies away to catch up with Lindsay and Wesley, her thick halo of corkscrew black hair wavering as she goes.

"Please tell me she doesn't actually care this much about a meaningless theme," Sammie says as we follow our friends to student parking. He's towered above me for a while now, ever since his growth spurt halfway through freshman year, but I always forget just how tall he is until he's right beside me. A consequence of being friends since infancy, I suppose. It's just hard to reconcile childhood Sammie, awkwardly lanky with a bush of untamable black curls, with young adult Sammie, endearingly spindly with soft spirals of hair framing his narrow face.

"Depends on which *she* you're referring to," I reply, cocking my head for emphasis and to see his face better.

"Both of them," he replies, but I watch his eyes track Lindsay as she bounces between Agatha and Wesley, telling a story with her entire body. I look away, the yearning in his eyes too much. "Agatha's disdain has been made abundantly clear, but she'll get over it once she refocuses on the bigger picture: getting to judge everyone's fashion choices." He laughs. "But I don't want this Little Mermaid bullshit keeping Linds from enjoying herself."

"You know what would really help Lindsay enjoy herself?" I ask, nudging him with my elbow. "Having a date. I hear Wesley is interested if you want to help him ask her out."

The funny thing is, when Wesley transferred here halfway through junior year, he and Sammie actually got along pretty well at first. Lindsay tutored Wesley in math and invited him to sit with us at lunch because he didn't have any friends yet. And while Sammie had never complained about being the only guy in our group of friends, I could tell he felt relieved by the company.

The problem is that for as long as Sammie and Lindsay have been friends, they've had pretty obvious crushes on each other. And by obvious, I mean obvious to everyone *but* each other. Their flirting was never serious enough to cause real tension in the group and not enough where either seemed willing to act on it, but it was there. For years, Agatha and I waited for the day our group would be rocked by the intensity of intragroup dating, but every time it seemed like they were ready to commit, they dropped the ball. Lindsay would start dating a guy on the track team, so Sammie would get jealous and kiss another girl at one of Lindsay's parties, and our fears would subside for the time being.

Sammie finally seemed ready to ask Lindsay to the Valentine's Day dance last year, but she asked Wesley before he got the chance. After that day, Sammie brooding at the punch bowl as Lindsay and Wesley slow danced among card-stock hearts and glimmering pink streamers, the budding bromance was no more. Just like my minor crush on the shy new boy, as Wesley went from stake-free fantasizing territory to Lindsay's unforeseen romantic interest.

This year has basically been a ticking time bomb of passive-aggressive comments between the boys while we all wait to see who'll finally make a real move before we graduate. Though truthfully, Wesley is all passive and Sammie is almost exclusively aggressive.

Sammie smirks, taking my taunts and jabs in stride. "Don't rush my process, O." He even has the audacity to wink.

"What happens when Wesley asks her out before you do? Should I get some tissues ready? Ask my dad to prepare some of those cream cheese pastelitos for you?" I poke him in the side. "Just give me the word and I'll tell him to cue up the heartbreak canciones."

He rolls his eyes. "I'll just take you to prom to make her jealous."

"Wow." I pause, fanning my eyes to dry imaginary tears. "I've waited all seventeen years of my life for this moment. I can finally, *definitively*, say I will be used by a man. Thank you for making my dreams come true, Samuel. Truly, it's an honor."

He flips me off. "Whatever. You don't have to worry about it because I got this. You'll see." We finally catch up to our friends as Agatha pulls a dingy orange flyer promoting cap and gown sales off her windshield, gagging at our class color.

"Now they're just mocking me." She balls it up and tosses it to me. "For your roses."

"You can't use colored paper as compost!" I shout as she blows several kisses, gets in her car, and leaves. I pocket the flyer anyway.

"I better get going too," Linds says. "I have to grab my car and pick up the twins from soccer practice."

"Where'd you park?" I ask, looking around for her signature red whatever-you-call-small-square-shaped-cars car that's normally parked right beside Agatha's white whatever-you-call-small-round-cars car.

"I actually didn't drive today," Linds replies casually, but her eyes flash quickly to Sammie, then back to me. "Wes gave me a ride."

"That's cool," Sammie says in a voice that says he very decidedly does not think it is cool. Lindsay smiles, and she and Wesley leave for the other end of the lot.

Even with as limited car knowledge as I have, I know Wesley's car is *nice*. I don't know what Mr. and Mrs. Cho do for work, but Wesley's cashmere sweaters and polished loafers don't exactly hide their salaries. All things considered— rich parents, muscular body, handsome face—he should've turned out to be a massive tool. I suppose I should be more grateful for his silent demeanor, given the potential alternative.

"You're drooling again," Sammie snaps as he stalks toward his car and opens the passenger door for me, tugging on it since it sticks no matter how many times he oils the hinges. He worked two summers at the vegan burger joint down the street from us to save up for his car, but his parents chipped in as long as he promised to help drive his sisters around. Instead of investing the additional money in, I don't know, a car with better doors, he bought an entire set of encyclopedias that he keeps in the back seat. He's a massive history nerd and uses them to pick his next personal research project.

"Am not." I wipe my face with the back of my hand while he isn't looking. Wesley is cute, sure, but definitely off-limits.

"Do her sisters even have soccer practice today?" he asks.

"How am I supposed to know?" I get in and toss my bag onto the *O–P* volume.

"You spent half of last year at the soccer fields watching Lucas's games," he says before starting the car. The engine sputters but eventually roars to life. "Didn't you run into Linds all the time?"

"His games were on Saturday mornings, not Friday afternoons. I have no idea when the twins have practice."

Sammie must notice my irritation, because he takes a deep breath and says, "Hey, I'm sorry about my Snooze-cus comment earlier."

"I don't care that you think he's boring."

"You mean your love life doesn't hinge on my opinions? Color me shocked." I make a face. "Seriously though, sorry."

"It's fine." I shrug, deciding it is. "I just wish Lindsay wouldn't have brought him up like that. She acts like it's some *tragedy* Agatha and I are ending high school single."

"You know I'm contractually obligated to point out the Shakespearean tragedy reference you just made, right?" he jokes. "But come on, you know she's just trying to help."

"I get that. But she's forcing it. I want someone to *want* to take me to prom."

"If I didn't know better, I'd ask if there's a guy you'd *want* to *want* to take you."

"And why do you know better?"

"Because there's no way you'd have gone this long without yapping about him if there were," he says, laughing. "Is it mean to point out that this is probably your record for the longest you've gone without liking a new boy? I mean, ignoring the usual daily drooling. Are you holding out for the influx of crush-worthy boys you'll meet in the fall?"

"It wouldn't be mean, but it would be incorrect."

He laughs and rapidly drums his hands against the steering wheel. "Do you need me to pull out receipts?"

"I really wish you wouldn't," I moan, but his shit-eating grin tells me he's beyond stopping.

"Let's start with the infamous Ezekiel incident from second grade, shall we?"

"We shan't."

"I, personally, will never forget the look on Ms. Leigh's face when she knocked over your pencil box and found literally dozens of doodles you'd made of you and Ezekiel as adults surrounded by your adorable children."

"I was seven! And he shared his big pack of crayons with me . . ."

"I'm letting that euphemism slide because I love you," he says. "Okay, let's see, how about in eighth grade? Nathan from PE? Remember how he offered to tie your shoes before the mile run that you ended up *failing* because you were too busy mentally picking out what roses you'd use as centerpieces at your wedding?"

"I'll have you know I picked out my bouquet flowers, thank you very much," I correct, wringing my seat belt in my hands.

"Forgive me," he chuckles. "You could always see if Marty still needs kissing practice." He waggles his thick black eyebrows.

"That's not fair! That was freshman year, and everyone was having their first kisses. Can you really blame me for thinking his offer meant something?"

He slaps the steering wheel. "Yes! Yes, I can!" He's laughing so hard I'm scared he'll veer off the road and we'll crash into a tree. Though given the topic of conversation, I'm not sure that'd be such a bad thing. "O, he literally asked Lindsay to practice kissing *a week* before he asked you. You were there!"

"Okay, okay, I get it. At least I didn't actually say yes."

"Yeah, because he moved on to Velly Jackson before you got the chance."

"I seem to remember this starting off as an apology."

"You're right," Sammie says, but he's fighting back a smile. "I am very sorry you depleted your adolescent dating pool options this quickly while I sat by, unknowingly complicit."

"You're genuinely the worst best friend ever."

"At least you still got Ags," he says. And it's true. When

Sammie temporarily ditched me in middle school because the pressure of Why Would A Boy And A Girl Even Speak At This Age If They're Not Dating got to him, I stumbled upon a friendship with Ags and, by extension, Linds.

"Good, because at this rate, it looks like she's going to be my prom date."

"As her date, at least try to talk her down from sneaking in Parisian decor to replace the inevitable fish cutouts."

"I kind of hope she enlists me to hide berets to replace the scuba masks they'll probably have for the photo booth," I say. "Oo! We can speak in French accents too!"

"Oui, oui, mon petit croissant," he adds, and I about lose it.

As he parks along the strip of sidewalk between our houses, I'm grateful, not for the first time, that Sammie and I haven't grown tired of each other after this many years of friendship. Middle school weirdness aside, we've been glued at the hip for as long as I can remember.

Dad's parents passed away when I was a baby, and Mom's parents live on the East Coast. We visit them every couple of years, but some of her family never exactly warmed to her marrying the son of two Cuban immigrants. I didn't pick up on it as a kid, but recent political elections finally cued me in. I've had little interest in seeing anyone but Grammy and Pops Kennedy since.

The point is, with no real extended family around, my childhood got lonely at times. Inversely, Sammie has three younger sisters and one older one, let alone dozens of cousins and aunts and uncles. So my big, empty house became his refuge, and his big, full family became my extended one by proxy.

"Want to come over? Mom's making her chicken biryani." Sammie's voice pulls me from my thoughts. He grabs our bags from the back seats, knocking over the *T* volume.

"Tempting," I admit as I take my bag and get out of the car. His mom's Pakistani cooking is to die for. "But my parents are making ropa vieja, so I've got Cuban obligations. Save me some for when we work on those sample DBQs tomorrow?" We've got the same teachers but different periods for most of our classes.

He winces. "Shit, O. I totally forgot. Linds and I are seeing that new horror movie tomorrow. You know, the one about the lady who murders all her daughter's boyfriends to protect her from heartbreak?" He pauses. "You can come if you want . . ."

"I've got too much work to do. Besides, you know I can't handle horror." I shudder dramatically to hide my hurt. "You guys have fun though." I muster up what I hope is a convincing smile as we split off toward our individual houses.

"I'm home!" I shout as I slam the front door behind me. I dump my backpack on the end table in the foyer and pointlessly shuffle through the stack of mail. College acceptances have been out for weeks, and most of them came by email. Plus, Sammie and I already committed to North Coast State a few weeks ago, a state school only an hour drive from home. Botany for me and general history for him until he decides on a specific focus. Lindsay is off to

Chicago, Ags to LA, and Wesley to San Francisco. Still, I've yet to kick the daily habit of checking for a new cheesy postcard promising me an enriching future for the low cost of never-ending student debt.

"Hola, mija," Dad says, sitting on a stool as I enter the kitchen. The island is crowded with half a dozen cookbooks and glass spice bottles, the smell of them a little overwhelming.

Mom frantically stirs a pot on the stove, brown sauce dotting her pale face. "I thought we agreed yelling wasn't the most effective way to announce your arrival," she says as I kiss her cheek, avoiding the sauce below her eye.

"Careful with your word choice, Professor," I reply. I sit beside Dad and kiss his cheek too. "Its effectiveness was never called into question."

"Claro que it was the annoyance being debated," Dad contributes.

"Y tú, Miguel?" she says, wielding her dripping spoon. "Siding with your daughter over the love of your life?"

"She's got my hair and last name, but that attitude of hers is all you, my love." He leans over to scrunch my nose.

He's joking, but he's not wrong. Dad gave me his brown eyes; dark, wavy hair; and unquenchable love of papas rellenas. My sarcasm, only somewhat ironic love of Shakespeare, and the light smattering of freckles across my cheeks and nose are all Mom.

Mom purses her lips but doesn't argue. "Why didn't you invite Sammie in for dinner? We're going to have plenty of leftovers." She tosses a bowl of peeled and chopped potatoes into the pot before snatching a spice bottle from Dad to shake generously into the mix.

"Friendly reminder that if you actually want Sammie over for dinner, you might want to buy halal," I reply as I break off a piece of the hard bread set out to go with dinner. "Like I've told you a million times."

"Make sure to chew that," she says, ignoring my reminder. Dad rolls his eyes and grabs a piece too.

"¿Y cómo está tu novio?" Dad asks, looking knowingly at Mom in the least parentally discreet way possible. Parents with the delusion their daughter's boy best friend is their future son-in-law really shouldn't give an extra house key to said boy, even if it's just for emergencies.

"Cálmate," I scold. "He's ditching me to hang out with Lindsay tomorrow."

"Are he and Wesley still fighting over that girl à la Cold War style?" Mom asks.

"Bringing up the Cold War at dinner with two Cubans is a bold choice," I joke. She rolls her eyes, and Dad claps his hands twice as he chuckles. "But yes, of course they still are." I tell them about the bet.

"Warms my heart to see my daughter treating her friends' romantic lives with the utmost sensitivity," Mom says.

"Speaking of tomorrow, you've got your graduation photos in the afternoon." Dad nods toward the rose calendar hanging above the sink.

"No te preocupes, I haven't forgotten," I reply, but Mom

scrambles over to the calendar with a scowl. "What's wrong?" I ask her, trying to keep a straight face as Dad vigorously seasons the food behind her back.

"I have to look over my students' final papers this weekend if I'm going to get their grades in the system by the end of the week." She sighs, running her hands through her straight, light brown hair. She's an English professor at the liberal arts college just outside town, specializing in Shakespearean texts. It's not hard to imagine who chose my name, even without knowing Dad is a paralegal. At least they didn't name me Malfeasance. "I don't have time to take you, honey. I'm sorry."

"It's fine. I can just ask Agatha to take pictures of me in the backyard next weekend. You know, like I wanted to in the first place." Mom and Dad share a look over my head. "Parentals? I can still see you."

"You know I think Agatha is incredibly gifted and the sweetest soul to walk the Earth. But the last time you two did a photo shoot in the backyard, you were wearing orange eye shadow and a sparkly green tutu."

I groan loudly. "Mom, that was an editorial shoot for her designs. She knows how to take boring pictures of me."

"Mija, your mom already made the appointment," Dad says. "Though I'm golfing con Alberto mañana, entonces no te puedo dar un paseo tampoco."

"Well, Ags has her cousin's wedding, so I guess Uber or Lyft it is."

"You are not getting in the car of a stranger from the

internet," Dad says swiftly. I'm beginning to regret taking a study period instead of driver's ed last year. "Especially not after that news clip my prima shared on Facebook—didn't I send it to you?"

I really should put parental controls on the computer. "I'll figure something else out then." I visibly cheer myself up for their sakes. Bright smile, voice pitched higher. "I swear, it's not a big deal. I'll get another friend to take me."

I leave the room and head upstairs before they can say what we're all thinking: I don't have any other friends.

❊ ❊ ❊

I spend the next half hour scrolling aimlessly through Instagram while toying with my new rose-printed duvet, the bright pink flowers complementing my lavender bedroom walls. I see so many promposal pics that I actually start to miss college commitment posts. Until I see Jeffry Adebayo got into Harvard, and then I just miss classic selfies and faux candids.

I toss my phone aside and get up to splash water on my face, the anxiety of encroaching prom, graduation, and college making me feverish. I tuck my hair behind my ears, the length almost reaching my shoulders now, and hold back my bangs before wetting my face. Pushing aside long-term thoughts, I refocus my attention on how I'm going to get to my grad pics tomorrow.

When I reopen my phone, I see Wesley shared a post from Zaq, advertising his photography services for senior portraits and prom pics. I scroll through the post, all gorgeously framed shots of our classmates, then click on Zaq's profile. I freeze on the most recent photo.

It's Talia, smiling brighter than I've ever seen her, looking directly into the camera. I don't know who I'm more jealous of—her for looking so stunningly happy, or Zaq, behind the camera, who got to be on the receiving end of this smile.

An idea hits me, and I'm suddenly extra grateful that Talia and I exchanged numbers after that initial icebreaker in government. I type the text before I can talk myself out of it, dropping my phone on my bed like it's on fire as soon as I hit send.

hey, sorry if this is weird, but is there any chance you'd be able to drive me to get my graduation photos taken tomorrow?

I adjust my top, suddenly feeling exposed. It was just a text. It's just a favor. I don't really have a choice unless I want to ruin my parents' dream of savoring their only child's high school graduation for years to come.

"Ophelia! Dinner!" Mom shouts from the kitchen.

"Coming!" I yell back. Parents forget that *someone* had to teach us our bad habits.

I'm halfway out the door when I hear my text tone. I practically pounce on my bed, ruffling through the bedding until my fingers find the cooled glass screen. I yank my phone to my face.

Sure, what time?? Talia replied.

THREE

"Smile naturally."

My cheeks burn as I smile wider, eyes watering under the bright lights.

"Better," the photographer says as she snaps ten photos of me grimacing. Can't wait to have this plastered all over the house for the rest of my life.

Somehow sweating and borderline crying in a steaming room while this photographer snaps at me every five seconds for not smiling authentically enough—shocking that I can't do that while being yelled at—is less painful than the car ride over here was. When Talia picked me up in her endearingly run-down white truck this morning, I had an entire mental notebook full of thought-provoking questions and witty commentary about our classmates prepared. But my mind went blank the second I got in her car, her GPS's voice command the only sound punctuating our silence during the ride.

She's currently waiting on the sidelines of the studio, arms wrapped tightly around her stomach. I look away from the camera for a second and catch her eye. She bares her teeth and widens her eyes in a grotesque exaggeration of what the photographer is asking of me, drawing a laugh out of my stomach. I look back to the camera right as the flash bursts.

"Perfect! That was the one," the photographer says, then dismisses me to go change out of my fancy black dress. It's decorated with little white and yellow daisies. I picked it out to wear for graduation months ago, in an uncharacteristic act of preplanning. In addition to her freckles, Mom blessed me with her gift of procrastination, so I can hardly be blamed for my genetic predisposition for avoidance. Case in point: She's spending her weekend grading papers last minute instead of driving me today. Not that I'm complaining.

Talia follows me to the dressing room and hands me my phone and change of clothes. "Your phone keeps buzzing. I wasn't sure if it was an emergency."

I have five texts from Sammie, all about what shirt he should wear to the movies with Lindsay, and three from Agatha, all complaining about how boring her cousin's wedding ceremony has been. I chuckle and tell Sammie to go with the maroon button-up before telling Agatha to hang in there and give her cute older cousin, Trey, my best.

Talia clears her throat. "Everything okay?"

"Yeah, just Sammie and Agatha being . . . Sammie and

Agatha." I laugh. "But thanks. I should probably change before I get it all sweaty." I close the door and reach for the zipper at the back of my dress, but it doesn't budge.

I swing the door back open. "It's stuck," I say helplessly, awkwardly twisting my arm as I keep trying.

"I can—uh." Talia takes a step forward, then back.

"Oh yeah, uh, thank you." I move my not-even-in-the-way hair aside just to give my hands something to do and hold my breath as she jiggles the zipper and eventually unzips the dress halfway. It's low enough that she gets a glimpse of my back and white bralette. The air is freezing on my exposed skin. "I probably would've sprained something trying to do that on my own."

Talia coughs out a laugh. "I'll wait outside," she nearly whispers, and vanishes. I quickly undress and slip back into my clothes, denim shorts with daisies embroidered on the cuffs and a lacy white tank top.

I'm determined not to let today be a complete dud, so when I meet Talia back in the main office and she lifts her dark eyes, I ask if she's hungry. And, thank goodness, she smiles and nods.

The photography studio happens to be in the same out-door shopping center as the best, and only, Cuban restau-rant in town, Ollas Amarillas. The promise of food fills the empty spaces in our conversation. She's like a whole new person, going off about the brilliance of the alcapurrias from a small cuchifritos place by her house, slipping back and forth from Spanish to English with an ease I'm still struggling to master. Words come easier now, but we're still walking nearly two feet apart.

"They're *so* good. Bueno, yo sé que no son las mismas que hacía mi abuelita, pero . . ." She stops herself. "I'm sorry, I'm talking a lot."

"No! No, it's fine!" I reply, awkwardly adding, "Está bien." When you've had the same friends for this many years, you forget how much work goes into your first one-on-one time with a new one. "It's actually refreshing to talk to someone so fluent in Spanglish." Though her Puerto Rican Spanish slightly differs from the Cuban Spanish I'm more familiar with.

I'm conversationally fluent in Spanish, and can even understand Dad's rapid conversations with his friends about the shit they used to get up to when they were my age (though he doesn't need to know that). But I didn't grow up with a big family like Dad did, and he's one of the only other Cuban Americans I know. Plus, I don't know any other Latines who celebrate Saint Patrick's Day like Dad and I do for Mom. For me too, I guess.

But when we step inside Ollas Amarillas and Talia admits she's never actually had Cuban food before, I gain the confidence I've lacked all day.

"You've been seriously missing out," I tell her as she scans the glass display cases of pastelitos de guayaba and de jamón y queso. I swear saliva trickles from her lips when she reaches the thick chocolate cakes dripping with cherry drizzle. I watch Julio, the cute waiter I used to drag Agatha and Lindsay to Ollas Amarillas just to stare at, as he presses fruit into the white cream frosting of a tiny spherical pound cake.

The place is small, with a half-circle glass counter that leads to the kitchen built into the middle of the back wall. The walls are painted a pastel yellow near the base, building to a deeper golden shade at the top. Small, white-clothed tables decorate the black-and-white-checkerboard floor. Posters displaying vintage cars and tanned, leathery men smoking cigars outside white stucco buildings hang from the walls.

"Everything looks so good," Talia says as she turns away from the food display. "What do you recommend?"

I crack my knuckles. This is an element I'm well versed in. "If you're in a savory mood, you can never go wrong with a medianoche or Cubano, just depends on the type of bread you're into—sweet and soft or salty and crunchy. The bistec empanizado is my dad's favorite, but be prepared because they go really hard on the breading here. Ropa vieja is a staple of Cuban food, but you can get that anywhere, same with arroz con pollo." I shake my hands out, antsy with excitement. "My personal favorite though, which isn't *technically* a meal, according to my mom, are papas rellenas. They're like little magical breaded balls of mashed potatoes and beef." *The closest you'll ever get to tasting heaven*, Dad used to say. Julio is still a cutie, but papas rellenas are my main reason for coming here now.

"Some people pack them with onions and bell peppers, or, God forbid, raisins." I shudder. "But here, they keep them sweet and simple. Meat with light veggies."

"Wow," Talia says, mouth slightly agape. "And I thought I was passionate about alcapurrias." She laughs and presses a finger to her lips, considering. I watch the way the muddy pink flesh dips under the pressure of her fingertip, her bright, flashy nails contrasting with her makeup-less face. "I can't exactly pass up on the papas rellenas after that recommendation."

I leave to place our order as eloquently as I can manage with Julio, insisting I pay for the food since she drove me to my appointment, and ignore the tingling sensation in my stomach from hearing her talk about my favorite food.

"Can I ask you something?" she says as she chews a bite of her second papa rellena. I dip my third into the creamy pink sauce, half wishing we also had some oniony ají. I nod, mouth full. "I'm just—I don't want this to sound like an insult or anything—but I'm surprised you asked me to drive you today."

"My parents and friends were all busy," I answer honestly, then kick myself for making it sound like *we* aren't friends.

"Oh," she says, eyes focused on the last bite of her papa. She takes a long sip of pineapple soda.

"But also," I say, quickly going for the recovery. "You and I never hang out outside of school. I thought, I don't know, it might be kind of nice to do something together."

She smiles at this, and I hold back a sigh of relief. "I don't have many girl friends," she admits, and I nearly choke on my soda, mishearing her for a second. "I mean, I actually don't have any. I don't have many friends in general, but I'm especially lacking on the girl front." She laughs nervously and downs the rest of her soda, avoiding eye contact.

"Well, you've got one now," I say cheesily. She doesn't cringe the way I feared she might. "Is it lonely hanging out with just guys?"

"No, of course not." Her reply is rushed. "It's not even about their gender—I shouldn't have brought that up. I love them both, but Wes is closer to Zaq than me. And Zaq, well, he's not exactly unpopular. It's just nice to, uh, have a friend of my own. Separate from them, I mean. Though I guess you and Wes are friends, so never mind." She stares at her fingers as they move to trace invisible designs on the tablecloth, laughing at herself.

That ache, the one I felt at Lindsay's party all those months ago, burns in my chest again. She's watching her moving hand, but the other is just sitting on the table, and everything in my peanut brain is screaming out for me to hold it.

But all of a sudden, I hear someone calling Talia's name from behind me. Her head shoots up as she hears it too. I watch as her expression shifts from confusion to something resembling a deer caught in headlights.

I turn around and see a girl approaching who looks about our age. Her face is young, but her neon red lips, sharply cut black hair, and cheetah-print stilettos make her seem more mature. She struts over, arms full of shopping bags. I'm tempted to take her photo and send it to Agatha for a fashion-inspo board.

"Prima," the girl coos once she reaches our table. Now that she's up close, I recognize the familiar shape of her round nose and wide-set eyes. She's lighter than Talia, with much straighter hair, but the resemblance is there. "¿Cómo estás? It's been so long." Something about the squint in her eyes and tapping of her nails on the table tells me she doesn't think it's been nearly long enough.

"Hi, Dani," Talia replies tightly. "What's up?"

"Oh, you know me." Dani laughs. "Just shopping around." She lifts her bag-heavy wrists. "My brother just started dating this Cubana who said this place makes amazing pastelitos, so I decided to give it a try." She pauses, but when Talia doesn't speak, Dani turns to me, running her eyes slowly over my sitting body. "Who is your friend here?" she asks.

Talia clears her throat. "This is my classmate Ophelia," Talia replies mechanically. "Ophelia, this is my cousin Dani."

"Cute name," Dani says with a smirk, then nods to my garment bag hanging over the empty seat between Talia and me. "What's in the bag? Did you finally change your mind about that silly little suit?"

"Suit?" I ask Talia.

"Oh, she didn't tell you!" Dani clasps her hands together. "She didn't tell me herself either—don't be hurt. I heard from her dad that she's wearing a *suit* to prom." I look at Talia out of the corner of my eye. She's gripping her soda bottle so tightly, I'm worried it might shatter. "They barely got her into a dress for her quince, so we shouldn't be surprised."

"I'm sure she'll look beautiful," I say sincerely. Dani smiles, tight-lipped, her intensity startlingly similar to Talia's. Her thick false lashes cast deep, sharp shadows across her heavily contoured cheekbones. It's a little dizzying how similar the two of them look, while still looking nothing alike. Talia is all curves and curls, while Dani is all angles and edges.

I'm tempted to tell her she's got lipstick all over her front tooth.

"Pastelitos para Danielle?" the abuelita at the counter shouts. Dani waves her hand in her direction.

"I should go grab that," she says. "But I'll see you soon, Talia, sí? It was nice meeting you, Olivia." Dani blows a kiss, then leaves, her echoing steps making me wince.

We sit in silence for a minute before Talia speaks. "Sorry about that," she says, poking the final papa with a fork.

"It's okay," I say, because I don't know what else to. "She seems . . . nice."

Talia snorts, and the tension of the moment dissipates. "No, she doesn't." Talia, midlaugh, strands of curly hair falling into her face as she toys with my favorite food, looks a little bit more like the girl I saw in Lindsay's basement again. "Some of my family is a little . . . traditional."

I think of Dani's crop top and cheetah heels. "How so?"

"They have a very specific idea of what they think women and men should be like. Machismo and double standards and all that. You know what I mean."

"Yeah, totally," I lie. I hate feeling like there's some monolithic Latine culture, because there isn't and it's reductive of me to pretend otherwise, but I foolishly wish I did know what Talia meant, given that I've hardly been around enough Latine families to know.

"Me wearing a suit to prom freaks some of them out, basically," she explains.

"But, I don't understand that," I admit, hoping she doesn't realize my contradiction. "You get great grades and stay out of trouble. Why does it matter how you dress to a school dance?"

"Thanks." She smiles. "But it's more than just the suit. It's also my boots." She wiggles her feet beneath the table, nudging mine and sending a shot of adrenaline through me. "And my plaid shirts and cargo pants, and only hanging out with boys. And honestly, my mom being half Black probably plays a part in all their criticisms too." She rolls her eyes, but it's obvious she's downplaying the hurt. "They're not all like Dani though, I promise. Most of my dad's family is great, but Dani and her mom and some of my dad's other sisters are a little more vocal about their opinions. The day I come home with a tattoo will probably be the final straw, but at least by then I'll hopefully be settled at UPenn."

"Does this hypothetical tattoo have a design yet?" I ask, to avoid thinking about her being all the way in Pennsylvania in the fall.

"Don't laugh," she says, her shoulders rising as she tucks her head down. It's like watching a turtle pop in and out of its shell with her; one second she's implying her cousin is a bitch and telling me about her sexist and racist family members, then suddenly she's afraid of me again.

"I won't."

"The quadratic formula," she says without blinking. I crack a smile. "You promised!"

"I said I wouldn't laugh, and *technically* I haven't," I say, but I can't deny my growing giggle. "Would you mind telling me why the hell you're getting the quadratic formula, of all things, literally stabbed into your flesh?"

"Why don't you tell me what you'd get a tattoo of first, since you're so high and mighty about it."

"Way to avoid the question," I say. I wait a moment, letting the chatter of the other patrons fill the space between us. "Probably a little garden of my favorite types of roses, maybe with a quote from *Hamlet*. But I don't think I'll ever get a tattoo. Needles freak me out." I shudder.

"Can I actually ask you something I've been wondering about?" She's playing with the half-empty saltshaker.

"Okay." I swallow the lump in my throat, thinking of Linds's party immediately.

"So your name is Ophelia," she says slowly.

Relief. "So I've heard."

She smiles. "And I don't think I've ever seen you wear an outfit that doesn't involve some type of florals," she says, then cocks her head and looks up, thoughtful. "Correction—I *know* I've never seen you wear an outfit that didn't involve florals."

"I'm still not hearing a question," I reply evenly, but it takes effort to control my voice when her playful eyes turn back to me.

"And you're obsessed with roses," she notes.

"I wouldn't say I'm *obsessed*."

"Okay, how about super talented at rose gardening for someone our age?" she says. "I mean, isn't that a little funny? It's like someone being named, I don't know, Prospero, and being super into books and amateur magic."

"That was the best example you could come up with?"

"I got a C minus on my *Tempest* essay last year," she laughs. "But seriously, Ophelia with the floral print and the rose garden? It can't just be a coincidence, right?"

"Okay, well, technically Ophelia didn't have any roses in the play unless you count rose*mary* . . . which literally no one should. So do you want the long version or the short version?"

"How about whatever version you can tell me on the walk back to the car? I promised my dad I'd be home in time to set out chicken to thaw." She stands up from the table, and we gather our trash. I feel my face warm when Julio shouts a goodbye as we leave.

"I've told you my mom is an English professor before, right?" I ask, and she nods. We walk down an empty sidewalk, warm spring breeze tickling our bare arms. "Well, she loves Shakespeare. Like, I mean, *loves* Shakespeare, especially the women in his plays. She says they inspired her to pursue becoming a professor in the field. Anyways, Ophelia is one of her favorites. She's written, like, hundreds of papers analyzing her role in *Hamlet* and how she's been represented in various interpretations of the play. I definitely had a leg up in our Shakespeare unit last year." Talia laughs. "She told my dad when they first started dating that it was one of her life goals to have a daughter named Ophelia, Miranda, or Viola one day."

"Aw, so you're her dream come true?"

"I guess." I shrug bashfully. "She hadn't decided on my name when I was born, but someone accidentally delivered a bouquet of daisies to her hospital room, and she swore I smiled when I saw them. Which Sammie says is impossible because my eyes were probably still closed. But she swears on her life I did. So she named me Ophelia and thought it was cute to dress me in floral prints when I was little because, you know, she was an English grad student at the time and lived for that sweet, sweet symbolism.

"But for me, dressing in florals eventually became less about my name and more about me just liking flowers. My parents let me start dabbling with gardening when I was in elementary school, and I started my rose garden a few years after that, with their help. I mean, I mostly used the internet and old gardening books from thrift stores, but they always supported my love of roses, even if it kills my mom that I'm not going to follow in her footsteps and study English in college."

"But why roses, then?" Talia asks. "Why not rosemary or . . . whatever flowers Ophelia actually had in the play."

"Rosemary, pansies, fennel, columbine, rue, and daisies," I reply automatically. "Like I said, my mom wrote a *lot* of papers on Ophelia." Talia snorts as she unlocks her car for us. We both slip inside. "As for me, I just always liked roses. I've got a soft spot for them. Like, they're a huge symbol of romance, and a contradictory cliché because they're seen as a special sign of affection but also as this overrated capitalist representation of love. People love to hate them and hate that they secretly love them. I respect them for that. Takes guts."

"That's really cool," she says, so softly I almost don't hear her over the rumbling engine. I feel suddenly exposed in the confined space.

"They're also not as difficult to grow as everyone assumes they are," I joke, trying to relieve the flutter in my chest. "But don't tell Sammie or Lindsay I said that. They're generally unimpressed with it, but I've still got them convinced I'm some type of gardening prodigy. Agatha sees through the bullshit though, as per usual."

"Your secret is safe with me," she laughs.

Maybe it's the way the light streams through the trees and windshield to decorate her skin with flickering golden beams, a gorgeous imitation of Lindsay's harsh, yellowy basement light, that makes my questions about that night maneuver their way back to the front of my mind. Or maybe it's just that Talia's spoken more today than I've ever heard before, and I'm worried this could be it. If I don't ask now, maybe I never will.

I open my mouth to do just that, but it disobeys and instead asks, "What about you and the quadratic formula, then? What's the story there?" *Coward.*

"Well, unfortunately I wasn't named Pythagoras, or Euclid, or Muḥammad ibn Mūsā al-Khwārizmī, but . . ."

"I don't know who any of them are, but I feel like I'm being sassed."

She laughs smoothly. "I guess that formula clicked for me the way gardening did for you. I was always units ahead of my classmates in math, teaching myself the next chapters out of boredom. I was even accused of cheating freshman year because Mr. Smith couldn't believe the Black and Puerto Rican girl in the back of the class could possibly be earning one hundreds on every test on her own." Her eyes narrow and lips turn sourly at the memory, and I make a mental note to scratch Mr. Smith out of all my yearbooks. "I almost feel the same contradictory cliché thing you said about roses. But about math, obviously."

"Elaborate on that, please?"

"Math is just so universal. It's seen as useless and annoying by a lot of people, but it's so necessary for everyday life. And people hate taking math classes but love when they do a math problem right. Plus, there's always one correct answer even if there are multiple ways to get there. I like that complicated simplicity. It's always been a breeze for me. Just don't tell Zaq. I've been tutoring him for years, and he's convinced I really am the next Pythagoras."

I watch her ruffle her curls while she drives one-handed. They bounce softly around her face in symmetrical coils. She looks like an equation done right.

"Your secret is safe with me too."

FOUR

"I swear I'm going to pay one of my cousins to get a divorce so everyone will stop making jokes about me being next in line to get married," Agatha groans over the phone, muffled sounds of throwback R&B in the background. I'm grateful for the familiarity of her complaints, distracting me from my buzzing skin. I've been fidgety since Talia dropped me off hours ago.

I'm painting my toenails silver, and I adjust my foot atop old geometry homework I had lying around as we talk. "Is it really that bad?" I ask, messily dabbing silver onto my tiniest toenail.

"Yes!" she exclaims, and I'm grateful she's on speaker-phone or that would've blown my eardrum. "Seriously, I need to dye my prom dress or get a new one or something because if my great aunt sees me wearing white, I will never, ever, hear the end of what a *beautiful* bride I'll be one day." I make out her talking to someone while a toilet flushes. "Ugh, that was my cousin asking why I'm not out there dancing with the groomsmen. She knows I'm barely eighteen, right?"

". . . Are the groomsmen cute?"

"Watch it, Rojas."

Agatha's always been opposed to the idea of getting married. Ironically, her parents are just as sickly in love now as they were when they were high school sweethearts, or so I hear, so it's not like she never had good role models for healthy love. She claims she doesn't see the appeal past tax benefits, which I suppose is fair enough. Sammie jokes that my abundance of crushes is the universe's way of balancing out Agatha's lack thereof.

"Don't let your mom post any pictures online and you'll be fine." I finish up my final coat, then stand to open my window and air out the dizzying polish fumes.

"Oh yeah, like that'll work," she scoffs. "You've met my mom."

I toss aside my curtains and push my big windowpanes open, letting the night breeze in. Sammie's bedroom light is on, and I watch, frozen, as he swiftly kicks his trash can, sending crumpled paper scattering across the carpet. The gap between our houses is close enough that I can see his fist twist in agony. I don't doubt that if his windows were open, I could hear him swearing up a storm.

"Earth to Ophelia?" Agatha says as I watch Sammie pace his room. When he reaches his bed and spins around, he looks up and sees me staring. I wave stiffly. "Are you still there?

Great. First I don't have enough bars to FaceTime, and now I can't even hear you. The service in this bathroom sucks."

"Sorry." I turn away from the window while Sammie crouches onto his bed, head falling into his hands. I grab my phone off the floor and turn it off speaker. "Sammie just got home, and he's looking a little rough."

I open my mouth to say more, but stop. Sammie's often aloof about what's going on in that beautiful head of his, but on occasion he lets me in. And though he didn't exactly have a choice in letting me bear witness to this meltdown, I still can't bring myself to betray his trust. Besides, Agatha's only ever seen Goofy, Nothing-Bothers-Me Sammie, despite being friends for years now, so I wouldn't even know where to start with describing this version.

"Texting Linds for details now." I hear her acrylics tap against her phone. We're all best friends, but at the end of the day my loyalties are with Sammie and hers are with Lindsay. We're only True Neutral with each other. "Does this mean I'm winning the bet?" she adds while I wonder if Sammie's parents and sisters heard him storming around.

"Let's see what Lindsay has to say before we start calling winners, all right?" The bet leaves an icky feeling in my chest suddenly. I hear sharp tapping again and think it's Agatha still typing before realizing the noise is coming from my room. Several small, round objects are gathered on the floor by my window. I flinch at another tap as one ricochets off the side of the house. I look up and barely dodge one hitting me in the face.

"Shit, sorry," Sammie nearly yells. His voice doesn't carry as well as whatever he's throwing.

I kneel down and pick up one of the round things. "Is this a popcorn kernel?"

"What?" Agatha's voice booms in my ear.

"Yeah," Sammie replies nonchalantly, reaching toward his desk and revealing a nearly empty movie theater popcorn tub. He tosses a partially popped, burnt kernel into his mouth and makes a pained expression as he chews it.

"Hellooooooo?" My phone vibrates in my hand.

"Ags, I think Sammie needs me right now; I'll talk to you later," I whisper into the phone.

"Fill me in tomorrow?" she asks.

"Uh, yeah, sure," I mumble, already knowing I won't. Loyalties over gossip.

Sammie leans out his window, shaking the popcorn tub before tipping it over and letting the remaining kernels sprinkle onto the concrete below.

"Do you need to talk?" He shrugs, refusing to look at me. "Meet outside in five?"

He nods after a second. I close my window, throw on my shoes, and run downstairs, stopping to make a mug of hot chocolate.

Careful not to spill it as I step outside, I watch Sammie pull himself up and over the brick wall dividing our yards. It's ridiculously low near the back, but neither house has ever minded the lack of privacy, considering how well we get along with the Nasar family.

He stumbles toward the closest rosebush to the wall, fingertips grazing a vibrant yellow rose, following the lines of the veins until he hits the red edges of each petal. I suppress an embarrassing shiver at watching the intimacy of his movements.

"I'm doing well this season." He plucks a petal off the rose and rubs it between his fingertips until it turns to mush. "Very hardy."

"You won't be for much longer if you keep picking off the petals like that," I scold, and pass him the hot chocolate. "Drink."

Last year, after the Valentine's Day dance fiasco with Lindsay and Wesley, Sammie was a mess. For a week, he was either eerily quiet or snapping at anyone who tried talking to him. On a particularly bad day after his attitude caused a fight with one of his sisters, he stumbled into my yard while I was gardening and sat, silently watching me while visibly fighting back tears.

He was so attentive and quiet that I decided to confess I'd started "assigning" different rose breeds to each of our friends. It was the one thing I'd ever kept hidden from him, Ags, and my parents, but something about his gentle vulnerability made me want to share the secret.

I took everything into consideration: flower shape, fragrance, disease resistance, ease of growth, blooming season, etc. Any information I could find about the rose was noted before I made my final decision.

Sammie had been a Tequila Sunrise rose before I'd even

decided to assign the flowers. They were one of the first roses I'd ever learned about, even though they're a newer breed. A stunning blend of rich sunshine yellow and deep red, bold and reliable, lightly fragranced like the mist of cologne always lingering on Sammie's lanky frame. Average resistance against diseases—sturdy but not invincible.

His eyes trace his Tequila Sunrises before shifting to Lindsay's Fragrant Clouds—intense, coral-red roses that bloom easily with glossy, heavily scented petals. They're easy to handle when you get past the intimidation of their beauty.

He moves past my fenced-in roses to sit on the concrete bench bordering the lawn. I sit down beside him as he sips the cocoa, the surface cold on my bare legs. I hug my knees to my chest and lean my head on his shoulder. "Do you want to talk about it?"

He shrugs, knocking my head off his shoulder before I roll back into place. We've spent many a night sitting just like this while he's cried about Islamophobia from kids at school, his relationship struggles, his worries about his future in academia, and more. And I've cried to him about diaspora-baby problems, mean boys with pretty smiles but ugly words, floating between identities and cultures that always feel two steps away from fully being mine. We become open books with each other, but right now he's slammed completely shut.

"Would it help you talk about it if we made fun of my bad romantic encounters first?" I say, and feel his shoulders relax with the relief of postponing his vulnerability. "We could talk about Jamie from fifth grade, how I cried for two hours when he refused to sign my yearbook because he was 'dating' Jen Russell."

"I prefer remembering him crying for two hours when I pushed him in the mud for not signing your yearbook," Sammie laughs, rocking me slightly.

"And then you signed my yearbook so big that you took up the entire page." Sammie exhales with the memory.

He scoots off the bench and drops onto the grass, patting the space beside him. I join him, jealous of his jeans and long sleeves as the grass prickles against my skin. We lie back at the same time, twisting our necks to look at the minimal stars visible in the sky. Chirping crickets fill the otherwise silent moment.

I clear my throat. "Sammie, what happened tonight with you and Lindsay?"

"I think I missed my chance," he says quietly, like he's afraid of me hearing him.

"Was your nondate really that bad?"

"No, that's the worst part," he groans, throwing his arm over his eyes. "It was completely fine, completely normal."

I sit up on my elbows. "Then why are we lying in wet, cold grass at nearly one A.M.?"

"Because nothing's changed between us! Nothing! We didn't talk about anything important, not like I do with you or like she probably does with Wesley. We talked about her sisters, my sisters, what grades we got on the English test last week . . . nothing that actually *mattered*. I just thought maybe now that we're getting ready for prom with graduation just around the corner, I don't know, that we'd click somehow. That we'd have some super deep, important conversation, and at the end of it she'd just smile and say, 'Sammie, please be my boyfriend.'" He pauses, then groans. "What kind of weirdo gets this hung up on someone they've never even hooked up with?"

I smile tightly and point a finger at myself. To be fair, given their individual track records with hookups, it is kind of wild that their intimacy with each other has never gone beyond a tight hug.

"Ugh, I'm turning into you," he whines.

"Sammie, Sammie, Sammie," I sigh, and lie back down, ignoring his dig. "You were basically on a date already. Why didn't you just finally tell her how you feel?"

"Because I'm scared. It's always been like this weird tightrope walk with us when it comes to our feelings. I know we've been at this for years, but if I fuck up and scare her off . . ." His voice trails off. The backyard feels so still. He takes several shaky breaths and pulls at his hair. I tell myself it's because it's late, this time of night bringing everyone to their most vulnerable. Because the alternative, that he's really fallen this deeply for Lindsay when this whole time Agatha and I have been treating their flirtationship like a joke, is too heavy to accept right now. Maybe I just haven't been paying close enough attention. Maybe Sammie didn't want me to.

He clears his throat, and when he speaks again, his voice

sounds deeper. "Whatever, I'm probably just being a little bitch about this," he says, falling swiftly back into his role as my cool and collected best friend.

"Hey, be overemotional all you want, but don't drag us *actual* little bitches into this," I reply. He takes the out and rolls his eyes, wiping them quickly as I pretend not to notice their dampness.

"Whatever. Did you finish your DBQs?"

"No," I say, my heart beginning to pound. "I actually went to get grad pics done . . . with Talia."

"Talia Sanchez?" This time Sammie pops up on his elbows. "Wesley's Talia? I didn't know you guys were friends."

"First of all, she's not Wesley's," I reply harshly before I catch myself. "And yeah, we're friends. I've told you we have gov together."

"Yeah, but I didn't know you were, like, *friends* friends."

"It's not a big deal; she was just helping me out." I'm grateful the darkness conceals my hot, lying face. "I was thinking of asking if she wanted to join us for prom pictures."

"Noooo," Sammie whines, falling back onto the grass. "Then Wesley is going to want to come."

"Wesley is already invited."

He springs right back up. "What? Since when?"

"What do you mean 'since when?' Sammie, we sit with him at lunch almost every day. The invitation was implied! And he's obviously closer with Talia and Zaq than he is with us, so I might as well invite them too."

"When did you become such a Wesley apologist?" Sammie turns his face toward me and frowns. The moonlight casts shadows over his features, turning his eyes dark and sunken.

"I'm not," I insist. "But Talia is cool, and I think it would be nice if she and Zaq joined us. If Wesley happens to benefit from that, then so be it."

"Whatever," Sammie says. "Honestly, I wish it was just the four of us snapping pictures with those pride roses the way we'd always planned." He waves floppily toward the white roses growing along the back wall of the yard, the only roses of mine that aren't corralled into a makeshift garden fence. Dad built a crisscrossed, white wood arch in front of them that I plan to decorate with fairy lights, just for our pictures.

"They're actually called Honor roses," I correct, and Sammie smiles like he already knew that. "And I get you wanting it to be just the four of us like the old days, but it'll be fun having a big squad. It's our last dance, like, ever. So the more the merrier."

"You did not just use the word *squad* to convince me Wesley Cho's presence will improve my senior prom."

I give up. "It'll be good practice for graduation."

"Ugh, he's going to be in those pictures *too*?"

I roll my eyes. "*Yes*. So behave yourself, please. For me?" I give him a pouty face, and he huffs loudly, telling me I've already won. If Wesley doesn't come, I doubt Talia will.

I stand up, brushing grass off my butt before offering Sammie a hand.

"You're lucky you're my best friend," he sighs before

taking my hand. He does most of the work pulling himself up though; the hand-holding is all for show. "Whatever, I promise to behave. Scout's honor."

"You quit the Scouts in fifth grade."

"I guarantee you half my troop grew up to believe fishing is a personality trait. I think I'm better off." He cracks his neck. "I did tie a damned good knot though."

"That you did."

He pulls me into a hug and kisses the top of my head. It's sloppy and a bit awkward, but I squeeze him tighter regardless. "Thanks for being my favorite ear."

"You're stuck with me."

"No matter what," he says, smiling. He hops over the wall again, with more flair this time, his goofy bravado returned. But as I head upstairs to get ready for bed, I wonder if he actually feels better or just decided he has to pretend to be.

FIVE

Gardening is all about routine. Monotonous, repetitive routine. Because roses don't care if you're bored of watering every single plant with approximately one and a half inches of water every Sunday while your friends are sleeping in. They don't care if rotten banana peels gross you out or if you ruin your manicure collecting tree leaves for mulch. Roses care about surviving, and if you care about their survival, you have to be prepared to love a routine.

My friends claim they're joking when they call my routine excessive and weird, but I think they genuinely don't understand why I subject myself to this. I always want to point out that Lindsay runs around in circles every day of the week during track season and Ags spends hours measuring and cutting and pinning patterns before she can even start sewing. But sure, I'm the weird one.

There's something about the way my mind numbs when I garden. I can let my thoughts wander or allow my head to fill with white noise and not worry about overwatering or missing any leaves when clearing the dead ones off the bushes. I'm most at peace when I'm gardening. Sometimes, it's just what I need to keep it together.

It's also nice to feel needed by someone—or I guess some-*thing*. Disastrous past experiences, like Dad overwatering my roses when I slept over at Ags's or Mom throwing premature compost down when she got tired of the smell, prove my roses don't just need attention, they need *my* attention. No one gets them the way I do, and in a cringeworthy way I'd never admit to anyone else, no one gets me the way they do either.

Basically, I'm seventeen with no license and the inability to cook anything more advanced than a quesadilla, so it's a nice change of pace to know that without me, they would die. So I spend three long hours every Sunday feeling needed by something beautiful. I don't think that's so strange.

My garden takes up an entire half of our already smallish backyard, and the lawn takes up the rest. While the white Honor roses get to line the back wall more freely, all my other bushes are corralled behind a white picket gate, organized in five rows that started out much more precise than they are now. Some of the bushes have grown tall enough to pour over the edge of the fence, colorful bulbs bobbing above the grass, Sammie's Tequila Sunrises among them.

I pop in my headphones, then click my bubbler attachment onto the hose, once again wishing I could just leave it on all week long. But Dad is a hose purist and hates using the softer stream on the grass and trees. I let the water run over my hands, shivering with the crisp coolness of the flow, before opening the gate and beginning my watering routine, letting muscle memory take over.

I water Sammie's Tequila Sunrises, then Agatha's gorgeous lavender and ruby Paradise roses before moving on to Lindsay's Fragrant Clouds. Once my friends are all settled, I take care of the rest.

All my roses are hybrid-tea breeds, the easiest to grow, because like I told Talia, I'm not actually an expert. Like, I'm not the Gordon Ramsay of roses, but I'm definitely not the Gordon-Ramsay's-victim of roses either.

I give my remaining flowers their inch and a half of water, naming them as I go. Golden Midas Touches, sunset yellow and pink Garden Parties, the soft yellow Maid of Honors, crimson Olympiads, blushed-gray Silverados, and flushed-ivory Pristines. They glow with the fresh water and still-rotting banana peels from Sammie. I give slightly less water to the few newer roses that are still in pots outside the gate, since I've been too indecisive to plant them yet. The cacophony of pinks, oranges, and yellows that make up the Voodoos and intense raspberry edging on the white Suffolks make them too bold to place at random.

The next hour floats by. I pick the dead leaves and browning petals for compost, brush off spiderwebs and pests that are threatening my babies, and mark down in the notes on my phone which bushes I think would be best to harvest from for everyone's corsages and boutonnieres. I don't realize how much time has passed until Mom pulls off my headphones, scaring the crap out of me.

I whirl on her. "Shit! Don't sneak up on a girl with a pair of trimmers."

"Language," she scolds, and I bite back a remark asking if she'd prefer I curse in Spanish. She takes a seat on the same bench Sammie and I sat on last night and pulls out a can of the Materva Dad picked up from the store last weekend.

"What's the occasion?" I ask as she hands me the can. I crack it open and take a long sip of gingery, bubbly goodness. Dad tends to ration the Cuban soda, since it's a rare find anywhere but the supermercado half an hour away. Mom says it's for the best, given how caffeinated they are, but I say it's all the more reason to up the Cuban population in NorCal.

"You've been working so hard out here, I figured you could use the reward." She pulls her hair into a ponytail. "Plus, you look flushed. 'O Rose, thou art sick.'"

"Please don't quote William Blake at me at this hour."

She perks at my recognition.

"Would you prefer William Carlos Williams? 'The rose is obsolete but each petal ends in—'"

"'—an edge,'" I finish. "Don't make me recite the entire poem; you know 'The rose carried weight of love but love is at an end—of roses' gets me every time."

She sighs. "You're every English professor's dream."

I offer her a sip of the Materva to veer away from her attempt to guilt-trip me about my future major.

"The roses look great," she says, handing me back the soda after only a light sip. She's more of a tea person.

"Hopefully they look as good in photos." I wipe sweat off my forehead. "Agatha will kill me if dead roses wreck her aesthetic."

"I still can't believe you're already a senior. My baby girl, getting so big. Soon you'll be off at college, moving out, getting a husband and having kids of your own—"

"Whoa there." I sit beside her and wrap my arms around her stomach from behind, resting my chin over her shoulders. "I love the idea of my happily ever after being around the corner too. But I'm still right here."

"I know, I know." She bends her neck and kisses my temple. "My sweet, boy-crazy Ophelia." She laughs and wipes her nose, standing up and stretching out her pale arms. "Sorry, honey, preemptive empty-nest syndrome. I'll let you get back to work. Just don't tell your dad I gave you that." She nods to the Materva and winks before heading back inside.

I turn my music back on, airy female vocals blending with soft ukulele strumming, but I don't get back to work right away—can't, actually. I fiddle with one of the newly bloomed Olympiad roses, the petals a vibrant, bloody red. With misty water droplets resting atop them, they glitter in the sunlight. Like sparkling red nail polish.

Mom's words echo in my head. *A husband . . . boy-crazy Ophelia.*

I drop the flower and get back to work.

SIX

Chatter fills the halls on Monday morning as potential prom-court-candidate names are tossed around left and right. The official ballot won't be announced until next week, but by now we all know who actually has a shot at winning. Anyone who has their eye on those plastic crowns should've been preparing since freshman year, because at this point people either know you or they don't. And people know Lindsay.

Star sprinter of the track team two years running (literally), math tutor to basically half our graduating class, holder of a 4.1 GPA, early acceptee into the undergrad math program at the University of Chicago, and guaranteed invite to every party, even the ones thrown by students she's never spoken to. In every way, Linds is the type of person you're expected to pay attention to, and people do, so she's a shoo-in for prom queen. If only she weren't so opposed to the idea.

"How many times do I have to say I'm not running

before you realize my answer isn't going to change? I'm not going to waste a chunk of one of our final months of high school begging for people to give me a useless crown," Lindsay huffs at Agatha as we all take our seats for first-period homeroom. From the minute we all pulled into the student parking lot this morning, Agatha has been back on her bullshit trying to sway Lindsay. So far, she hasn't done much but annoy her.

"How many times do I have to list the reasons why you *should* run?" Agatha replies. She takes her seat beside Lindsay, in front of my and Sammie's desk.

"I'd like to hear the list again," Sammie says as Lindsay sighs and drops her head. Wesley pats her on the shoulder on his way to his and Zaq's desk, and Sammie stiffens beside me.

"At risk of further encouraging this debate," I start as Lindsay lifts her head, "do you think winning prom queen would compensate for losing Best Hair?"

"Oh my God, you little floral genius!" Agatha screeches. "I didn't even think about the superlative!"

We all, naively, assumed Lindsay's bright red locks had Best Hair in the bag come senior year, but Danica Peters's rainbow hair swooped in at the last minute and won. Lindsay and Sammie ranted about the unfairness of unnaturally dyed hair winning, but Sammie's frustration was, at best, a lackluster attempt at flirting. Truthfully, I admired Danica for her dedication to her wild hair. Lindsay hasn't exactly worked for her locks, but I still felt bad about her disappointment. Especially after she stood up when they announced the winner at the senior assembly last month before realizing they hadn't called her name. She had to pretend to give Danica a standing ovation. It was rough.

"Everyone, settle down," Mr. Greggory calls as students scramble into class last minute. First-period homeroom used to be lax when we were all A students who did our homework the night before. But senioritis has everyone procrastinating and rushing to finish shit before next period. I don't even want to think about this carrying over to college.

"Fine," Lindsay says quietly. I freeze while pulling out my chemistry worksheet, sneaking a peek at Sammie. He looks at me with wide eyes before looking to Linds.

"Fine . . . what?" Agatha asks with a creeping smile.

"Fine . . . I'll run for prom queen," Linds sighs. We all explode in cheers, even Wesley and Zaq. Agatha squeals, listing off the next steps to guarantee Lindsay doesn't lose *this* title. Forget fashion, Agatha should work in political campaigning.

We may not be the closest, but I know Lindsay. And while I'm willing to believe she'd risk embarrassing herself again if it meant making up for the loss of Best Hair, I'm not sold on her giving in to Agatha this easily. Unfortunately, I don't have time to dwell on that before the unforeseen consequence of this victory quickly arrives.

"Does this mean you're running for king now?" Zaq asks Wesley, poking him until Wesley cracks a smile.

Sammie turns to Zaq and bats my hand away when I try to pull his face back toward me. "Good idea, Zaq—that way Wesley will lose at least one thing that night," Sammie says, winking. Wesley looks down at his notebook, blushing furiously. Zaq sits up, looking ready to give Sammie several choice words he very much deserves, but Wesley nudges him until he sits back down. They start sketching, and it's only then that Sammie turns back to me with a pleased smirk.

I smack his arm with my chemistry homework.

"What was that for?" he seethes, rubbing his arm.

"I could ask you the same thing, pendejo."

"I'm pretty sure when your dad said he'd like you to practice your Spanish more, calling me an asshole isn't what he had in mind."

"I asked you to *be nice to him*. Not comment on his virginity." I'm tempted to hit him again. "You promised me."

"And you promised me I'd be in on your and Ags's next bet," he says. "Doesn't feel good, does it?"

"Very mature, Samuel."

"Just go back to Spanish insults if you're going to full-name me."

"Mr. Nasar, Miss Rojas," Mr. Greggory says from his desk, brows raised. He stumbles over both our last names. "I'll gladly give you papers to file for me if you don't have anything else to do."

"No thank you, sir. Sorry," I reply, looking down at my worksheet until he goes back to his computer. I elbow Sammie. "Leave Wesley and his potentially existing virginity alone," I whisper sharply. "Don't be *that* guy."

He exhales loudly but doesn't reply, so I lose myself in balancing chemical reaction equations until I stop fuming. It only half works.

One hour and one sloppily finished chemistry worksheet later, homeroom ends and our group splits ways.

Except for Wesley and me, who have chem together. We partner up on occasion for experiments, but only speak as much as our lab necessitates. The best part about it is that Lucas is in our class and seems jealous whenever Wesley and I finish early. We normally walk in tangibly awkward silence or make small talk, the kind that feels like when you run into someone you're acquaintances with in public and have to do the whole song and dance of pretending like the obligatory chatting isn't painful for everyone involved. But today, he goes for a different approach.

"I wanted to thank you for texting me yesterday. For inviting me to your house for prom pictures."

"Of course, Wesley," I reply, a little caught off guard.

He rubs his hands together, watching them as we walk. "I just wasn't sure I would be. Because of all the Sammie stuff," he says, eyes downcast on his polished leather shoes.

"Sammie is my best friend, but you're a part of this friend group too."

Wesley chuckles, nervously running a hand through his straight black hair. Sammie does the same thing, but it's usually when he's flirting or furious. I don't think I've ever seen Wesley flirt or be angry even once in our acquaintanceship. "Lindsay told me I should be more assertive and talkative with you guys. Especially since we're graduating soon and everyone will just forget about me if I never speak up."

"Lindsay said that?" I'm both shocked and not.

"Maybe not the second part," he laughs. "But I could fill in the blanks."

We shuffle up the steps leading from the lower courtyard to the sciences classrooms. "It *would* be nice if you talked to us more," I admit, leaving out that we could probably make a better effort to talk to him too. "But we could never forget you."

We step into chemistry, still smiling, and my hand brushes someone else's as we reach for our lab instructions off the front table at the same time. My heartbeat spikes when I look up to see it's Lucas. I feel flushed as I watch him walk back to his desk, and thankfully Wesley speaks again before I can lose myself in the memory of Lindsay saying Lucas still needs a date to prom.

"Is it okay if Talia and Zaq come too? I'm sorry to ask because I don't want to impose, but—"

"Of course they can come," I interrupt. "Talia and I actually hung out this weekend, but inviting her slipped my mind." A lie, but fortunately he doesn't know me well enough to catch the lilt in my voice that would tell him that.

"Thank you, Ophelia. Seriously." We sit at our lab station in the back. His small smile stays firmly on his face even as he turns away to get our supplies ready.

We work in our typical silence for a few minutes, pouring chemicals into various test tubes and counting our powder tablets for the experiment. Usually our silence is stark and professional, but today it feels comfortable. Had I known it only took one text to turn Wesley around, I would have formally invited him to prom pictures months ago.

"Can I ask you something . . . kind of serious?" he says out of nowhere as he hands me a slender test tube of murky brown liquid.

"Sure," I reply, my attention focused on carefully placing the test tube in the rack. I drop a tablet inside. He passes me an eyedropper, which I cautiously squeeze until it's full.

"Is Lindsay expecting prom night to be . . . *special*?"

"Special how?" I raise the eyedropper above the test tube.

"You know, uh, like—like the clichés?"

"Uh, I guess? I mean she's running for prom queen now, so there's that." I laugh, but his face isn't amused. I turn back to the experiment. "I'm not sure what you're asking me."

"I mean, like, what Sammie said . . ."

"'What Sammie said'?"

"Is Lindsay expecting to have sex after prom?" he asks in one breath, loudly. Loud enough that I'm startled and accidentally squeeze the eyedropper too hard, overflowing the beaker with the second chemical. I move my hands away from the spill as a thin, wispy cloud of smoke twirls around us. I wave my arms, coughing.

"Ophelia! I said *one* drop," Mrs. Waitley scolds as she approaches our station and pushes us aside to contain the reaction. I'm tempted to correct her. Technically, she didn't say anything; she just left instructions on a table and hoped for the best. But I'm too busy coughing the mysterious smoke out of my lungs to be sassy. I should be relieved Mrs. Waitley isn't concerned enough about the smoke to make us evacuate the room, but maybe that's more indifference toward me than anything else. I did break five beakers this semester.

"I'll go get breathing masks," Wesley says, scurrying off as I finally register his question. I turn to follow him, unsure of what exactly I'm planning on saying, but Mrs. Waitley steps into my path before I make it very far.

"Clean up the spilled mixture and finish your post-lab report," she says sternly. "You two are lucky none of these chemicals are dangerous." She walks away before I can apologize for the mess.

I look around at a few tittering faces. Whether they're laughing at Wesley's question or my failure, I can't tell. I focus on wiping up the table to block them out.

"Don't sweat it," someone says behind me. I've missed that voice, missed it calling me pretty, or asking if I wanted to grab pizza after school, or come over to watch him and his friends play *FIFA*. "Waitley burned the sleeve of her coat during that first experiment back in September, so who is she to judge?"

I look up. Lucas looks older than he did last year. Substantially so. I unfollowed him on all social media and usually only allow myself quick glances at him during class, so until now I hadn't noticed his longer hair or sharper jaw. His curls look like golden leaves in the fall and his eyes look like wet mud after a fresh watering routine cycle. He smells earthy, like he just finished playing a soccer game, minus all the sweat. My brain is turning to mush. And he's still waiting for me to say something back.

"Yeah," I exhale in reply, hating myself instantly.

"I'm sure Cho will forgive you." He cocks his head toward Wesley, who is now fumbling with the paper towel dispenser. Lucas leans on my desk while his annoyed partner glares from behind his shoulder. "We should catch up sometime."

"Yeah," I coo. He flashes me a lopsided smile, forcing me to look at his lips.

Wesley returns with a surplus of paper towels, mopping up the liquid while avoiding eye contact. I get the distinct feeling he doesn't want to talk about his question, at least not right now.

I don't know what I'd even say, to be honest. Like, Linds probably wants to have sex after prom . . . but who am I to really know? Why is he asking me and not, I don't know, *Lindsay herself*? Virginal as I am, my golden sexual-advice rule is that if you can't talk about it, you probably shouldn't be doing it. Seriously, be a little mature.

Granted I just fell apart like a flaky pastelito when Lucas so much as uttered two sentences to me. So, kettle, meet pot, I guess.

The bell rings as Wesley tosses out the sopping paper towels, and he grabs his stuff and bails before I can get a word out. I consider chasing after him to let him know being a virgin isn't anything to be ashamed of and to talk to

Lindsay about this, but figure I can pull him aside at lunch to clear the air.

I head to trig, and it's only once I've sat down and pulled out my bullshitted homework that I realize with a terrifying jolt that Lucas and I really talked. For the first time. In nearly a year. And he wants to catch up, right before prom.

I can't stop myself from thinking that maybe my dream prom is still within reach.

❋ ❋ ❋

I never get the chance to talk to Wesley about his Lindsay-prom-sex question though, because when we arrive at the bench for lunch, he's nowhere to be seen.

"Where's Wesley?" I ask as Linds, Ags, and I sit in our usual configuration. Sammie shrugs before reaching across the table for one of the vegetarian empanadas Dad made me for lunch today. I slap his hand away.

"Can you text him, Linds?" Agatha asks as Lindsay offers Sammie a consolation bite of her vegetarian pot pie. "I need to tell him we're having a prom-campaign photo shoot at his house after school on Friday." Lindsay turns suddenly, pie crumbling off her fork and onto Sammie's lap. I laugh as he brushes the wasted morsels off himself.

"When did Wesley offer up his house?" Sammie asks sourly, returning to his own snack of thick grapes. He looks to me with furrowed brows. "And why are you asking about him?"

"More importantly," Linds interrupts before I attempt

to stumble my way through a believable excuse, "when did I sign up for a photo shoot? I said I'd *run*; I didn't say I'd turn into a pageant girl."

"When will you people learn to trust me?" Agatha sighs. "I know what I'm doing." The confidence in her voice sends me back to every surprise party and beach trip she's whipped up last minute over the years. But my moment of silent praise slips away when I see the taglines she's writing down in her notebook. She catches me staring and quickly covers the list with her hands.

"They're not bad," I lie—badly—and Agatha groans.

"I was hoping Wesley could also help me with ideas for slogans, but of course he's AWOL the one day I actually need him."

"How exactly is Wesley going to help with slogans?" Sammie asks with a scoff.

"Wesley can be funny," she says, sounding unconvinced.

"Are we talking about the same Wesley? Tall Korean American guy with big muscles and no sense of humor whatsoever?"

"He's creative, okay!" Agatha says. "I'm sure he could come up with something funny."

"Did you just say Wesley has big muscles?" I ask Sammie.

"He draws little cartoons—he's not a stand-up comedian," Sammie says, ignoring me. He tosses several grapes into his mouth, then snatches the list of slogans from Agatha while she's busy reapplying her purple lip gloss. "Although I think even he could do better than this." He grows progressively less stoic as his eyes scan the page.

"They're not that bad!" Agatha whines.

Linds smacks Sammie in the stomach and takes the list from him as he tries to calm himself down. But even she can't bite back her laughter after reading the first few.

"Okay, screw both of you." Agatha leans forward to grab back the list, but Lindsay dodges her with ease.

"Come on, Ags! 'Linds is in'? Even the twins could've come up with something cleverer," Lindsay laughs.

"Is *cleverer* even a word?" Sammie adds.

"Yes," I reply. "And 'Lindsay Hawk is worth the talk' was my personal favorite."

"You too, O?" Ags says.

"What? I'm being genuine! It's cheeky!" I'm ready to admit that "Say Hey for Lind-Say!" is actually pretty catchy when I notice a familiar figure out of the corner of my eye. Talia is standing a few feet away, shifting her weight back and forth between her booted feet. She sees me looking and waves weakly with the hand that isn't holding her big stack of books topped by her lunch tray.

"Sammie, you still think Snooze-cus is funny, so let's be real, who the hell are you to—" Agatha starts, but I don't hear the rest. I get up and head toward Talia, who stops fidgeting as I approach. Saturday suddenly feels like it was years ago, like it happened to another girl in another life.

Today she's wearing a loose gray *Ghostbusters* shirt, ripped jeans, and her typical work boots. I feel my mouth go dry.

"Hey," she says softly as I finally regain moisture in my mouth. Gross.

"Hey. Are you okay?" I ask.

"Yeah, yeah. I'm fine." She struggles to balance her books and lunch. "I couldn't find Zaq and thought maybe he'd be here with Wesley and you guys." She nods to my friends, who are now engaged in a grape war.

"I don't know where either of them are. Sorry," I say. "But you can sit with us if you want."

"Are you sure?" She looks warily over my shoulder as Lindsay and Agatha team up on Sammie, filling his curls with grapes.

"I promise to protect you from their grapes of wrath," I laugh, relieving her of some of her books and lunch.

"You guys know Talia," I say awkwardly as we sit at the table. Agatha scoots over to make room for the both of us.

"To what do we owe the pleasure?" Sammie drawls with a smile.

"Ignore him," Agatha says.

"We all try to anyway," I add. Sammie spits a grape at me.

"Did that hurt?" Agatha touches her own nostril, then points to Talia's nose ring. Agatha's wanted a septum piercing forever and claims her mom would kill her, but I've met her angel of a mom, and we both know it's her own fear of needles, not any maternal obstacle, that's keeping her from biting the bullet.

"A lot, actually," Talia replies, tension leaving her hunched, toned shoulders. How does someone who spends their free time doing math proofs and hanging out with two cartoon-ists get so toned? She and Wesley have to be on a secret workout plan together. "My friend was the one who pierced it in their bathroom though, so it probably would've hurt less with a professional."

"Badass." Lindsay nods in approval.

But Talia doesn't have any friends besides Wesley and Zaq, or at least according to what she said on Saturday. And if either of them had done it for her, wouldn't she have just come right out and said that?

"Something wicked this way comes," Sammie mutters as Wesley and Zaq approach.

"I will hurt you," I whisper. He rolls his eyes and mimes zipping his lips shut.

Lindsay had shown no sign of concern over Wesley's absence, but her face is suddenly aglow with what looks like relief.

"Where were you?" Talia asks softly. She's feigning casual, but there's obvious hurt in her voice. She's staring more at Zaq than Wesley, but I imagine it's because she expected Wesley to sit with us and not her today anyway. Zaq keeps his eyes on the table while Wesley apologizes for finishing up a piece for AP drawing. Talia looks unconvinced, but Wesley takes his usual spot beside Lindsay while Zaq crams in on our side beside Talia.

"Are you still in a creative mindset?" Ags asks, hesitantly passing her notebook over to Wesley and Zaq. "Lindsay's prom campaign is in dire need of a slogan."

"I think we can help you out here," Zaq says with a cautious smile. "Wes and I created an online comic strip, and one of the supervillains talks exclusively in rhymes and puns."

"Sounds *super* cool," Sammie mumbles.

Zaq ignores him and immediately starts scribbling down ideas. Ags asks about his septum piercing and studded, two-toned leather jacket, and he laughs like she's done it a million times. I forget sometimes that they're already friends from the Black student union, so maybe she has.

"So, when are you going to pierce my nose in a bathroom?" I ask Talia as she takes a bite out of her sandwich, hoping to get more details about this mysterious friend. She smiles tightly as she chews, her expression seeming performative now that I know what an Authentic Talia Smile looks like. Without replying, she looks away, toward Zaq and Agatha's conversation about the importance of cadence in a good rhyme, so I swallow another bite of empanada and turn away as well.

When the bell rings, we head to government together and she drops the weirdness of the moment. But I'm still left wondering about this mystery friend. I ruefully add it to the growing list of unanswered questions about Talia that I'm too afraid to ask.

Despite the somewhat rocky ending to lunch, Zaq and Talia join us again the next day. Zaq comes by to drop off more slogan ideas for Lindsay's and, more importantly, Agatha's approval. Wesley brings up, in as casual a manner as he can, that it'd be cool if they started sitting with us every day.

So it's no surprise when we're together again on Wednesday. Talia wraps Agatha into an enthusiastic conversation about the importance of geometry in fashion while Zaq argues with Lindsay and Sammie over some new video game's graphics. Wesley and I chat about *King Lear* since he's considering creating a comic adaptation of it, and we actually start talking when we walk to chem together. And though Lucas constantly watches us from across the room, shooting me those sparkling smiles whenever our eyes meet, he doesn't further our earlier conversation.

Despite that, everything starts to feel like it's falling into place. Two groups become one, I get to spend more time with Talia, my ex-boyfriend seems jealous, and Sammie and Wesley—by the miracles of the universe and/or Zaquariah Field's constant interference—get along, even as prom approaches at an unreal speed. All the beautiful high school clichés senior year promised me, falling perfectly into place. Or so I hope.

SEVEN

I came over to Agatha's after school to work on home-work, but two hours in all I've done is organize her collection of fabric swatches in rainbow order. In my defense, it's impossible not to get distracted in her room.

I've never been particularly crafty outside of the occasional floral arrangement and corsage, but being in Ags's room is like visiting a craft supply store. I suddenly want to pick up needlepointing and beading and quilting, all at once.

Everything about her room—the bright orange walls and white shag carpeting, animal print–patched bedding and faux diamond chandelier, the vaguely opaque tubs stacked in each available corner that hold everything from scaled swim-suit fabric to fiery red tulle—feels brimming with life and creativity.

"In your professional opinion, how realistic does this look?" Ags holds up a rose made of neon green satin so shiny that it looks wet, her highlighter-yellow acrylics a stark contrast of color.

"Well," I start, taking the rose from her. "I mean, technically a real rose wouldn't be a bunched-up ball like this." I'm careful not to completely unravel the fabric as I pick at the folds. "If you really want to be accurate, you'd have to cut and sew together dozens of petals."

She pouts and sticks out her cupped hands. I suppress a laugh as I place the rose back in her possession.

"If it's any consolation, I doubt your future costume design professor will care about your seventeen-year-old friend's scientific accuracy assessment," I tell her. She turns to pin the rose back on the neckline of the simple makeshift gown draped against her dress form. For her eighteenth birthday back in February her parents got her a custom, plus-size dress form with her exact measurements to make the sewing process a little easier.

She's been working on her portfolio forever. I thought she would've eased up a little after getting accepted into her dream school, the Fashion Institute of Design & Merchandising, but if anything, she's amped up her productivity.

"You don't get it, O," she says, and I feel a jolt of defensiveness rise to the surface. Agatha and I have always bonded over having the most unstable career aspirations of our friends—with Sammie's dreams of academia in history and Lindsay's love for mathematics making them seem miles more reasonable than the two of us. "I've been stalking my future classmates on Insta and Twitter." She thrusts her phone in my face. It's open to an Instagram page covered in photos of elaborate dresses that look like the clothing equivalent of a love child between Marie Antoinette and Titania from *A Midsummer Night's Dream*. "I thought I'd have a monopoly over glitter and neon glamour, but half these kids are doing the exact same shit as me." She pauses. "If not better."

I snatch her phone from her and throw it across the room onto her bed.

"Hey!" she shouts.

"How many of those designers have size-inclusive designs?" I ask.

"Ophelia, I—"

"Answer the question, Agatha. How many are plus-size designers?"

She sighs. "Like, two of them."

"And do those two also hand bead all their designs and refuse to work with premade accent pieces like store-bought fabric roses?" I ask, motioning to her dress form. "Did they spend an entire summer studying color theory or ask for extra tutoring sessions in geometry just to better under-stand the math behind design?"

"Okay, okay. I get it."

"No," I tell her. "*I* get it. I get how talented you are and how hard you've worked for this. Don't psych yourself out—you earned your place."

She makes a weird noise, a combination of a laugh and sigh. Impostor syndrome is a bitch. Agatha will rightfully compliment herself all day long and boost the rest of us out of our pits of self-loathing, but try to give her a genuine compliment and she'll very nearly shut down.

I'm going to miss her so much in the fall.

"Thank you," she finally manages, but still doesn't look at me. She fetches her phone from her bed.

"You can thank me by designing my wedding dress one day." I flop back on her bed the second she moves away from it and goes back to pinning roses.

"Like you can afford me," she laughs without turning around. "What'd you have in mind?"

"I used to picture a princess-cut during the Nathan-crushing years, but moved toward mermaid while dating Lucas."

"And now?" I see her turn ever so slightly out of the corner of my eye.

"Low cut and flowy. Maybe a little off-white."

"What about the boy?"

I sit up. "What boy?"

She finally faces me. "You know, the one you need standing across from you at the altar. The one who'll brush away tears after you've walked up the aisle and handed off your bouquet to me and Lindsay in our *stunning* bridesmaid dresses." She spins back to her dress. "I was thinking mauve. Should complement both our color palettes."

I pick at the sequins on one of Agatha's pillows. "There isn't a boy."

"Still stuck on Lucas?"

I kick off my shoes and tuck my socked feet beneath me. "I guess? I mean, when I picture my happily ever after, I don't really picture him anymore."

She freezes again and looks at me over her shoulder. "No?"

I shake my head.

"Hmm," she says, shrugging, then moving a rose from the neckline to the waistline.

I wait for her to ask if there's someone else. If I still picture myself being loved by someone specific, butterflies hatching in my stomach every time I see them. But she doesn't. She asks me if the roses look better pinned to the neck or waist of the dress.

"The neckline," I tell her, then change my mind. "Actually, I kind of like them at the waist. Maybe both?"

She tilts her head and puts her hands on her wide hips. "Really?"

I change my mind again, because I can. "Everywhere," I say. "I think the roses should go everywhere."

EIGHT

Talia parks on the street outside a property lined by thick, towering bushes. The two of us are the last to arrive, so we hurry out of the car and over to the keypad gate where everyone else is already waiting, the shrubbery bordering the property towering above them.

Wesley hesitates as Agatha, Sammie, and I wait breathlessly. For the three of us, this'll be the first time seeing Wesley's house. In between reminding everyone all week to nominate Lindsay for prom queen, we joked about finally being welcomed into the Cho Mansion. Wesley did his best to scold us for overexaggerating, but if Talia's, Zaq's, and Linds's anticipating faces are any indication, our joke isn't too far off.

"Wait," Wesley says, turning to face us. "Can you three just, uh, just promise me you aren't going to be weird about this?"

"I promise," I say as Agatha says, "I will make no such promise." Sammie just shrugs.

"Wes, just get it over with," Zaq says, nudging Wesley's back. He sighs, then finally types in the key code, and the gate swings open.

"You've got to be fucking kidding me," Sammie says.

Wesley's house isn't a mansion; he was right about that.

It's a palace.

Three stories of shining white stone and a steep roof guarded by elaborate granite gargoyles loom before us. Two cars, looking equally as expensive as Wesley's, if not even fancier, sit around a fountain in the circular gravel drive before the porch. And waiting on the steps are two people who I can only assume are Wesley's parents.

"You've got to be kidding *me*," Wesley echoes, trying to reach his parents before the rest of us, but failing miserably as we speed-walk after him like giddy schoolchildren.

"You must be Wesley's other friends. We've heard so much about you all." Mrs. Cho beams, her glossy black hair cut in a blunt bob. Her white jeans and flowy blue blouse don't have a single crease in them.

"It's so nice to finally meet you," Mr. Cho says. His build and face look so similar to Wesley's that he looks more like his older brother than his father.

"Who knew Wesley had hot parents?" Sammie mutters, just to me, but when Wesley turns bright red, I assume he heard too.

"Of course, we've already met you three," Mrs. Cho says, smiling at Zaq, Talia, and Lindsay. "But I wanted to formally welcome *you* three." She turns to Agatha, Sammie, and me, giving us each a quick but warm hug. "Would you like a tour around?"

"They're fine," Wesley says tightly. "Zaq is just taking some pictures of Lindsay out here, so . . ." He twitches his head and widens his eyes.

"Oh! Oh, of course," Mrs. Cho says, wringing her empty hands. "Well, if any of you need anything, don't hesitate to ask." She heads for the front door, Mr. Cho on her heels, but she turns around at the last second. "And Lindsay, you look lovely as usual."

Lindsay's face turns as bright as her hair as she fumbles to thank her. Who would've thought all it took to get Lindsay Hawk to blush was a genuine compliment from a sweet mom.

Zaq pulls out his professional camera while Sammie and Talia help Agatha unpack her bag of props for Lindsay. She said taking photos outside a fancy house with nice cars would be ideal for promoting Lindsay as a true queen, but I wonder how Lindsay really feels about all of this. Her family isn't struggling the way they were when we were in middle school, but most of her clothes are secondhand, and her bedroom isn't much bigger than Wesley's car. I'm honestly surprised she insisted on paying Zaq for taking photos and Agatha for doing makeup today. Though I'm relieved they're getting compensated beyond "exposure."

We wait for Lindsay to change into one of the gowns Agatha designed for a small formal collection she made last year. According to Ags, Lindsay wearing her real prom dress would make prom itself way too anticlimactic, about which I actually agree. Mrs. Cho silently sets several trays of snacks on the porch steps before Wesley shoos her away again, to Sammie's and my amusement.

Zaq and I kick a rock back and forth while Sammie and Talia nerd out about the history of mathematics in the Middle East, combining their two aspirational fields of study. I'm about to ask Zaq if he thinks we can Hacky Sack the rock when Linds finally emerges.

Sammie and Talia are struck silent, mouths open, and Wesley stops chewing his apple slice midbite. Agatha smiles knowingly in approval. Zaq is the only one completely unfazed.

My mouth feels dry and thick, my tongue heavy, as I try to form complimentary words. Linds's soft curves are on full display in the tight, plunging black satin gown. She let her hair down, so it settles around her pale shoulders, the ends tickling her bare, freckled arms.

I've seen Lindsay in a dress before. I've seen Lindsay in *this* dress before, when she modeled it for Agatha's portfolio. But suddenly I'm thinking of homecoming, freshman year. Lindsay in her short red tank dress, applying cherry-scented lip gloss in the bathroom. I shouldn't, but I remember the moment she caught me staring and smirked at me before puckering her lips again. I didn't speak to her for the rest of the night.

Think of something else. But now it's Agatha running product through her hair during a sleepover sophomore year, the haze of exhaustion giving her eyes a smolder as she asked if I wanted her to brush and French braid my hair before bed.

Talia's arms on the steering wheel, muscles taut, as she drove us here today.

"Ophelia?" Agatha finally snaps me out of my trance, literally, snapping her fingers before waving two plastic tiaras in front of my face. Everyone else already stopped drooling and moved back to their conversations and snacks. "Which one will look better for the photos?"

"Just go with the silver one. Silver is classic," Zaq says. He snatches the plate of apple slices from Wesley and winks before Wesley kicks him.

"I like the one with the little seashells," Sammie says, pointing at the opposite crown. Zaq frowns and Wesley takes the apples back.

"Isn't the seashell thing a bit much though?" Lindsay complains. I don't let myself look at her as Agatha tells her to get off her high seahorse and just put the crown on.

I jog up the steps, mumbling something about needing the bathroom. I don't wait for directions, too desperate for a moment alone.

I shut the front door behind me, and the cooler air instantly clears my head. Leaning against the door, I close my eyes and catch my breath. When I open them, I see the foyer walls are covered with artwork. I'm so busy walking around and studying each piece that I don't notice there's someone behind me until she speaks.

"Wesley made those," Talia says, and I jump, startled. "Sorry." She winces. "I just thought you might get lost. I did my first time. And my second."

"Thanks," I say, the jitteriness from outside starting to return.

The corridor expands into a large room that splits into three hallways, with two staircases leading to the next floor. The paintings cover the walls in every direction, all bright, active scenes. A family riding bikes, a packed swimming pool, dogs running in a park. But each is comprised of thick, heavy strokes of acrylic, making them alive and unworldly all at once. "I knew Wesley was talented, but this? This is . . . wow."

"I know, right? He and Zaq both," she says with a smile, walking past me, down the nearest hallway to the left.

"How did you three become friends anyway?" I ask as she leads. She pauses, because of my question or directional confusion, I don't know.

"What did Wesley tell you?"

"Nothing. I never asked," I reply, following her past a sharp turn. We end up outside a pale blue bathroom tucked in a corner, the first sign of color in the house besides Wesley's paintings.

"It's not that interesting," she says, leaning against the wall beside the door.

"Tell me anyway."

She shrugs, and I start to feel like she's avoiding the question because of something other than an underwhelming answer. "We just have stuff in common. Zaq and I had a few classes together in middle school and didn't really know anyone else when we got to high school." She tilts her head, and I clench my hand so I don't reach out to tuck the curl that's dangling over her forehead behind her ear. "When Wesley transferred, they met in Digital Media and realized they read the same comics and manga. Wes and I have the same taste in music, K-pop and indie stuff mostly." She clears her throat. "What about you guys?"

"Long story short: Agatha saved me from being friendless in middle school when Sammie was busy being annoying, and she and Lindsay were a package deal. Sammie's the boy next door that I've known forever."

"That had to be nice, growing up next to your best friend," she says.

"It definitely has its perks." I absently stretch my leg into the space between us, nearly reaching Talia as she scoots herself more directly in front of me. Her lips look dry but soft in this light. I quickly look away.

"Is one of those perks having an automatic meet-cute story to tell your grandchildren?" she teases, eyes flicking to the ground.

"Sorry to disappoint the hypothetical grandkids, but Sammie has been a little busy with a very different love story. I mean, you noticed how he reacted when Lindsay came out in that dress, right?" I instantly regret bringing up the dress as I feel my cheeks heat. I need uglier friends.

"I noticed *you* noticing it." I can't tell if she means me noticing Sammie or me noticing Lindsay.

"Sammie and I are just friends," I say quickly, trying not to choke on the words.

"That's probably for the best. He has enough to worry about with Wes stepping up his game. I can't imagine that love triangle turning into a square," she says, eyes still on the ground.

"Is that the only reason you're asking?" I say boldly. She flinches, finally looking up.

"What do you mean?" There's an edge to her voice, and she straightens, leaning less on the wall.

"Oh, nothing." I laugh nervously. "Just checking that you don't have a crush on Sammie or anything. You two *were* talking up a storm," I say awkwardly, internally cringing.

"A storm about . . . mathematicians overlooked by Euro-centric history?"

"That's basically foreplay for Sammie." *Kill me.*

"Oh—uh, no." She laughs stiffly.

I will my mouth to apologize for the awkward comment, but come up silent.

"Anyway, here's the bathroom," she says before I can fix this conversational mess, mechanically motioning to the room we've already been standing beside for several minutes. "I'll, uh, see you back out there."

She walks off quickly. I wait until I hear the front door shut before stepping into the bathroom. The tiny, sanitized space feels more costly than my entire house. I sniff the lavender soap, instantly calmed by the scent, and pull my hair back with the tie I always keep on my wrist. I meet my reflection's eyes in the mirror and sigh.

"Ophelia, you're a clown."

* * *

Hours later, after Lindsay's arms are sore from posing and Zaq's are sore from holding the camera, Sammie and I ride home, windows down, cricket songs filling our silence.

"Agatha is going to run her own modeling empire one day. The way she got Lindsay to pose and work those crowns today? I don't think Lindsay has ever 'smized' before," Sammie finally says, squinting and pursing his lips to impersonate Linds.

I laugh, swatting him until he relaxes his face again. "But do you think it's, I don't know, weird that Ags has been pushing so hard for Lindsay to run and win instead of running herself?"

"Prom queen doesn't really seem like Agatha's thing. Plus, elephant in the car: Lindsay is way more popular," he says. I shoot him a look that he barely catches, given that he's driving. "Come on, Linds just knows more people. You know I wouldn't have a shot as king, any more than you or Ags would have as queen."

Even though I agree, and have never even wanted to win prom queen, it stings a little. "Thanks."

Sammie scoffs. "Sorry. Why are you talking to me about

this though? You and Ags are the queens of gossip—just ask her."

"I don't want to make it seem like I'm judging her or think she has some kind of ulterior motive though."

"She's your best friend—just ask her."

"You know, out of context I could shoot that sentence right back at you regarding Lindsay and your *feelings*."

"Haven't you done enough meddling for the week? Do you have a quota or something?" he asks, taking a sharp turn. My shoulder knocks into the car door.

"Ow," I say, rubbing my arm. "And if you're referring to merging the Wesley groups two months before graduation, I think it's some of my finest work yet."

"All right, Rojas, I'm going to drop you off on the sidewalk if you start going around saying we're one of Wesley's groups. If anything, our friend group is totally mine."

"How, exactly? If anything, *I'm* the one who brought us all together."

"Maybe," he concedes. "But I'm clearly the glue."

"Samuel, please enlighten me." I cross my arms and lean against the window so I can get a good look at his face. The setting sun and dim streetlights glow in the spaces between his curls like soft embers beneath burning wood.

"Gladly." He nods. "You and I are obviously good friends."

"Oh, obviously."

"Agatha and I are tight enough that she turns to me for help with bra shopping when you're too busy talking to your plants in your backyard," he continues, and if he weren't driving, I'd throw one of his encyclopedias at him. "And then, of course, Lindsay and I have our tragically slow-burn, but still budding, romance." He gives me a quick, satisfied smile. "Get it? Budding?" He leans over a little, eyes still on the road, and lowers his voice. "Because you like flowers."

I push him back toward his seat. "I got it. But I've identified a few problems with your theory."

"All good theories are controversial." He beckons for me to proceed.

"Well, for starters, you went bra shopping with Ags *one time* when I had pneumonia and you two were already at the mall."

"A minor discrepancy."

"Secondly, I would not precisely call your 'budding romance' with Lindsay something that is unifying the group because, my third point, where does Wesley come in?"

"Easy," he says as we stop at a red light. I try not to let the color remind me of Talia's nails. "Wesley is my counter-opposite in the group."

"Please explain what the hell a 'counteropposite' is?"

"Wesley is quiet and likes to drive a fancy car and doo-dle with his beefy arms. I am loud and use my spindly legs to dance and drive my admittedly cheaper, but ultimately cooler and more hipster-esque, car," he finishes as we turn down our street.

"You've been talking a lot about Wesley's beefiness lately."

"Attacking me personally won't invalidate my theory, Ophelia."

"Well, I can't argue with that foolproof logic."

"Thank you." He smiles as he parks between our houses and kills the engine. "Don't hold this against me, but I actually think Talia and Zaq are pretty cool. Even though I'm pretty sure Zaq wants to kick my ass half the time."

"Don't worry, that's just a requirement for being in the group." He hugs me goodbye, then flips me off, and I laugh my way out of the car and up my front yard.

"Mom? Dad?" I call out as I step inside the house, wary of the unlocked front door combined with all the turned-off lights.

"Up here!" Mom replies from upstairs. I lock the door behind me and fumble my way through the dark.

"Front door was unlocked," I say as I give them both a kiss on their cheeks. They're sitting up in bed, watching a monotone British documentary on Fidel Castro. Mom's glued to the television, but Dad is scrolling through recipes on his phone. I can't tell if he's genuinely uninterested because of the documentary's seemingly impersonal framing and narration, or feigning it because of his own complicated diasporic feelings about Cuban history.

"I wasn't sure if you took your keys to school," Mom says before pausing the documentary. "How did the photo shoot go?"

"It was fun." I smile and Mom reciprocates. "Lindsay looked . . . nice."

"Is she any closer to picking her date?"

"Still could be anyone's game."

"Chismosas," Dad mutters, still on his phone.

"And what about you?" Mom asks cautiously. "Still no one you're interested in?"

"Mo-om," I whine. Dad looks up, clearly fearing an argument brewing.

"I'm sorry, honey," she says. "But you've always got some little crush fluttering around in that heart of yours. I'm just surprised you don't have your eye on anyone, that's all. What about that boy Zaq you mentioned. He is spending time with you and your friends now, right?"

I want to roll my eyes, but to be fair Zaq *is* cute. I remember having a brief, teeny, tiny crush on him when I ran into him and Agatha once during sophomore year, but I was swiftly distracted by a guy in my English class, Henri, who could quote most of *Twelfth Night* verbatim. Liking Zaq now would make me a hypocrite for judging the intra-group drama of the Lindsay-Wesley-Sammie love triangle. I pointedly don't think about Talia.

"She could always fight Lindsay for Samuel," Dad says before I can reply to Mom. I throw the pillow by his feet at him. "Aye, cálmate!" he laughs, tossing the pillow back to the end of the bed. "I like Samuel; he's a good young man. What makes that roja better than my Rojas?"

I roll my eyes, although in this light I doubt he notices. "I agree with your father," Mom starts. "Plus, you know how much we love the Nasars. It'd be nice to know we wouldn't hate your in-laws." They're both smiling, looking like giddy chismoses rather than parents. I know I should play along with their teasing, laugh and promise to marry Sammie as soon as Lindsay is done with him, but I can't help myself.

"What if I didn't end up with someone like Sammie?" I ask, enunciating each word slowly as I force them from my mouth.

"No entiendo," Dad says, sitting up straighter as he senses the seriousness in my voice better than Mom, as per usual. "What do you mean?"

I take a deep breath. "How would you feel if I didn't end up with a person like Sammie?" I wait a beat before adding, "Or like Wesley?"

"You can date a short boy," Mom jokes before noticing neither Dad nor I am laughing along. Her eyebrows crease in concern, her face pale in the frozen television light.

"I'm not sure we know what you're asking us, mija," Dad says.

"Never mind," I say, equal parts relieved and disappointed. "I'm just tired. All the stress of prom planning has been getting to me," I lie, waving off the implications of my questions.

Mom's concern deflates as she wishes me a good night and unpauses her documentary. But I feel Dad's dark eyes watch me as I leave the room, closing the door and conversation behind me.

I scrub away what's left of my makeup in the steaming

shower, feeling oddly drawn back to my parents' room. I stay firm in the hot water though, letting the worry fade as I aimlessly run my finger through the condensation gathering on the lavender tiles.

My parents love me; I know this for sure. But I also know they love weddings and grandchildren and the expectations they have for me. They love the daughter they know, but what if I stop being that daughter?

My sweet, boy-crazy Ophelia.

I scrub and scrub until my skin feels raw and the red flush of heat and friction, alongside the water rushing down my face, hides the tears that fall of their own volition.

NINE

"Another cup?" Mrs. Nasar asks, poking her head into Sammie's room for the third time this morning. Her tunic is a soft yellow, adorned with white beading along the cuffs, and billows around her thin frame as she's hit with a gust of wind from Sammie's fan.

"I'm good, thank you," I reply, sipping the last of my chai. I'm really not a tea or coffee person, but Mrs. Nasar serves her chai with thick globs of honey and cinnamon from the local farmers market, making it my guilty pleasure. Though I'm still getting over the embarrassment of calling it chai tea until I was thirteen and one of Sammie's younger sisters, Hana, called me out, telling me I was basically saying tea-tea. Mrs. Nasar never had the heart to say anything, and Sammie thought it was too funny to put an end to.

"You're going to run up the electricity bill," Mrs. Nasar says to Sammie, yanking on his ceiling fan until it switches to a lower setting. She looks at me, sitting at Sammie's desk, where I'm highlighting passages from *Northanger Abbey*. "Look at Ophelia, taking notes and doing homework on a Saturday while you're sitting on your phone."

He tosses his phone onto his pillow. "Mujhe maaf kardo," he says. It's one of the few Urdu phrases I can recognize, but given the tight smile on his face, I can tell his request for forgiveness isn't sincere.

She ignores him, smiling at me instead as she brushes long curls out of her face. Sammie's height definitely came from his dad, but he's the spitting image of his mom. All long lashes and sharp cheekbones. She rests her hand on my shoulder gently. "Another cup? I made plenty." She grabs my cup before I can refuse, snatching Sammie's up from his side table as she passes.

He clenches his hands, suppressing a snappy comment after she leaves, only shutting the door halfway behind her. He gets up to shut the door all the way before his sister Jani walks by.

"Doors stay partially open when girls are over, lover boy," she coos, effortlessly cooler than I was at fourteen.

I turn a laugh into a cough unconvincingly.

"Keep laughing, nerd," he says as he plops back onto his bed. "That isn't even for homework, is it?"

"I'll accept your insult if you can swear to me you weren't using your phone to do history research. For fun."

He holds my gaze for a long moment before breaking. "The Inca Empire isn't nerdy, okay?" I cackle while he flips me off. "I'm compensating for my Eurocentric education. You're reading an old white lady book."

"Did you know Jane Austen called watering roses a 'heroic enjoyment of infancy'? She really was ahead of her time."

"I need new friends."

"Listen to this: 'I have no notion of loving people by halves; it is not my nature.' I'm feeling so valid right now."

Sammie groans, pulling his pillow out from behind his head and pressing it into his face. His words come out mumbled. "Is it too late to retract my commitment to North Coast?"

"Technically, no," I reply, shutting my book and lowering my voice. "But then who is going to take care of you when you get all sad and wall-punchy in college?"

Sammie lifts the pillow off his face. "Is this you attempting to segue into an emotional bonding moment about last weekend, or are you just giving me shit for it?"

"¿Por qué no los dos?" I ask. Sammie groans again, dropping the pillow. "Fine, fine. As much as I'd love to pick 'just giving you shit' . . . your Wesley jokes have been getting a little meaner lately." I pause and nod at his now-dented trash can. "Is there a correlation to last weekend's . . ."

"Lapse in judgment?"

"I was going to say minor breakdown, but that works too."

"I'm fine." He sits up, curling around his pillow in his

lap. "It was one time. I just had a bad night and got caught up in my head."

"It might make you feel better if you talk to Lindsay about all of this. Or maybe your parents, I don't know. I'm not trying to lecture, but—"

"Then don't."

I hear Mrs. Nasar downstairs, the clink of ceramic cups and hum of her talking to Sammie's dad in Urdu. Sammie always made an effort to learn basic Spanish, not just because it was a language requirement for school, but because he knew I felt lonely growing up without a real Latine community. And yeah, he's got a ton of sisters and extended family who emigrated from Pakistan a couple of generations back, but I feel a snake of guilt coil around my stomach knowing I couldn't speak a word of Urdu if I tried.

"Can I ask you something?" I break the silence. He nods. "Would you have talked to me about how upset you were if I hadn't seen you?" He starts to sigh and shifts on his bed, so I quickly add, "Or talked to anyone? Your parents or your sisters?"

Sammie runs a hand over his face before leaning over to check that neither his mom nor any of his other sisters are coming. "O, we're not all besties with our parents."

I wilt. "I know."

He straightens his back, his face clear of any of its usual amusement. "So you know they don't want to hear about some pointless drama."

"I was just trying to—"

"Understand, I know," he finishes for me, slumping. I bite my nail. "I get it, you love telling your parents all our chisme and talking about your feelings. But that's not me. I'm fine, okay? What happened last weekend was nothing. Please, just move on."

He clears his throat as Mrs. Nasar comes back in, handing each of us a piping hot cup of chai. She offers us almond cookies on a platter that we refuse, but knowing her, she'll be back with the whole box in a few minutes. Sammie and I sip in silence.

The thing is, Sammie has to be wrong. I look at the carefully prepared cups of chai and how artfully his mom stacked those cookies for us. Maybe she's not sitting down on his floor and asking what's the latest with him and Lindsay, but his mom cares about his well-being. And I'm sure his dad does too.

Which means the problem here isn't that Sammie doesn't have a willing audience. It's that he thinks he doesn't need one.

"All right, what we're not going to do is be weird now," he finally says. He sets his cup on his side table. I curl my hands around my own so I won't move to put a coaster under his. "Anyway, don't you have to get ready for your mom's bougie English department party soon?"

"Shit." I pull my phone out of my pocket and check the time. I was supposed to head home fifteen minutes ago. "I should go. You still down to help me scout roses for everyone's corsages and boutonnieres tomorrow?"

"I am a man of my word." He takes my chai and lightly

bumps my shoulder with his before reaching around me to pick up *Northanger Abbey*. "You're only reading this to impress your mom's colleagues despite swearing you have no interest in studying English in college, aren't you?"

"Go drink your chai." I snatch the book back and race home.

❊ ❊ ❊

Ags started a group chat this morning with herself, Lindsay, Talia, and me to tell us about some big makeup sale in case we needed anything new for prom, so I figured why not send them a selfie in my Sophisticated Ophelia outfit? I'd normally send a picture to Ags and Linds anyway.

It took me a few tries to get a good shot that wasn't embarrassingly blurry, sitting in the back seat of Mom's car, but I finally get one as we park. I stare at it for longer that I'd like to admit, worrying my eyes are uneven or my smile looks too forced, but we're here, so it's now or never.

I slip my phone into my purse after sending the photo and straighten my dress as we get out of the car, determined to make it through tonight without feeling like a baby or a disappointment. Or both.

I managed to get out of coming to these events for the past two years, but couldn't find an excuse this time around. At least this year I'm almost the same age as some of the attendees, so it'll be like practice for the fall.

My pale blue dress with the white collar studded with tiny, flower-shaped pearls shifts in the early evening breeze.

I run my hands over the several buttons lining the front of the chest.

Feeling girly and pretty, but still classy, I take the bottle of wine my parents brought from my dad as he knocks on the front door. Mom's colleague, an older Black man named David, opens the door, and I'm met with the sight of dozens of mingling college students behind him, all wearing casual ripped jeans, band tees, and the occasional yoga-pants-and-sweatshirt combo.

"So glad you could make it," David says as he pulls Mom into a hug and shakes Dad's hand. He hugs me too, and despite knowing him since I was a kid and feeling comfortable around him, I'm annoyed Dad gets away with a handshake whereas I'd be rude for rejecting the hug. "Ophelia, it's great to see you. What grade are you in now, tenth?"

Dad stifles a laugh. I forcefully hand him back the wine. "I'm actually a senior."

"No way!" He gasps in that classic I'm An Adult And Cannot Process You Aging At The Same Rate As Me For Some Reason way and turns to Mom. "Stella, you didn't tell me she was getting so big."

"I know, it's astonishing," she sighs.

"David, where should I put this?" Dad interrupts, lifting the wine.

"Oh, let's go ask Susan where would be best," David says as he beckons Dad to follow him, chatting about how potent the wine is or how dried the grapes were or whatever it is people actually say about wine, leaving Mom and me in the foyer.

She's quickly swarmed with greetings. Students and faculty alike crowd us. And I know she's not forgetting me and no one here is ignoring me. But I wonder if we looked more alike, if people would stop and ask if I was her kid rather than another student waiting for the chance to speak with the illustrious Professor Rojas.

I step into the open living room and quickly spot a table covered with chips and salsa, crackers and cheese, and fruit platters. I'm stacking up my plate with watermelon cubes, hungry after an afternoon surviving solely off chai and Sammie's sarcasm, when someone bumps into my shoulder.

I spin around, annoyed, only to see an attractive white boy standing beside a shorter blond girl with freckles. The boy adjusts his thick hipster glasses and smiles at me. "Sorry about that. Gotta get to the salsa before people start double dipping."

"No problem," I say, praying my tight voice doesn't betray how cute I think he is.

"I'm Jeremiah." He sticks out his hand, and I shake it despite feeling my palms begin to sweat. "This is Coleen." He nods to the girl beside him, who smiles and takes a sip of her drink.

"I'm Ophelia," I reply, instantly regretting it. Their eyes widen like they're children on Christmas morning before they glance at each other as if to say *did you hear that?*

"Dude, are you Professor Rojas's daughter?" Coleen asks

excitedly. "Your mom is, like, the *coolest* professor I've ever had."

"Seriously." Jeremiah nods in agreement.

"That's me," I admit, already regretting the recognition I craved just minutes before. The last thing I want to be is the professor's little kid, especially in front of a cute boy. I wonder if I could bring up *Northanger Abbey* now. I'll even recite some Blake if that's what it takes to move on.

"You know, I actually get the name thing now," Jeremiah says before I can speak.

"The name thing? Oh yeah, well, you know my mom's super into Shakespeare, and she always loved Ophelia—"

"No, not *your* name. Your mom's last name. I mean, she's white as hell," he says in a way that feels like he's ignoring that he's also *white as hell*. "It makes more sense looking at you."

"Jeremiah," Coleen huffs, rolling her pale eyes.

"What?" He furrows his brows at her. "What, do you want me to pretend not to see color or some shit?"

"It's okay," I lie, voice weak. I don't have the energy to play the whole Yes, My Mom And I Have Different Skin And Hair Colors, What A Concept game today. Not to mention explaining the vast array of Latine skin tones and hair types in the world. "I look a bit more like my dad."

Jeremiah nods, looking satisfied. I grab some punch, which I hope is virgin, and follow them to some seats off to the side. The living room is crowded with mismatched tables and sofas, and most of the attendees are clustered in little groups, snacking and chatting. It's been so long since I've come to one of these, I guess I played up the age difference in my head. Swap out the classical music David is playing for some rap or EDM and it might as well be one of Linds's kickbacks.

"You're older than I thought you'd be," Jeremiah says as we sit, and I'm painfully aware of the way my dress is riding up my thighs. He seems to be too. "The way your mom talks about you, I thought you were, like, twelve."

I laugh nervously. "I'm graduating high school in a few months." I hoped I'd sound mature, but it comes out defensive. "I didn't know she talked about me that much."

"Oh yeah, she bragged about you and your rose gardening all the time," Coleen chimes in. "Every time we read anything with floral imagery, she had to remind us." Her words sound a little catty, but her smile says otherwise. I watch her eyes flicker between me and Jeremiah. "Sounds like you've got an impressive green thumb."

"She also talked about your 'little crushes,'" Jeremiah adds. My bite of watermelon lodges itself in my throat, and it takes several seconds of coughing before it plops wetly out of my mouth and onto my plate. I don't even have time to be embarrassed about it.

"What?"

"Oh, leave her alone," Coleen says, but it's not very convincing. "She never said anything bad, just mentioned you being a big romantic—and not in the literary sense." She laughs at her joke, and I'm reminded why I'm staying away from this field of study.

"So, are you coming here next year?" Jeremiah asks.

"No, I'm going to North Coast for botany," I reply, grateful for the change of subject.

"That's a major?" he asks, astonished. I nod. "That's so sick."

"But a shame," Coleen says. "We could seriously use another Rojas around here next quarter. The entire English department is teaming up with the drama department to host a series of Shakespearean adaptations. We're actually working on *Hamlet*, funnily enough."

Jeremiah rolls his eyes and makes an angry, throaty noise. "That sounds cool," I say. "Are you doing anything special with it?"

"Oh, just wait until you hear this," Jeremiah says. I look at Coleen, confused.

She ignores him. "My team wants to cast Hamlet as a girl. You know, make him and Ophelia lesbians." She makes a weird, shaking motion with her hands when she says "lesbians."

My heartbeat picks up. "Oh?"

"Yeah, it was our director's idea. She's the head of our school's gay club, or whatever, and wanted to play up all the homoerotic potential. I'm cool with it, you know, 'cause it'll make us stand out and probably attract publicity around campus."

"Oh come on," Jeremiah groans. "The only reason your team agreed was because you guys know more people will show up if they get to see some girl-on-girl action onstage.

Plus, if anyone criticizes the production, your director can just blame it on homophobia instead of her shit directing." He downs the rest of his drink.

"You're just mad that your proposal to make the play take place after World War II wasn't selected by the committee," Coleen teases while I try to calm my breathing. Suddenly, the chatter in the room sounds like buzzing.

"Whatever," he scoffs. "I'm just pissed that the committee is pandering to a bunch of queers instead of focusing on *actual* creative ideas. Seriously, it's just a bunch of PC bullshit. Besides getting to watch two chicks rub up against each other onstage in tight corsets, what's the point of making the characters a couple of dy—"

I'm not sure what happens. One second, I'm sitting beside Jeremiah and Coleen, feeling his leg press against my bare skin as he speaks. The next, I'm standing and he's cursing me out, soaked in punch.

"What the fuck is wrong with you? Jesus Christ." He flicks his hands, and red splatters against the floor. The scent is sweet and fruity, floating off his white shirt.

"Hamlet would be a great lesbian," I say before running out of the room and out the front door. I feel eyes on me as I leave, only realizing how quiet the room was when I hear Coleen call after me. In anger or concern, I'm not sure.

My forehead is pressed against Mom's car window, and I finally let go of my now-empty cup. I don't hear anyone come outside, but I still don't jump when I feel a familiar hand on my shoulder.

"¿Qué pasó con ese gringo?" Dad asks evenly. "Did that boy do something?"

I ignore his questions. "Is Mom mad?" I ask, and my voice comes out so high, I'm surprised it doesn't crack. He pulls lightly on my shoulder, forcing me to face him.

"Mija, what happened?" He takes a shaky breath. "Did he touch—"

"No! No. I'm fine," I lie. "I just, I really don't want to—can we go home?"

He doesn't look satisfied, but when the first tear spills over, he softens his expression and nods. Promising to be right back, he runs inside. I count the seconds until he returns with his jacket and a frown.

"Where's Mom?" I ask as he unlocks the car. I hesitantly get in the passenger seat.

"David offered to give her a ride home," he says as he starts the car. The hum of the engine fills the car's silence, and I pick at a drop of dried punch on the hem of my dress. I wonder if Agatha knows how to remove stains.

"Is she mad?" I ask again once he starts driving.

"She's not happy," he admits, sighing. I watch him out of the corner of my eye. Dad's skin has never looked more lined with wrinkles. I swear every day his thick, once dark, head of hair and thin beard grows peppered with more gray. Even now, he smells like coffee, the kind he buys at the mercado forty minutes away because he says real Cubanos can't drink just any old bean water. I've always considered myself more like Mom—romantic, sarcastic, honest—but something in his exhausted eyes makes me pause. He looks the way I feel.

"I'm sorry."

"I trust you had a good reason," he says, always too generous to his only daughter. "I'm sure Mom does too."

I stare at the street, empty and pocked with shadows between the reach of the streetlamps. They shine so brightly, bathing the asphalt in harsh orange.

He takes a hand off the steering wheel and rests it, palm up and open, on the divider. I place my hand in his. "Tú eres mi luz, lo sabes, ¿verdad?" *You are my light; you know that, right?*

I nod, tears threatening my eyes again. I'm lucky to have the parents I do. Agatha, Lindsay, and Sammie get along with their parents just fine. But like Sammie implied earlier, they think I'm weird for telling mine about my love life (or lack thereof), my friends' drama, my bad grades, and bad days. I tell my parents everything.

Almost everything.

I never found our relationship weird or unusual. I always feel like I'm bursting at the seams with feeling, always physically incapable of keeping emotion in. I've needed confidants from the time I could first speak and realized my heart would chase after every pretty thing—every pretty boy—it saw. So who better to fill the role than the people who brought me into this world?

It's that trust, that instinctual need to share with them, that tells me I owe Dad some explanation, even if he doesn't ask for one.

"That boy, Jeremiah . . . ," I begin as we stop at a light. The car turns scarlet in the glow of the red light as I turn to Spanish because, somehow, it feels right to. "Dijo insultos homofóbicos."

Dad's grip on the wheel tightens. He inhales and removes his hand from my shoulder.

"Thank you for telling me. I'll talk to your mom tomorrow," he says.

"Wait—" I say. "Please, just . . . don't tell her."

He looks at me for a beat, eyes searing into mine, before nodding once.

The light changes. We don't talk the rest of the drive home.

TEN

My alarm for Sunday morning gardening woke me up hours ago, but I promptly shut it off and tried to fall back asleep. I heard Mom come home a few hours after Dad and me last night, and I'm in no mood to learn what their hushed whispering means. So it's not hard to imagine my annoyance when I'm in that foggy, not-quite-asleep-not-quite-awake state, thinking about what the floral arrangements at prom will be like, when my bedroom door flies open.

"Rise and shine, O. I've got things to see and people to do," Sammie sings as he tosses my curtains open, allowing the bright morning sun in.

"It burns," I whimper, pulling my sheets over my head and burrowing deeper.

"Wakey, wakey."

"What awful thing did I do in a previous life to deserve this?"

"I'm a ray of sunshine brightening your morning, so shut

it." He yanks my blankets off my body, folding them at the end of my bed before sitting atop them. "I'm also requesting your forgiveness. Although, why the hell are you still sleeping? Aren't there thirsty roses and thirstier boys you should be attending to?"

"We really need to talk about your apologies," I moan, avoiding the question. I try to dig deeper into my pillow, but it's unfortunately impenetrable. Eventually I give up and turn over.

Sammie's curls are long and loose around his face, shining with dampness. He smells good, better than usual, like he doused himself with his best cologne. And he's wearing a dark color for once, a black T-shirt that deepens his eyes. "So, I need your help winning the love of my life."

"It's nine A.M."

"No, it's *romantic*," he replies.

"Elaborate."

"On the definition of romantic? Well, well, well. How the tables have turned."

"Samuel."

"Okay, okay. So, you know how I agreed to help you with corsage crafting today?" he asks slowly, long fingers playing at a loose thread on my sheets.

"I remember you *volunteering* earlier this week."

"Okay, so about that . . . ," he begins, then stands to look at photos of us from our middle school graduation plastered on the wall above my dresser. "Damn, I really looked bad with braces, didn't I?"

"Sammie."

"You didn't look too hot either, but maybe that had more to do with those awful highlights you begged your mom for. Seriously, light hair was not the move for you."

"For the love of all that is good, please tell me why you're in my bedroom insulting me this early in the morning." Before he can even fully open his mouth, I add, "And don't you dare ask what time of day I'd prefer you to insult me at." He closes his mouth, lips still curled in amusement.

"Lindsay asked me to come to the twins' soccer game after her morning mass," he admits, moving back to the bed. "She's never invited me before. This is a good sign. You get it, don't you?"

I do, unfortunately. The amount of times I ditched Sammie last year to watch Lucas's games more than cancels out him bailing on me today. Still, last night left me in a funk, and I wish he would've at least let me sleep through this betrayal.

"Go," I sigh, waving him off. "Have fun. Fall in love. Eat a snow cone in my honor."

He leans over, ruffling my hair in a brotherly manner. It makes me feel even worse. "You're the best."

I check my phone after he leaves. Talia texted me a few minutes ago, asking for pictures of our government notes that she missed a few weeks back. As I dig through my backpack to find them, I feel slightly relieved that she texted. After Friday and Saturday, I needed this tiny victory.

I send Talia the pictures, getting ready to crawl back into bed when Dad walks by my open door. Damn you, Sammie.

"You're awake," he says, leaning in the doorway with crossed arms. "Are you feeling okay?"

"You know, *most* teenagers sleep in this late on Sundays."

"You're not most teenagers."

"I don't have the time to unpack how much I hate that statement."

He laughs, and tension I hadn't noticed in my shoulders until now softens. "I thought I heard Samuel up here."

"You really should be more concerned about me having strange boys in my room. Honestly, Sammie should be banned as punishment."

"He woke you up, didn't he?"

I drop my backpack and flop into bed. "I'm going back to sleep."

Dad clears his throat. "Your mom wants to talk to you when she gets home. She went out to brunch with David and Susan to celebrate the end of the quarter. They should be done in an hour or so."

I watch my finger as I trace the outlines of petals on my duvet. "Is she mad?"

"She'd be less mad if you told her what you told me. But she said that boy is graduating next quarter and isn't taking any more of her classes."

"Will she get in trouble for what I did though?" I ask, unsure if pouring punch on someone's head counts as aggravated assault. Dad's lack of pressing concern, as a paralegal, comforts me.

He steps into my room and kisses the top of my head. "No te preocupes," he says. *Don't worry.* "She'll be fine."

"Okay," I reply, feeling small.

There's no chance I'll fall back asleep now. When Dad leaves, I grab my phone again. Talia thanked me for the notes, and Agatha texted, asking how my roses are doing.

I need to get out of here, but I can't be with someone who knows me enough to notice how upset I am. So I send two texts, one saying *they're looking perfect!* and the other saying *Could I pull you away from studying for a bit?*

❋ ❋ ❋

"I feel so cheated. This is the second time I've picked you up, and I still haven't seen your garden," Talia complains. Her wet hair is up in a bun, and she smells like Irish Spring bodywash. I tug on the frilly ends of my navy romper decorated with pink tulips as I adjust my seat belt.

"Sorry," I reply, and leave it at that. I know Mom wouldn't chew me out in front of a guest if she came home, but the idea of introducing Talia to my parents right now makes my stomach queasy.

"It's all right." She shrugs as she drives away from my house. "I'll see the big reveal at prom, I guess."

"So what's the plan for today?" I ask, pretending I'm not the one who invited Talia to hang out. She looks at me out of the corner of her eye, clearly unable to ignore that fact.

"Well, I was originally going to go hiking before I got to studying."

"I love hiking!" I lie. "Hiking sounds great."

"Really?" Talia looks at my outfit skeptically.

No. "Yeah! You know how I feel about flowers. I love nature. Can't get enough of it."

"Well, I showered already, but I can just shower again tonight, I guess." *Do not think about her showering.* "I should turn around so you can pick up a change of clothes though."

"No!" I yell. Talia jolts. "I mean, uh, we don't want to waste any more time and miss the prime hiking hours. Wouldn't want to go when it's hot out, right?"

She purses her lips. I look away. "Good point. You can just borrow something from me, since my house is on the way." She turns on the radio, and we hum along to indie pop songs, both of us singing in that awkward talk-speak way you do in elementary school for recitals. Guess we're not at the Belting Badly And Comfortably stage of friendship yet.

The drive is shorter than I expected. It feels weird to think Talia's only lived fifteen minutes away all this time. Her house is small, square, and painted a rusty orange that reminds me of half of Sammie's wardrobe.

"Sorry in advance for my messy room," she says as we step inside.

"I should be the one saying sorry for imposing," I reply, and run my eyes over the family photos in the hall. They're mostly childhood Talia, a few with a man who I assume is her dad.

"Please," she scoffs. "At least now I have a hiking buddy. Zaq always refuses to come with me. He doesn't like to get sweaty."

"What about Wesley?"

"Him too," she laughs. "They usually ditch me to doodle."

"I know the feeling," I reply, thinking of Lindsay and Sammie.

We reach the end of the hall, where the final door is painted off-white with a red *T* in the center. I don't mean to hold my breath as she opens the door, but when the room inside is revealed, I exhale deeply.

Like the rest of the house, it's small, but the belongings scattered about make it look well lived in rather than cluttered. Clothes are strewn across her bed, but yellow sheets and a white comforter peek out from beneath the piles. All but one wall are painted dark green, the last one paler than the rest. The wall across from the door catches my eye first, as it's covered in photographs with sparse spots where only tape and bits of torn pictures remain. The only things on the palest wall are a few doodles that look fresh compared to the rest of the room, most signed with a *Z* and a few others signed with a *W*.

"Like I said, it's a mess in here," she laughs with a self-conscious shrug. "I wasn't expecting company."

"I like it," I say, hating the breathiness of my voice. "These photos are so cute." I motion to a shot of Talia, Zaq, and Wesley that looks like it was taken last year during spirit week. They're all wearing our school colors, red and black, but Zaq also has bright red streaks painted on his cheeks. My eyes drift to a photo sitting on the dresser below it, a faded shot of childhood Talia and another little girl.

"Is that you and Dani?" I ask, fingering the edge of the photo.

"Yeah," she sighs, eyes lingering on an empty spot on the wall where only a strip of tape remains. "Yeah," she repeats, louder, eyes focusing. "That was from Noche Buena when I was like, hmm, maybe six?" She points at their matching red dresses. "She's a year older, but my abuela loved dressing us like twins."

I'm ready to turn away, scared of overstepping, but then I see a picture that's still on the wall of her and Dani bordering a third girl who doesn't look anything like either of them. She's got dark red hair, much deeper than Lindsay's, and has both of her pale arms slung around Talia's and Dani's shoulders.

"Who's that?" I ask, but when I look at Talia, she's frowning. I instantly wish I could take back my curiosity.

She turns away before replying. "She's an old friend. The one who pierced my nose, actually." She tosses clothes off her bed, searching for something. "This should fit you," she says, handing me a graphic tee with the Puerto Rican flag on it and a pair of leggings that look twice the length of my legs. Her wide eyes scan my body but don't meet my eyes.

"Thanks," I reply, thoughts racing to catch up with what she just said.

We stare at each other before she jolts with realization. "Oh right, you can change in here. I'll go change in the bathroom." She grabs a pair of leggings and a green tank top from her bed before leaving the room without another word.

I wonder if that means anything, her leaving while I stay

here to change. Lindsay strips in front of Ags and me regularly, often in spite of my insistence I can leave and give her privacy. Agatha never complains, never seems to mind. But my eyes always feel glued to the carpet to avoid her bare form while Ags still chats like normal.

Sometimes I wonder if I missed out on learning these girl codes when I was younger, just me, Sammie, and my parents. There are all these unspoken rules that I feel I'm still catching up on, always seven steps behind everyone else.

I quickly slip out of my clothes, taking a moment to stand there, in Talia's bedroom, naked down to my bra and underwear. A chill runs up my spine as I take a deep breath, goose bumps running up my bare arms.

"You done?" Talia asks, knocking on the door.

"One sec!" I shout back, hastily throwing on Talia's clothes, trying not to think of them pressing against my bare skin as they previously have hers. As I finish, I ball up my own clothes and hug them against my chest.

"Ready!" I call. Talia opens the door and smiles as she tosses the jeans and shirt she was wearing earlier onto the mound of clothing on her bed.

"You can put that in the car if you want," she says, pointing to the clothes I'm still clutching like a security blanket. I nod, momentarily unable to speak.

I follow her out of her room, keeping my eyes on the walls to get one last look at her childhood photos and definitely not so I won't look at Talia's body in those leggings. We get to the front door, and she motions for me to give her a second, jogging toward the other side of the house.

I hear tidbits of Spanish floating through the thin walls, Talia and her father, I guess. I didn't even realize he was home. And maybe it's the wall dulling their tones, but their words sound empty, hollow. I can't imagine my parents and me ever sounding like that, even when just talking about mundane things like needing more toothpaste or passively commenting on the weather. Then I think of seeing Mom's disappointed face for the first time after what happened last night, and it feels a little more imaginable.

❊ ❊ ❊

"So what's the deal with Sammie and Lindsay?" Talia asks as we begin our incline. She brought us to a hiking trail near the outskirts of town where my elementary school once came on a field trip. I suppress the memory of Sammie threatening to put worms in my lunch if I didn't stop ogling our classmate Milo Wu, who picked me a poppy on the way to the junior trail.

"What do you mean?" My breath is already coming in shallow and dry, and we've barely begun walking.

"Well, you said you guys have been friends for a while, and feelings like theirs don't just appear out of nowhere." *They don't?* "But they're also both so . . . what's the word?"

"Bold? Charismatic? Flirtatious?"

She laughs. "Yes. Yes to all of that."

"I'm going to let you in on a little secret," I say, leaning toward her conspiratorially and lowering my voice. "It's all a front."

"Their feelings or their cockiness?"

"The latter," I reply. "They're both the type to talk about masturbation or sex without a hint of shame, but ask them about their feelings and they promptly shut down."

"They'd probably save themselves a lot of time if they were more honest about their feelings. They'd save Wesley plenty."

"Ah, so this isn't just chisme you're looking for." I point my finger at her. "You're sneaky."

She mock gasps and presses a hand against her chest, her tank top darkening in the spots where it touches her sweaty skin. I trip over loose gravel.

She reaches over a hand to steady me, but I quickly brush her off. "I'm good." I fan the back of my neck. "Just a little hot. As for Lindsay and Sammie though, trust me, Agatha and I agree. I think they're just scared of being that real with each other, you know? Risking their relationship changing and all that. Even though they obviously both know how the other one feels."

"I get it," she reassures me. "Even if you're close, going from friends to dating is so scary. Just admitting how you feel is such a gamble. But it's nice when you find people you don't have to worry about that with." We take a turn around a bend, and I'm grateful to see the ground flatten out a bit. At least the fresh air is crisp in my lungs, even as I heave it in ungracefully. "I mean, like, when you can be honest with someone, completely honest, and you trust them not to bail on you for being real." Her voice gets floaty, eyes glazed and staring far off toward the tree line. She recovers immediately, snapping back so quickly I may have just imagined that look on her face. "Not just about romantic feelings, of course. Just, people you can be up-front with."

"Yeah, that's the best," I reply awkwardly.

"You've got that with your friends though, right?" she asks, adjusting her bun as a coil of hair escapes from her scrunchie.

I hesitate, only for a second as I catch my breath, but that second hangs heavy on my chest as I half-heartedly say, "Yeah."

She pops her eyebrow, clearly having noticed the moment of uncertainty.

"It's just . . . ," I begin too quickly, words lost before I can even think of them. I start over slowly, careful not to let the words pour out too suddenly. It's easier now that the trail is inclining again. "I've known them for so long. And they know me. We repeat stories and anecdotes and finish each other's sentences."

She smiles. "That sounds nice. I love Zaq and Wes, but we don't have that much history."

"Yeah, it is nice." I pause, collect myself, and maneuver around my thoughts. "But sometimes, when you've known someone for years and they build up this image of you, it's hard to talk about things that mess with that image. It feels like you'd be breaking some bond of trust between you and that person by being different than you were before. I don't

just mean subtle, slow changes. I mean, like, the big things that they never saw coming." I inhale long and slow, the words suddenly exhausting me more than the hike. "Do you know what I mean?"

"Completely." She nods, her eyes so wide that she almost looks frightened.

I wait a moment before asking what's been on my mind since we left her house, the moment too perfect to let it pass. "Were Dani and that girl from the photo like that for you?"

"Like what? People I could be honest with or people I worried about being honest with?"

I wipe sweat, and probably a layer of foundation, off my forehead. "Either."

She stops to retie her sneaker, propping her foot up on a rock. When she rises, her eyes look glossy. "That other girl was the first. Dani was the latter."

"Can I ask what happened?"

She doesn't reply right away, but we keep moving. We come across a bench overlooking a grassy area where a family is playing a game of soccer. Talia nods to the bench, and we sit. For a few seconds, the crunch of gravel, our heavy breathing, and the family's laughter are the only sounds between us.

She runs her hands over her thighs. "Her name was Victoria, but Dani and I called her Tori. Actually, Dani called us her papas." She snorts and smiles wider when she sees my confused expression. "It's silly. I'm Ta-lia and she was To-ri, so we were Ta-To. Like po-Ta-To. Papas, potatoes." She laughs even harder, and I'm torn between feeling grateful I get to see her this happy and feeling like I'm third wheeling with her and her memories.

"Anyway," she continues, laughter settling, "we did everything together. Dani was older, so she was like our ringleader, but when she got busy with high school, Tori and I started hanging out just us two." She hesitates, watching the family as one of the kids scores a goal and the father hoists her onto his shoulders. "We got . . . close."

"Close how?"

"We shared clothes, slept in the same bed at sleepovers, had secret matching rings we didn't tell Dani about. We'd sneak over to each other's houses when we had nightmares and pierced each other's noses." She touches her nose ring almost subconsciously, fingers barely grazing the metal. "She started off as Dani's friend, but in the end, she was more mine than Dani's."

"I'm guessing Dani didn't like that," I say.

"No." Talia smiles again, but sadly. Her lips look torn between turning up or down. "Dani *really* didn't like that."

"So what happened? With Tori, I mean. Did you stop being friends just because Dani was jealous?"

"Not exactly." She sighs, knee bouncing. In a moment of adrenaline, I reach my hand out to touch hers on the bench, barely skimming the tips of her fingers before nodding her on.

"Tori's mom got a better job offer in another town. They were set to move about a month before we started high school. At that point, Dani was always busy with her new, older friends, so I didn't expect her to show up the day that

Tori was leaving." Talia looks down at her hands and picks at a layer of her vibrant nail polish. "You know, Dani was the one who bought me this nail polish color. When our abuela passed away, she left us each a brooch shaped like a rose." I perk at the mention of roses, and Talia's quick smile tells me she noticed. "The first time you told me about your roses, I immediately thought of our brooches. Dani's is blue and silver, and mine is red and gold, so Dani bought us matching sparkly nail polish in the same colors. I hardly even know where the brooch is anymore, but the nail polish stuck for some reason." She peels off the entire coat of red polish on her pointer finger, letting it flutter away in the breeze. "Isn't it funny how some things become routine like that?"

I think of my clothes. My roses. My friends. My crushes. "Yeah."

Talia exhales, seeming to come to some conclusion. "Dani walked in on Tori kissing me goodbye."

"Oh." My stomach drops. Here it is, the story she began all those months ago.

"Someone let her in hoping to surprise Tori before she left. We didn't hear her coming, even after she opened the door. We just heard it slam shut and saw her racing down their front yard from the window."

Talia looks at me, eyebrows turned up in question. Her knee is bouncing faster, and she's already peeled off another two nails' worth of polish. I stare back, unsure what she's waiting for, my heartbeat pounding faster as I feel myself lean forward.

My reaction, I realize, freezing. She doesn't know how I'll feel about her having kissed another girl.

Which means she doesn't remember Lindsay's party like I do.

"What did Dani do?" I ask, hiding my disappointment because I don't want her to perceive it as discomfort.

She stares at me for a second longer before looking away again. "Tori and I never finished our goodbye. I knew Dani and our family, and knew she wouldn't keep the kiss a secret. By the time I got home, my dad and tía already knew. Dani's mom stopped letting her come around, not that Dani seemed to want anything to do with me anymore. My dad never talked to me about it, but I could feel him watching me around the house. It was like he wasn't sure who I was anymore."

"I'm so sorry," I say, because what else can I. This explains Dani's thinly veiled callousness, her curiosity toward what Talia and I were doing together when we ran into her, the way Talia and her dad spoke when we were leaving.

"It's okay," she says, like she knows it isn't but accepted it long ago. "My dad stopped being weird about it after a while, and we were never close to start with. I just lived with him because I didn't want to move to Seattle with my mom after the divorce and leave my family behind." She laughs a little bitterly. "Lot of good that did me."

"Does your mom know about Tori and your family?"

"She does, but she didn't care the way the people in my dad's family did. She was actually pretty cool about it, and so

❀ 133 ❀

were my grandma and grandpa on her side when they heard. They had it pretty rough as an interracial couple back in the day. Knowing that and that the people who stopped wanting me around after finding out about Tori were the same ones vocally opposed to my dad marrying a Black woman when they were still together, my mom said she'd never want to put me or my future partners through the same bullshit." She lets out a long, slow exhale. "I apologized to Dani *so* many times for what happened with Tori. But it was just one kiss when I was fourteen. I never apologized for kissing boys. I shouldn't have had to apologize just because she and her mom and whoever else decided somewhere along the way that I wasn't the type of girl to kiss another girl. That photo you found of me and her at Noche Buena? It was still on my wall for the longest time because I kept thinking maybe one of these days Dani and I would go back to how we used to be. I took it down after we ran into her last weekend."

"Do you and Tori still talk?" I ask. Talia stands to stretch her legs, and I mirror her, feeling stiff while her movements look effortless.

"We send each other birthday messages, and I texted her a while back to see what her college plans are, but it was hard for us to keep in touch after she moved. Her parents heard about the kiss from mine but didn't even bat an eye. She actually has a girlfriend now." She looks away as she says this, like despite their distance now, emotionally and physically, it still wounds her to know Tori's with someone else. "I keep that photo of us on my wall, even though Dani is in it, because our friendship meant a lot to me. But we both moved on."

"Good for her," I say, but my sincerity falls flat.

"Well, now that I've definitely overshared"—she laughs nervously, and it makes me wonder how long it's been since she was able to talk to someone like this, about this—"want to keep going?"

I want to say that she didn't overshare and that I'd know what that looks like because I always do it. I want to say I'm glad she trusts me enough to tell me this, even if I already knew, more or less. I want to say that I wish I could've met Tori but also that I kind of hate her but also that I hate Dani even more. I want to ask what it felt like to realize a girl's lips could be just as nice as a boy's, that for some people maybe they all taste the same when your eyes are closed, and to know if it was scary or exciting or felt like scratching a bug bite after everyone told you not to.

Mostly, I want to ask if it was worth it. If that small moment between her and a girl who she shared beds and rings and nightmares with was worth losing the version of herself that her family had in mind from the time she was young, to let who she really was breathe for a minute or two.

But all I do is tighten my short ponytail and smile like the periods behind everything I ever thought about myself aren't slowly being replaced by question marks. "Yeah, let's keep going."

ELEVEN

Sammie, Ags, Wesley, and I get to school early to either congratulate or comfort Lindsay on Monday. I'm hoping it'll be the former. And not just because Agatha already printed out campaign posters and asked me to check them out post–jewelry shopping after school. Anything to stay out of the house and away from my mom.

The official ballot for prom court is being announced via our class Twitter account before homeroom, so we've been refreshing our feeds nonstop for the past ten minutes. Lindsay, whose default outfit is yoga pants and a cropped jersey, is wearing a blue sundress that I'm half convinced belongs to one of her sisters. That alone is enough to tell me this isn't just about pleasing Agatha anymore; she wants this.

"Oh my God, it's up!" Agatha screams. Lindsay gasps and reaches for Ags's phone. Their eyes race across the screen. "You made it!" Ags grabs Linds, and they start jumping up and down together, chanting, "Yay! Yay! Yay! Yay!"

Danica Peters passes by, eyes downcast. I guess winning Best Hair doesn't guarantee a shot at winning prom queen. If it's any consolation, the video she posted on Instagram over the weekend of Freddy Santos serenading her with an old Beatles song was the cutest promposal I've seen this year so far.

"Did we miss it?" Zaq says as he and Talia walk over. He shuts his notebook when he catches me trying to look at the open drawing, a flash of red nails catching my eye.

"You are looking at future prom royalty!" Agatha motions dramatically to Lindsay who, to my surprise, strikes a pose and flips her hair.

"Congrats!" Talia reaches out and gently rests her hand on Lindsay's arm. I feel goose bumps break out on my own.

"All right, that does it," Agatha says, beaming brighter than her neon yellow babydoll dress. "Screw our plans, O. We are all getting celebratory pizza after school. Wesley is paying." Wesley blushes and rolls his eyes.

"I actually have plans today," he says shyly, despite the sassy eye roll.

"I'll take you, Linds," Sammie says, speaking up after standing on the sidelines for most of the debacle. "My treat."

Lindsay smiles as he wraps his arm around her shoulders and first-period bell rings. The two of them walk ahead of us while Talia waves goodbye and Zaq comforts what looks like a jealous Wesley.

Agatha sidles up next to me, hooking her arm through mine. "Guess I'm not getting free pizza today." I console her with promises to buy her some at the mall as we make our way to homeroom.

❋ ❋ ❋

On our way to chemistry, Wesley and I are in the middle of a riveting debate about what color we hope our grad robes will be—my vote is white and his is black—when I see Lucas waiting outside. He nods when he sees us approaching.

Wesley looks between me and Lucas quickly. "Do you want to talk to him?" he asks under his breath.

"Yeah," I say. "Go ahead. I'll be in in a second." I walk over to Lucas with butterflies in my stomach.

"Hey," Lucas says casually, like we ran into each other at the mall instead of outside a class we've shared all year. "I heard about Lindsay getting on the prom ballot. Tell her congrats."

I adjust my backpack on my shoulder, careful not to accidentally yank down the embroidered neckline of my blouse. "I'll let her know." Given how much my friends still hate Lucas, I'll be passing his congratulations on to Linds privately.

We stand in awkward silence for a moment, his brown eyes too heavy on my slowly heating face. I remind myself that I've kissed this boy, plenty of times, so talking to him shouldn't have me this flustered. But the memory of his lips and hands on me just makes my cheeks blaze hotter.

"Wild how soon we're graduating, huh?" he says, brushing locks of his light hair from his face with calloused hands. I nod. "Puts shit in perspective, you know? Like, I'm guessing you don't have a date for prom yet, so I was thinking . . ." He pauses to pop a vape pen into his mouth and exhale a white cloud.

I cough and wave my hands, lungs suddenly full of sickly sweet smoke. That draws Mrs. Waitley's attention, and she steps outside just as the last of the vapor dissipates. She sniffs the air once. "If you two would care to join us, we have a lot to cover today."

"Sure thing, miss," Lucas replies, fist tight around his vape. He motions for me to enter first, pocketing the pen. I take my seat and try to catch Lucas's eye before he takes his, but he doesn't look my way.

"How was your chat with Lucas?" Wesley asks as he stops doodling what looks like Lindsay on the corner of his notes.

"I—I think he may have been trying to ask me to prom."

❋ ❋ ❋

I feel Agatha's eyes on me as I flick a pair of silver hoops in the jewelry section at the mall's secondhand store.

"What?" I finally ask, nearly knocking over the display as I turn.

"Ah, so you *are* in a bad mood."

"Is it too late to change your major to psych?"

"Okay." She cocks her head. "A really bad mood."

I turn back to the jewelry, plucking a pair of chunky plastic earrings shaped like pink lips. "These would match your shoes."

"Distracting me with fashion," she says as she takes them from me. She holds them up to her face in a mirror. "Smart move. But not smart enough to make me forget about your weirdness at lunch."

"I'm fine."

"Tamara Wilks asked Richard Baelish to prom via mini-flashmob *during* their sex-ed presentation in second period."

"Seriously?"

"Yes! And I already told you this at lunch! See? You're being weird." She hands me back the earrings, shaking her head. "Too flashy. I need something more understated."

"You're wearing a Marilyn Monroe replica dress; I think you're beyond understated," I reply, but keep looking. We scan for a few minutes, me in silence and Ags softly humming along to the pop song playing overhead.

I'm about to quit and suggest we hit up the next store when I spot them. "Ags!" I call as I grab the earrings and hide them behind my back, pulling them out once she's close enough for a dramatic reveal.

"Oh, I've taught you so well." She takes the earrings from me, thick faux pearl studs lacquered in hot pink glitter. "They're perfect—let's go." She tosses something I barely catch as she turns for the register.

I open my hands and see a pair of silver chandelier earrings, sparkling iridescently in the fluorescent mall lighting. They match my dress and shoes perfectly. She's good.

✵ ✵ ✵

"So, are we going to talk about it?" Ags asks once we're back in her room. She tugs Linds's campaign posters out from behind a stack of fabric remnants.

"Just stressed about school . . . and stuff," I reply, picking at her shaggy carpet.

"Ah, yes. *Stuff.*"

"We graduate in two months. It's my God-given, seventeen-year-old right to be ambiguously stressed out."

"If you say so," she singsongs, like she wasn't having a crisis of faith about her future less than a week ago. She unfolds a poster to reveal Lindsay in all her tight-dressed, glossy-papered glory. "Thoughts?"

"They look nice."

"Wow, don't hurt yourself with that enthusiasm." She turns the poster around and appraises it herself. "Definitely adding these photos to my portfolio. Speaking of which . . ." She tosses me the finalized fabric roses from last week. "Help me glitter these up?"

I hear someone walking in the hallway and assume it's Agatha's parents or little brother, but Lindsay, of all people, pushes the door open before I can reply to Ags.

"Aren't you supposed to be eating my pizza with Sammie right now?" Agatha asks, barely looking up as she hands Linds several flowers and a tin of golden glitter.

"He had to go pick up Hana from a friend's, so we cut out early," Linds replies, taking a seat on the floor against Ags's bed beside me.

"How'd it go?" I ask, and Agatha shoots me an annoyed look, either because I stole the question from her or because I'm finally choosing to speak, just not to her.

"Fine," Linds says, expertly coating her flower with fabric glue and sprinkling glitter atop it, somehow without making a mess.

"Just fine?" Ags presses, setting her glitter aside.

We stare at her until she accepts we aren't going to drop it. "Okay, seriously? What, do you guys need more material to gossip about when I'm not around?"

It feels like a slap in the face. Mostly because it's true.

"We just wanted to know how it went, that's all," I say, putting a lid on both my pot of glitter and my desire to get defensive.

"Well, I told you already, it went fine. And so did my study date on Saturday with Wesley and the soccer game with Sammie yesterday. It all went fine; everything is just *fine*! Should I leave now so you guys can talk about how I'm slutting it up with two guys who deserve better?"

"Whoa, whoa, whoa," Ags starts, immediately scooching closer to Linds and me. "No one is calling anyone a slut right now. I don't know what you two drank in the water at school today, but I need us to backtrack this conversation about ten steps."

"Ugh." Linds covers her face with her hands. "I'm just so overwhelmed. It's like I'm on the freaking *Bachelorette*, and I have to pick my husband in the next five minutes. Do you know how many people asked me today who I'm taking to prom? Because I lost count after third period. And my mom keeps reminding me that I should be spending more time with my sisters instead of Wes and Sammie since I'm moving halfway across the country in a few months."

"To be fair, most people were probably just making conversation," I say.

"Not implying you're a slut," Ags finishes.

"No, I know *that*. But you two, you know what's been going on. And Ophelia, you looked so pissed at lunch today, and Ags, you didn't even invite me over to help . . . do whatever this is." She knocks a flower aside.

"Babe." Ags places her hand on Linds's knee. "We don't think you're a slut. And whatever Ophelia's problem is, it had nothing to do with you."

"I don't have a problem—" I start to defend myself.

"We'll unpack whatever is going on with you in a minute," Ags interrupts. "Point is, even if you were 'slutting it up,' you're our friend. We don't care."

"We just don't want to see any of you get hurt," I add.

"Me either. They're both great guys," Linds says. "But I don't know, I think they expect a lot from me. I like them both, so much. But I don't want to be the girl walking into college already in love with someone back home. I want to be the girl who can walk into any party and find a guy to dance with or who can flirt with boys from class over coffee without any strings attached. I've already met some guys going to my college from incoming U of C freshman group chats I found online, and talking to them has been so exciting. It's like, there's this whole world of guys out there, really cute, cool guys. And it's nice to not worry about them wanting to marry me or see them looking at me the way

Sammie and Wes look at me sometimes." She folds in, face in her lap. "God, I do sound like a slut."

"You sound like a girl who wants to enjoy *her* life on *her* terms," I reply. I've been silently judging Lindsay for months because, okay yeah, I can admit it, I was jealous of her. And talking about it with Agatha the way we have, like it's a sporting match I actually enjoy watching, softened the blow. But I never want to be the girl who calls other girls sluts just because I can't get a boy to like me back. I don't want to contribute to a society that makes my friend feel bad for wanting to explore her options just because she has so many.

"Linds, you could sleep with a new guy every day of the week, and, I think O would agree, I wouldn't look at you any differently," Ags says, offering her hand. The three of us join our grips, like we're readying to perform a spell. "If doing what you want means being a slut, slut it all the way up."

"Thank you, Agatha." Linds smiles before looking at me. "Oh my God, Ophelia, are you crying?" she asks, laughing.

"Never," I say, wiping away my blackened mascara tears. We both turn to Agatha with wet, expectant eyes.

"What?" Ags shrugs, eyes dry as a bone. "I'm saving the waterworks for graduation and our moving-out days, when it really counts. And by the way, like ten people asked me who I'm taking to prom today too. It's not that deep, Linds."

Lindsay chokes on a laugh. "Thanks, Ags."

We go back to glittering our flowers. Lindsay cues up

some music on her phone and sings along, loudly and badly. Comfortably.

Agatha's sentiment lingers in my mind though, long after we move on to talking about the drama already cropping up in Lindsay's college group chats. It's weird to think about her having this whole other life already, but it's nice that she's welcoming us into it a little bit.

I imagine what it would be like to welcome them into mine. To tell them about Talia, the way we've been growing closer. But how do you say what you can't explain? How do I convey a heartbeat, a caught breath, the goose bumps on my skin when Talia hugged me goodbye in the confines of her truck on Sunday?

Things may be changing, but this change feels like too much.

What happens when you tell the girls who trust and love you that you realized you sometimes look at them the way they expect boys to? Does everything—every borrowed lipstick and shared dressing room and innocent cheek kiss—become suspect, corrupted by some illusion of straightness?

My stomach churns, and I swear I feel my heart stop working. I'm going to be sick all over Agatha's floor.

Illusion of straightness.

This isn't an illusion; *I* am not an illusion. I've liked boys, plenty of boys, and all this with Talia is just . . . closeness.

The same closeness she had with Tori. No. Yes. Maybe.

Was it worth it? Was Tori worth it? Would Talia be?

"O?" Agatha tosses a container of glitter at me, which I

narrowly catch before it can explode on her carpet.

"Huh?"

"All this glitter has me inspired." She zips open the dress sleeve hanging behind her door and pulls out her pristine, almost glowing, white prom dress.

Linds and I look down at the glitter and fabric glue in our hands.

"No way," Lindsay says, but she's grinning. "I thought you were going to deck it out in beads for that extra umph."

"What's the saying?" Ags asks, turning to me. "'¿Por qué no los dos?' Might as well finish off high school with a bang."

I'm still at a loss for words as I recover from my tornado of thoughts, but I manage to smile and nod, ready to help.

While Agatha starts brushing the fabric with glue, Linds nudges me. "So, what was your damage anyway?" she asks. "Now that I know my shit wasn't behind it, what was with the sad face at lunch?"

"I—um." *Tell them about Talia, Lucas, Jeremiah.* "Cramps?"

Linds pats me on the shoulder, and Ags offers me aspirin, which I decline. I tell myself I don't mention Lucas's potential offer because they'd laugh it off as me looking too much into his words, or call me out for crawling back to my ex. It's definitely not because there's a chance they might tell me to go for it. Or because there's a chance I might not want to.

TWELVE

Tuesday morning, I was ready to shed whatever residual weirdness I felt from yesterday and Saturday. But then Sammie whistled at Agatha and me when she leaned in to apply some of her lip gloss on me before class, Lucas ignored me in chemistry, and Lindsay snapped at me for hanging her posters too close to the trash cans. I abandoned the campaign efforts and headed back to the bench where Zaq, Talia, and Sammie were eating and watching over the rest of the posters.

"I think I just swallowed some glitter," Sammie croaks. After tackling Ags's dress and flowers, we had dumped the leftover glitter on the posters. Talia offers him a sip of water, but he shakes his head.

"Hey, Ophelia, Wes said you're making corsages and boutonnieres for prom. How much are you charging?" Zaq asks.

"Oh, uh, nothing," I reply, pushing the rice in my Tupperware around with a fork.

"Nothing? You know florists charge outrageous prices for those, right?" He grabs Talia's water and takes the sip Sammie refused.

"Yeah, I know." I put the lid on my rice, losing my appetite.

"We try to keep her humble," Sammie says, apparently done choking on glitter.

"By not paying her for her labor? Don't you want to do all that flower stuff professionally one day?" Zaq asks, a creeping edge to his voice. "You pay Agatha when she alters your clothes, right?"

"I mean, yeah, but that's different." I shrug. "Sewing takes time and money."

"And all gardening takes is dirt?" he asks. "Look, Lindsay paid me for taking her photos. Let me pay for my and Talia's flowers at least. I'm sure Wesley will pay for his and—" He cuts himself off when Sammie looks up from his lunch. "And Lindsay's should be taken care of. By *someone*."

I try to think of a way to thank him but still insist Talia's corsage is a gift to her, without having to actually say that. I settle on mumbling gratitude and picking at the hem of my skirt.

"Hypothetical question, would someone taking Ophelia to prom have to pay for her corsage, then?" Sammie asks before coughing again. "Ugh, this glitter."

"Jeez, just take some water," Zaq says, uncapping Talia's bottle and handing it to Sammie so forcefully that when

Sammie refuses it again, he accidentally knocks it over. Onto me.

My light yellow skirt instantly soaks through with water, and I thank myself for wearing undershorts today.

"Shit, the posters," Sammie says, using his sleeve to mop water off the now-bleeding ink.

"I'm so sorry," Zaq says to me, digging around in his backpack for a napkin.

I exhale shakily. "It's. Fine." I get up to go to the bathroom and clean off, ready to tell Talia she doesn't have to come. But she doesn't offer. So I spend the rest of lunch by myself with my skirt under the hand dryer. I'm walking back to the bench as the bell rings, seeing Agatha, Lindsay, and Wesley back there already.

Everyone, Zaq and Wesley included, is laughing over something Sammie's saying while Agatha braids a section of Talia's hair. I go to government without waiting for Talia and spend the rest of the day saying as little as possible so I don't bite anyone's head off.

So when Wesley offers to give me a ride home so we can finish the last of our chemistry set on the drive, I take the opportunity to spend time with the one person who didn't piss me off today.

I finish the set of equations while Wesley drives, grateful that I'm impervious to car sickness. He pulls up to my house as I put our names on the top of the sheet and shove it into my backpack.

"That was weirdly efficient," he laughs, despite having

contributed little to the work. I think being in a bad mood makes me better at chemistry.

"Mm–hmm. Thanks for the ride." I'm gathering my stuff when Wesley reaches to stop me, pulling back halfway.

"Uh, are you . . . are you okay?" he asks. "You just, you don't seem like yourself today."

"How would you know?" I bite back too quickly. He flinches. "I'm sorry. That was bitchy."

He shrugs, but I can still see the hurt in his eyes. "Is this about Lucas?"

"You're more perceptive than I give you credit for."

The hurt finally leaves his face, and he cracks a smile. "Thanks. But you also told me about him trying to ask you to prom. I haven't heard Agatha or Lindsay say anything about it though. Which makes me think you didn't tell them."

I sigh. "It's complicated." *Because it's not just about him or prom*, I want to say, thinking of my hasty departure from the kitchen when Mom came in for breakfast this morning.

"I'm sorry."

I shrug it off, surely just as unconvincingly as he did. His phone goes off from where it's sitting in the cup holder. I can't help sneaking a peek. It's a group text from Talia and Zaq, both of them asking when he's coming.

Wesley and I look up at the same time. "We're just study-ing," he says quickly, almost choking on the words.

"Cool," I reply, confused and relieved that he didn't call me out for reading his texts. I get out of the car without saying anything else, anxious to get inside, but also not.

Besides meaningless comments during meals, Mom and I still haven't talked since Saturday.

I'm halfway up my driveway, nearly out of earshot, when Wesley calls my name. I turn around to see his bulky frame awkwardly hunched across the front seats so he can get close to the passenger window.

"We aren't actually studying today. We don't even have any classes all together," he says quickly, like a child admitting a wrongdoing to a parent who likely wouldn't have otherwise caught them.

I shift my backpack and suppress a smile. "Then why did you tell me you were?"

"I didn't want to tell the truth about where we're going," he says plainly. His words shock me, not just because this means Wesley Cho is actually capable of lying to another human being, but because he trusts me enough to admit it.

"And now you do?" I ask, head cocked.

He shakes his head slowly, looking unsure.

I shrug. "Then don't."

"I just—I felt bad lying. Especially after you told me about Lucas," he admits. The heart in this boy is kind of unbelievable. I love Sammie, I really do. But, damn, I get it now, Linds.

"Don't," I say, sighing. "Everyone deserves their secrets."

❋ ❋ ❋

I'm in the middle of picking the dried petals off an Honor rose when a familiar head pops up on my left, startling me into accidentally yanking off a couple of perfectly fleshy, white petals along with the crusty ones.

"I'm busy, Sammie." I've been gardening for two hours since getting home, and I still feel behind on how the back-yard should look by now. I really shouldn't have taken Sunday off, even if I needed to escape the house. At least Mom has left me alone while I work.

"Sorry," he says, propping his elbows on the brick wall between our yards and leaning his chin into his palm. "You were just so quiet today. I mean, you were quiet yesterday too, and I would've asked after school, but . . ."

"But you and Lindsay were off in pizza heaven," I reply.

"I meant after school today. When Wesley gave you a ride home."

"We had to finish chem work."

"This isn't about what Zaq was saying at lunch?"

"Nope."

"Is it about what I said at lunch?"

"Nope," I reply, eyes still on the rose in my hand. "Nothing's wrong."

Sammie brushes dirt off the front of his yellow button-up. "Come on, O. You're a shit liar and you know it."

"I'm *fine*," I insist, voice wavering slightly. "I'm just over-whelmed. It's senior year, remember? And I've got a lot of gardening to catch up on."

He rolls his eyes. "You're really not going to tell me?"

"There's nothing to tell."

"Is this about Lindsay?" he says, looking like he regrets the words the second they leave his mouth. His eyes widen before shooting down to focus on the texture of the wall instead of my face.

"What?" I finally drop my rose and pull my hair into a ponytail, breathing heavier in the stale afternoon air.

"Sorry," he says, shaking his curls out of his face. "I meant, is this about Lindsay . . . and Wesley?"

"Still not following you."

"Look, just don't get mad."

"Oh, now you tell me." I rest my hands on my hips, waiting.

He hesitates for a moment. "Do you have a thing for Wesley?"

I cannot believe this. "You're joking, right? Where is this even coming from?"

"I don't know!" he says, throwing up his hands in surrender. "But you keep insisting you don't want a prom date, yet as soon as prom really starts rolling around, suddenly you're all buddy-buddy with him and making sure he's included in everything. Then after Lindsay wins the nomination and you and Wesley have chem, you're quiet all day, especially today when he chose to keep putting up posters after Linds snapped at you. Now he's giving you rides home instead of me? You guys have homeroom together and we're *next-door neighbors*. I took chemistry sophomore year; I know balancing equations isn't that pressing." He pauses, like he's really scared to say his next thought. "You've never gone this long without liking someone. But it would make sense if you didn't want to talk about liking the guy Lindsay is also into." I can tell it pains him to say this, but then his lips quirk slightly, like something just occurred to him.

"Hold on," I say, trying to break down everything he just threw at me. "Ignoring all your flimsy evidence about Wesley and me suddenly being besties just because we *walk* to class and do our literally *partner-assigned* work together, and the fact you apparently think I'm incapable of going more than five minutes without falling apart over some boy, please tell me you aren't hoping I like Wesley just so it'll make it easier for you to date Lindsay."

A beat of silence. "That's not the *only* reason, but you can't deny that it would simplify things for everyone."

He shrugs, like he isn't breaking my heart with every passing second. My best friend, the person I thought knew me better than anyone except possibly my parents, really can't wrap his head around me being upset about anything but a *boy*.

"My feelings don't exist to *simplify* things for you."

I don't let him say anything else. I remove my gardening gloves and grab my shears from the ground, lobbing them roughly into the bin by my feet. I burst through the gate around my garden and throw the bin down beside the back door as I storm into my house. Sammie calls after me, lazily apologetic like always, but I slam the door behind me, cutting off his voice.

I don't think properly about what I'm walking back into though, because suddenly I'm watching Mom stare at me from the living room sofa, glasses perched on her nose, holding her favorite collector's edition of *The Tempest*.

"Everything all right?" she asks, like I haven't been avoiding her since Saturday. I don't think I've ever gone this long without talking to my mom, but every time I think about it, all I feel is shame and anxiety. So I've tried not to.

But now I have no choice but to talk to her. I silently pray Dad kept his promise and didn't tell her what Jeremiah said.

"We really should move houses," I sigh, melting into our usual rapport. I miss my mom, and Sammie pissed me off too much to silently sulk. I've kept so much bottled inside lately that it feels impossible to keep quiet about this. "Our neighbors' son is abysmal."

She looks pleased at my vocabulary choice despite it being about my best friend, whom she probably still hopes I'll be marrying in the next five years. "I thought I heard Sammie outside," she says, closing her book and propping her glasses on her head. "What did he do this time?"

I don't even know where to begin, mostly because I'm scared she'll agree with Sammie's assessment. Maybe everyone in my life thinks I'm harboring a secret crush. Although if I'm being scarily honest with myself, are they really that far off?

"It's whatever," I say, dropping the moment. Mom visibly deflates. I feel bad about it, but I doubt I'll be able to get into everything Sammie said without getting into every-thing I refused to say. "I have homework to finish." I head down the hall toward the stairs, foot nearly on the bottom step, when Mom calls me back.

Cautiously, I tiptoe back into the room. She's placed her book and glasses on the coffee table and motions for me to sit. "Can we talk for a minute?"

"Is this an intervention? Because I swear I was only gar-dening that long because I missed Sunday's routine," I say, still standing, then realize I walked right into her next, inev-itable question.

"Dad mentioned he didn't see you out there on Sunday. Have you been avoiding me since the party?" she says, and part of me, the part that isn't scared about where this con-versation is going, finds it hilarious that out of context, this might as well be a conversation between teenage girls rather than a daughter and mother.

"I wouldn't call it avoiding, per se," I reply, finally sit-ting down across from her, folding my legs beneath me and adjusting my skirt before she can ask me to sit more ladylike.

"Stop using word-specificity arguments on me. It's a flimsy trick and a waste of linguistic studies." I resist the urge to roll my eyes. "Ophelia, I'm not mad at you," she says directly. I'm the one deflating this time, realizing there's no getting out of this. "I'm just disappointed that you embarrassed me in front of so many of my students and colleagues. I could've gotten in serious trouble if Jeremiah had complained to the dean about your little moment."

"My *moment*?"

"Honey, you threw a cup of punch on my student."

"At least I didn't *actually* throw a punch."

"You're not taking this seriously," she scolds. "I am willing to be understanding about the situation if you explain yourself and agree to apologize to Jeremiah via email."

"But I'm not sorry," I say without thinking. It's only once the words leave my mouth that I realize I wouldn't have done anything different if I were given a do-over.

Mom sighs and runs a hand over her face, pressing into the slightly wrinkled skin around her eyes. "I hoped you'd be less stubborn about this."

Of course. It doesn't even cross her mind that I might have had a good reason for doing what I did. Because maybe I'm well-behaved, get the grades my parents want, don't stay out too late or drink at the few parties I attend. But at the end of the day, I'm still me. Still *boy-crazy Ophelia*. And that negates everything else about me. That's my reigning personality trait, I suppose. So of course, whatever happened with that boy, it was me and my crazy heart's fault. Not his.

I know I'm being petty when I say it, but I can't help myself, not now. "What about how *you* embarrassed *me* when you decided my personal crushes and hobbies were fair game to talk about with all your students?"

She looks shocked, her face turning a bright pink. "Is that what this is about? Did Jeremiah say something about your crushes? You've never been embarrassed to talk about those things before."

"Yeah, with my parents! Or my friends! Not with your complete-stranger students! Do you know how uncomfortable that made me feel to know that anyone that has ever stepped foot in one of your lectures knows all my personal business?"

"Honey, there isn't a single teenage girl out there who hasn't had dozens of crushes on boys growing up. I didn't tell them anything they couldn't have already known about you," she insists, sitting up straighter and taking on the look of Professor Rojas more than Mother Rojas. I try to imagine her with this posture, publicly laughing about her foolish, predictable daughter.

I can't do this, can't break down how wrong her statement is and on how many levels. How do I explain to her that knowing she genuinely believes what she just said is fundamentally the problem with my life right now?

I leave the room, the second time in the past fifteen minutes that I've walked away from someone I love as they call after me, half-heartedly apologizing for their ignorant assumptions. But Dad is standing at the base of the stairs, arms crossed.

"Go back and talk to her," he whispers. "Tell her what you told me that boy called you and she will understand."

I pause. "He didn't call me those words; he used them against someone else." I watch Dad's face twist in confusion.

"¿Qué?"

"Jeremiah used slurs, but not at me," I repeat.

"But—I thought that was why you were so upset." He

frowns. "He wrongly accused you of being gay using hateful words, no?"

I'm frozen in shock, in anger. *Accused? Wrongly?*

A frustrated laugh escapes me. I really don't know my parents, and they really don't know me. "I can't do this right now." I move past him, and he lets me go without another comment. Upstairs, I shut my door more gently than I'd like to, and close my curtains, despite seeing Sammie in his room look up from his desk and try to wave at me.

I flop onto my bed and stare at the ceiling, waiting for my anger to burn off.

Eventually, the ceiling stops feeling therapeutic. I pull my phone out from my back pocket.

Why does everyone suck? I type, falling into the role of the cliché teenage girl everyone apparently expects of me.

Talia replies almost immediately. *You don't suck*

I smile at the message despite this afternoon and ignore the urge to go continue my gardening. *Can I call you?* I send before I lose the nerve.

A few seconds pass, and then Talia's name is lighting up my screen. I answer the FaceTime immediately. Then realize my phone is at a horribly awkward angle and scramble to sit up.

"What's up?" she says, propping her phone against her desk. Her laptop is in front of her, casting her brown skin in bluish light as she types.

I consider telling her the truth, that everything is going to shit and I just need someone to talk to. But that would open a can of worms I'm not ready to deal with. "Just bored. What are you up to?"

"Working on homework for English," she says, face focused on the screen. "We're supposed to write a letter to ourselves at the start of high school."

"What do you have to say to preteen Talia?" I ask. Despite pushing my own feelings aside, I half hope she'll bring up Tori again.

"I'm sure she's very surprised to know that she's sitting at the cool kids' table now," she laughs.

"There's *no* way you're talking about me, Sammie, Agatha, and Lindsay."

"Don't be humble," she laughs again, snort echoing over my phone's speaker. "Lindsay and Sammie know everyone, and Agatha dresses . . . well, like *that*." She pauses, and my stomach flips. "And you have your whole I Only Wear Flowers And I Don't Care thing."

"I didn't realize wearing floral print made me so edgy," I say, picturing myself batting down the butterflies in my stomach. "In fact, I don't even know why I'm on the phone with you right now. I've got cigarettes to be smoking in a garden while wearing shoplifted Urban Outfitters floral jellies."

"Ha-ha." She rolls her eyes and continues typing. "Tease all you want, but you know it's true. You're one of those people everyone will actually remember after graduating and going off into the 'real world.'"

It feels weird, knowing someone thinks this—something

I've only ever thought true of my friends, but never of me. "Lindsay and Sammie, certainly. And definitely Ags for her style. But I think I'll be in the back of that mental snapshot alongside Wesley."

"Come on, you were on my radar years before we'd ever spoken in government."

My heart stops beating. "What?"

She covers her face, smiling. Each second without further explanation feels like torture, even while seeing her so giddy. "You remember freshman-year orientation, right?"

I nod, at a loss for words.

"I saw you with Lindsay and Sammie, though I knew none of your names at the time." I remember Agatha missing orientation because of a sore throat. That day was the first time Lindsay and Sammie ever really spoke outside of the casual conversations Agatha and I had instigated over that summer. Because of Ags's absence and my parents' insistence on coming to orientation with me, Sammie and Linds discovered a shared love of sarcasm, bloody video games that made me nauseous, and flirting.

"You had on a graphic T-shirt of a raven surrounded by cherry blossoms that reminded me of Edgar Allan Poe. We'd spent half the school year working on it in English because my teacher kept saying we'd need to know about it in high school," Talia says. "Turns out, I did need to know, because I spent thirty minutes trying to come up with something clever to say to you about it, but forgot everything we'd learned."

I fight the urge to find that shirt from the back of my closet and put it on. "Why didn't you just say hi?"

"Talking to people has never been my strong suit, as you've probably realized." This time I'm the one who laughs. "I'd just lost Dani and Tori a few weeks before and was desperate for someone to talk to, but I couldn't talk myself into saying anything."

"So essentially, I'm a constant reminder of a shitty moment from when you were fourteen?" I ask, joking to distract myself from the mental image of Talia watching me wistfully across a crowded auditorium years ago. To distract myself from the fact that she still remembers the shirt I was wearing down to the cherry blossoms.

"More like a personified life lesson that good things come to those who overcome their fears. All this time, we could've been friends."

I think of the months of casual conversation after Lindsay's party, regret blooming in my chest over where we could've been by now if I'd only tried to befriend Talia sooner.

But then she chuckles to herself, typing furiously on her laptop again. "Better late than never though."

I hum in agreement, cutting off the regret, and sink back into bed, losing myself in talking to the girl who makes everything else—every fear and worry weighing on my chest—feel a million miles away.

THIRTEEN

During the ride to school the next morning, I'm flipping through songs on my phone when Dad taps me on my shoulder, forcing me to pull out one of my headphones and feign ignorance when he says, "¿Qué ha estado pasando con Samuel?"

"Nothing is happening with Sammie," I lie, wrapping my headphones around my phone and resting it in my lap. I'm wearing my lily pad romper today, the one Lindsay always insists I'm too old for because of the cartoon frogs. I'm in a slightly better mood after spending last night talking to Talia.

He exhales loudly through his nose. I pretended to oversleep this morning so I could avoid Sammie giving me a ride, but he left before I could even text him a bullshit excuse, leaving Dad as my only option. "You know I don't mind driving you to school, but I'd like your honesty in exchange," he scolds as he pulls into the drop-off roundabout.

"I told you, nothing is happening with Sammie," I repeat, tossing my phone in my backpack. "It's just pointless teenage drama."

"Isn't it always?" he jokes. My gut twists. I hardly mumble a goodbye.

I don't bother meeting my friends in the student parking lot, too worried about running into Sammie and having to deal with that awkwardness. It's weird fighting with Sammie like this, if I can even call it that, and being around our other friends in this state will only make it weirder.

I'm entering my locker combination when Agatha walks over, leaning against the metal with crossed arms and a raised eyebrow.

"Morning," I say, grabbing my chemistry notebook and flipping through it like I'm looking for something.

"Don't give me that."

I look around myself with wide, exaggerated eyes. "Is it not morning? I must have really slept in today."

"Is that why Sammie didn't give you a ride?" she asks, ever the gossip.

"Why don't you ask Sammie why he didn't give me a ride?" I reply in a fake cheery voice, slamming my locker shut.

"I tried, but he was too busy teasing Wesley about the purple sweater he wore today to notice," she says, finally opening her locker. She peels off her own striped sweater, revealing a black body-con dress, tight around her wide hips, that stands out against her bright pink sneakers. Only Agatha could pull off this look on a Wednesday morning.

"Sounds like Sammie," I reply.

"I think he's just mad that he tried on the same sweater last month at the mall but couldn't find one that suited him," she laughs, and some of my tension melts away.

"That *definitely* sounds like Sammie." First bell rings, and I think I'm in the clear with Agatha, but she hooks her arm around mine as I turn to head for homeroom, slowing me down.

"I'm only going to say this once, because you know I hate being sappy. But you know you can talk to me, right? About whatever it is that's making you wig out on everyone right now." She gives me one of her million-dollar smiles, white teeth bright against lipstick that matches her shoes.

"I know," I say, feeling less confident about the words than I expected to be.

The minutes in homeroom tick by slowly, painfully, but I manage to survive it without another fight with Sammie, so I consider it a small victory.

Wesley, in his admittedly lovely purple sweater, and I hardly speak on our way to chemistry, the memory of yesterday heavy between us. I'm so focused on maintaining our silence without acting abrasive that I don't notice Lucas approach our desk.

"Hey, Cho." Lucas nods to Wesley like I'm invisible.

"Hi?" he replies, shooting his eyes between me and Lucas as if asking my permission to continue the conversation.

"You care if I sit with Ophelia today?" Lucas asks, smiling to reveal his flawless, straight teeth. He never even had braces; he just got lucky. He still hasn't looked at me.

"Uh, are we allowed to do that?" Wesley asks.

"I doubt Waitley will care if we switch partners for one day," Lucas says, rolling his eyes and biting his lower lip. He finally looks at me, and I feel my organs flip inside out. "That good with you, Ophelia?"

I nod, suddenly unable to speak.

"Oh, okay," Wesley says, looking disappointedly at me before moving to work with Lucas's partner.

Waitley turns down the lights and starts up her lecture slides. We don't have a lab today, making it impossible for Lucas and me to talk. I sink into my seat, diligently taking notes about mole conversions when Lucas slides a folded paper onto my side of the desk. I look up at him before pulling it into my hand; a smirk plays on his lips while his eyes remain facing forward.

I unfold the note discreetly in my lap, years of passing notes with Agatha having prepared me for this. I'm convinced my eyes aren't seeing properly in the dimmed light, but the words are written in bold, blocky letters, clear as day.

Lunch tomorrow. Meet at your locker.

I look at him again, sure he'll snatch back the paper and say he made a mistake and meant for me to pass it to someone else. But he just flashes me another smile and, under his breath, says, "I've got a meeting with the team today at lunch."

Part of me is torn. He dumped me last year. He's hardly spoken to me this year. And on the few occasions he has, he's left me feeling confused and anxious, like I am now.

But this is Lucas, the boy I spent an entire summer heartbroken over. I owe it to that girl to at least give whatever this is a shot, don't I?

Plus, he's still cute as hell.

I jot down *yes* and pass back the note, but he slips it into his pocket without even checking it. He winks at me, sending a flutter through my chest. Before I can focus on the lecture again, I feel Wesley's eyes on me across the room. I flicker mine to meet his gaze momentarily before he turns away, his unreadable expression leaving me uneasy for the rest of the period.

✳ ✳ ✳

By lunch, Wesley's weird look has washed clear of my mind. But watching him laugh with Talia and Zaq while Sammie swallows a chocolate bar whole reminds me of the ordeal. I take my seat between Agatha and Talia and avoid eye contact with Sammie, which isn't too hard considering he's not attempting it.

"You're still coming over today, right?" Talia asks as she takes a bite out of a red apple. I sip my water as I wait for her to stop pressing her mouth into the crisp flesh, too distracted to speak otherwise. Eventually I settle on nodding.

"What are y'all getting up to?" Ags asks. I feel a surge of gratitude that she, unlike Sammie and Lindsay, has never been inclined toward jealousy. She's genuinely curious about our plans, not passive-aggressively fishing for an invite.

"Working on the end-of-unit paper for English," I reply, finally regaining control of my voice. Sammie scoffs, likely annoyed that I didn't offer to help him like I usually do.

"Oh, I was going to ask if you can look over mine for me," Ags says, digging around in her bag. "Shit, I forgot to print it out. Can you check it out tomorrow at lunch? I can just make the last-minute edits during my free period before English."

I'm about to agree when I remember Lucas's note. "Well . . . ," I say. Agatha looks up from her chaotic mess of a backpack.

"Well . . . what?" She tilts her head. Sammie goes still, watching us out of the corner of his eye.

"Can you just send it to me after school? I actually have plans tomorrow."

"During lunch?" Ags asks.

"Yeah," I reply, feigning ignorance about her curiosity. I quickly turn to Talia, who has nearly finished her apple while I wasn't watching, thank God.

"So is that a Fuji or Granny Smith?" I ask her.

"Granny Smiths are green," Zaq inserts.

Ags grabs my shoulder and turns me to face her. By now, Lindsay has also looked up from her cold lasagna and Sammie isn't even pretending not to watch us.

"Who are these plans with?" Agatha asks. "Do you have a

new friend we don't know about?" Her lips quirk in amusement.

"Oh, you know," I say airily as I take a bite of Mom's chicken, leftover from the dinner I refused to come downstairs to eat last night. "Just . . . Lucas," I mumble, loud enough to hear but quiet enough to hear my embarrassment even better.

"Lucas?" Sammie asks, breaking our radio silence.

"The plot thickens," Ags says as Lindsay clasps her hands together excitedly.

"I'm sorry, who is Lucas?" Zaq asks.

"Ophelia's ex-boyfriend," Talia replies, leaning past me to give him a pointed look. She doesn't meet my eyes though.

"Emphasis on the ex," Agatha says, looking straight at me. "He ghosted you and figures two months till graduation is as good a time as ever to hit you back up?"

Everyone stops eating, homing all their attention in on me. I know I should feel giddy, act flustered the way they expect me to with hope in my eyes and a cliché in my heart. But truthfully, I don't know what Lucas wants. I barely know what I do.

I thought I wanted him to ask me to prom, for us to get back together for a few sweet weeks before graduation inevitably drew us apart again. But talking about it now, aloud and with real possibility, I'm stuck. It's like when he's right in front of me, I'm under a spell. But the second I step away, the illusion shatters.

"I don't know," I reply, my answer carrying more

meaning than my friends could possibly know. "He mentioned prom, but . . ."

"Do you want to go with him?" Talia asks, finally looking at me. Her expression is just as unreadable as Wesley's, but where his left me uneasy, hers leaves me dizzy and spiraling toward conclusions I have no right to jump to.

"I don't know."

"Fingers crossed he asks!" Lindsay squeals from across the table, reaching to squeeze my hands briefly. I know her excitement is for my benefit, so I try to perk up. Agatha watches us both, a frown tugging at her lips, but she offers me a tight, closed-mouth smile when she catches me staring.

Wesley and Zaq awkwardly shift the conversation to helping Agatha with some designs she has for graffiti-printed evening gowns.

I wager a look at Sammie, who I expect to be furious over me entertaining romantic possibilities with Lucas again. But his expression is soft, almost patronizing in its gentleness.

"Be careful, O."

The bell rings before I can reply, but his words swirl through my head for the rest of the day.

❋ ❋ ❋

"I just don't *get* Barthes," Talia groans, lifting her laptop over her head and tucking her knees into her chest. She looks so small, even though she could easily curl her whole body around mine in that position.

We're sitting on her bedroom floor, the carpet scratchy

against my bare legs. We've been "working" on our papers for over an hour now, but all she's typed is her name and the title while I've barely made it past my introductory paragraph. Turns out we aren't the most productive pair, but I'm not complaining. I'd stay up all night writing both our papers if she asked me to, just to keep laughing at the random memes she shows me whenever I manage to write another sentence.

She doesn't ask me to write her paper though, thankfully, so I decide to do her one better and make good on my promise to be helpful. "All right, shut your laptop and humor me for a second."

She unfolds her body and watches me attentively, straight-faced, and I have to look away before I get stuck staring at her like this.

"Okay, so." I think of how Mom tried to explain literary theorists to me last year when I started looking into college programs and she was still convinced I could be swayed into studying English. Literary theory is surprisingly interesting, but I'll still take examining different forms of fungal root rot over it any day.

"Have you ever really, really wanted a piece of chocolate cake?" I start, and Talia's blank stare shifts into a suppressed smile. She doesn't stop me to tease though, so I keep going. "Like you've been thinking about cake all day, how it'll melt in your mouth and feel against your tongue and sliding down your throat? You think about the thickness and the moisture and the flavor until you're driving yourself mad with how much you *want* that cake?" I pause for her to nod, wanting to be sure I haven't lost her. "Roland Barthes said that what you really want is that want itself, not the cake. When you eat the cake, you don't really focus on all those things. You eat it, and you're left unsatisfied because the cake wasn't everything you wanted. Because it can't ever live up to what you built it up to be. You just wanted the act of wanting something."

She nods slowly, her lips pressed together. "What if I don't like chocolate cake?" she says, trying to keep her face serious. But her laughter gets the better of her. I throw a pillow at her, and she only laughs harder.

"What kind of cake do you like, then?" I ask mockingly, hands on my hips as I sit up. I feel like a parody of my mom.

"Tres leches?" she tries, shrugging.

"Feel free to retract my Latine card, but I've never been able to stomach tres leches," I admit. Now it's her turn to throw a pillow at me.

"You're lucky your love of papas rellenas and other Cuban food I've never heard of compensates for that cultural betrayal," she laughs, lying back on the floor and resting her head on her crossed arms. "I think I get it, but what about his whole *the lover is the one who waits* thing? That was him, right? Where does that play into all of this?"

I feel my cheeks flush as she says the word *lover* so casually, especially as we sit in her bedroom, even if we're several feet apart and on the floor.

"That's not really the same thing," I explain, lying on my back like her and focusing on the chipping ceiling paint. "I don't think we have to cover that on this paper; just stay focused on the desiring-desire theme and you'll be fine."

"Can you give me a non-food related example?" she teases, forcing me to arch my back so I can stick my tongue out at her.

"Fine," I say, trying to think of something specific that'll apply to Talia personally. I nearly say that her love for math could work as an example, that Barthes would say she loves solving equations because she wants to complete them, but that completing them doesn't quench that desire. But my brain short-circuits, and instead I say, "Have you ever wanted to kiss someone so badly it physically hurt?"

She sits up, her attention caught as she silently nods. I look back to the ceiling but feel the heavy weight of her eyes on me as I speak. "Barthes would say that you don't actually want to kiss that person; you just like the feeling of wanting to kiss them."

"Is that why people are so into emotionally unavailable people?" she asks drily. My stomach aches when my mind flashes to Lucas.

"I guess so," I reply. "I don't know if Barthes ever said that directly. But I think it applies."

"So we're all masochists?" she laughs, breaking the intensity of our words. I smile and turn my face toward her.

"Not necessarily. It's not that we like the pain of *not*

having something; it's more that the act of wanting gives us more satisfaction than the actual thing ever will. Less masochistic and more like we're all Goldilocks, getting off on constantly searching for the perfect whatever. But we'll never find it."

She whistles long and low. "Barthes seems like a bit of a downer." She turns over onto her stomach again, opening her laptop and staring at the blank screen. Her face is lit up by the white computer light, turning her eyes more orange than brown. "He has a point though."

"You agree with him?" I ask. I finally lift my head fully off the carpet and lean my back against her bed without breaking eye contact. She fiddles with her piercing, a chip of red nail polish fluttering off her finger and onto her keyboard. She doesn't notice.

"I feel like I'm always disappointed in things. I don't look at them as romantically as you do," she says, and I flush, torn between feeling complimented and insulted. "I love my birthday and Noche Buena and Easter. But without fail, by the end of the day, I feel let down. I think I like the planning and anticipation more than the actual day."

"Do you think prom will be like that?" I ask, the terrifying thought something I haven't dared to ask myself until now.

"Probably," she admits. "When I was younger, I imagined going with Dani and Tori, Dani and I wearing our matching rose brooches. I even pictured sneaking them in if we didn't end up at the same high school." She sighs wistfully, eyes drifting over to her wall. I imagine she's focusing on the empty spaces where the torn photos once hung proudly. "After all these years, I've let go of most of those little fantasies. But prom was always something I imagined us doing together, sort of like a prewedding, pseudo-group-quince thing." She snorts. "I'm not even wearing a dress," she says softly, like she's forgotten I'm in the room with her.

It makes me want to fix this, guarantee her the prom she deserves, even without her family's unanimous support and first love by her side.

"Be my prom date," I blurt out.

Talia laughs. But her smile drops when she tears her eyes away from her wall and sees how serious my face is. "What?"

I don't know where the words come from. They pour out of me before I can shut my mouth. "I don't mean like a date-date. Like, I'll make you a corsage—I mean, I was already going to make you a corsage, but Zaq doesn't have to pay for it now. We can save a slow dance for each other and take goofy, cliché prom-pose photos for our parents." I think of her family, how her posing with another girl wouldn't help their already messy situation. "I'd ask Sammie," I start, hoping to veer the conversation away from her drama and toward mine, "but he and I aren't getting along too well and he might still be Lindsay's date and anyway my parents would probably take us going together *way* too seriously but this way it'll just be fun and casual." I finally manage to stop, catching my breath. I'm breathing faster than is reasonable while Talia stares at me, mouth slightly pursed.

"I promise to be a shit date. I mean, it's not even like a *real* real date, obviously," I add, which finally breaks her passive expression as her lips quirk up. "You don't have to get your hopes up over a fake, silly date." I swear I will evaporate if she doesn't say something soon. "And it's not like either of us has any other options."

She laughs nervously. Good nervous? Bad nervous? "That sounds like fun," she says before turning back to her laptop. I wonder if I imagine the way she straightens her posture and refuses to look me in the eye the rest of the evening. But she flashes me a smile when she drops me off later, and it calms my racing thoughts.

Back home, I tiptoe through the front doorway and up to my room. I shut the door loud enough that my parents will know I'm home without my having to actually go talk to them. Though with the lights off and their room quiet, I wonder if they're even awake waiting up for me.

I stumble into my bathroom and stare at my reflection for a few moments, thinking back to this afternoon, when I kinda, sorta, half asked out Talia. My cheeks are still glowing and warm. My bangs are pressed to my forehead with sweat, and my eyes have never looked brighter, the rich brown hue sparkling in the fluorescent lighting.

I press a finger to my lips as they curl into a secret smile.

FOURTEEN

I wake up early the next morning, so I have enough time to apply more makeup than usual. But my stomach is growling before I can even finish combing out my eyebrows, so I head downstairs to grab a granola bar. Halfway down the stairs, I freeze when I hear muffled shouting from Mom and Dad's room.

"This is absolutely ridiculous, and you know it." Mom's voice is dulled by the closed door, but her anger is loud and clear.

Carefully, I tiptoe my way closer and lean against the wall so they won't see my shadow beneath their door. Mom and Dad yell every once in a while, but I haven't heard them get this riled up since one of Mom's old childhood friends made a "casual" inquiry about Dad's citizenship status last year. And even then, their shouting was in mutual anger at someone else, not at each other.

"Stella, I made a promise. I can't just break her trust like that," Dad replies, voice much quieter.

"Well, what am I supposed to tell the other faculty members? All my colleagues that were there? My past and future students? She poured a drink on one of my students, Miguel." My stomach bottoms out. "Do you know how humiliated and confused I felt? No, of course you don't, because you and Ophelia fled the scene before I could even process it."

I'm suddenly all too aware of my body—my slight tremor with each intake of breath, the way my joints rub together as I teeter slightly on the balls of my feet. My hands moisten with sweat.

"I apologized for that," Dad says. "Ophelia was distraught and crying. I had to put her first."

Mom scoffs, and it's just as biting from outside the room as I imagine it is inside. "Oh, so now you're the good cop and I'm the bad cop? Worrying about the consequences this could have for my career *is* putting Ophelia first. Lord knows her flower degree isn't going to pay for itself."

I flinch and clench my jaw to hold back the tears.

"In case you forgot, I have a job too," Dad says after a beat of silence. His voice is calmer than I'd expect, and I almost hate him for it. Part of me wants him to take a dig at me too, snap back at Mom, tell her what I told him, anything. At least then I could be angry instead of guilty. I could feel betrayed instead of unworthy. "Mira, Ophelia asked me to keep her reasons for acting out between the two of us. I don't like this either, but I have to keep my word."

"But why won't she talk to *me*?" Mom's voice breaks. I press a fist to my mouth to keep whatever is threatening to burst out of me buried deep inside.

"Stella—"

"It's fine," she says, but I hear a sniffle. "I should get going before I'm late for my appointment."

I hear movement and can't tell if they're moving toward each other or away, but I need to go before they see me here, eavesdropping. I move as quickly and quietly as I can back to my room and shut my door before I hear theirs open.

Sitting back down in front of my mirror, I stare at my reflection. *This is who you are now*, I think. *This is what happens when things change.* Graduation, college, getting older? I'm blameless there, just as wrapped up in the inevitability. But this? This was me.

❋ ❋ ❋

Sammie is standing at the bottom of my stairs by the time I leave my room, despite the forty minutes it took me to apply three coats of mascara, blush, highlighter, and iridescent lip gloss to complement the sequin flowers on my white sundress.

"Hi," I say, pausing halfway down the steps. I expected my lateness to lead to another ride from Dad, even after what I overheard, but his keys, as well as Mom's, are missing from the foyer. They both left without saying goodbye.

"Hey. You ready to go?" Sammie asks, obviously taking in my outfit. His nostrils flare, and I feel insecure about the amount of perfume I'm wearing.

I expect our ride to go by in silence, but Sammie seems determined to mend fences, because before he even starts the car, he turns to me and says, "I don't want to fight with you. About anything, least of all Wesley."

"Me either," I admit, and he relaxes.

"I'm sorry for making assumptions," he says gently, like he's worried he'll set me off again.

"It's a natural human flaw," I reply as he turns the ignition and pulls away from our houses. His comments still hurt, but it's Sammie. I can't stay mad at him, not with everything else going on. I need him by my side.

"I know, but you're so used to my perfection that it was obviously startling to see me in such humbling light," he says, lips tugging upward.

"Sammie, I watched you pee yourself at the shark exhibit during our third-grade class trip to the aquarium. I've never seen you as a perfect being."

His ears turn bright red from where they peek out in his mass of hair. "I would've thought you were too distracted by the cute tour guide to notice."

"He was a teenage boy who knew about aquatic plant life," I reply. "That is one instant love I will never apologize for."

"Don't apologize for any of them," he says suddenly. "I tease because I love you. But you wouldn't be Ophelia if you weren't in love with every boy you meet. Don't let any of our jokes change that about you."

My first instinct is to scream at him for saying "every boy." For still not getting it. But I notice the way his hands tighten their grip on the steering wheel. I realize, with a jolt, that Sammie is being sincere here. He's talking about my crushes seriously, without a hint of sarcastic judgment. Despite my annoyances, I don't fight the warmth his words bring when I let that reality sink in.

I'm just so used to apologizing for my heart.

"Thanks," I say softly.

Sammie nods, expression firm. We don't say anything else until we get to school, but we don't have to. We've said plenty already.

❀ ❀ ❀

Lunch comes faster than I'm prepared for. All day, my friends shoot me a combination of encouraging and worrisome glances. I keep quiet, trying not to think too much about what Lucas is planning on saying to me while also welcoming the anxiety as a distraction from the memory of my parents' shouting. Agatha and Lindsay can't stop staring at each other at our lockers, putting their books away at a comically slow speed. I'd call them out on it if I wasn't so nervous.

Agatha lets out a deep sigh, looking behind me. Which means Lucas is finally coming.

"Good luck," Lindsay singsongs, walking away before Agatha does. Ags doesn't say anything, but her raised eyebrows say enough. I think of Sammie yesterday, *Be care-ful*, and nod before she leaves to join Linds and our other friends. Our other friends, including Talia.

The girl I sort of asked to prom last night.

Before I can think too much about that, Lucas is in front of me, offering me a wilted dandelion, still yellow and spiky. No one will ever get to wish on it now.

"I picked this for you earlier," he says as I take it from him. There's a dead ant resting between the layers of golden fluff. "I remembered you love flowers."

"Thanks," I say, half-heartedly twirling it between my fingers. At least he tried.

"Shall we?" he says. I follow him outside, through the cluster of people still chatting at their lockers, until we reach the bench by the rusty water fountain that Sammie's con-vinced is haunted.

"So how have you been?" I ask, perching on the bench beside him.

"Hanging in there, you know."

"Do you know where you're going in the fall yet?" I ask.

"I ended up getting an athletic scholarship to UCLA."

"That's amazing! Congratulations!" I nearly place my hand over his, but stop myself.

"It's whatever," he says, and shrugs, letting his golden hair cover the satisfied smile on his soft, pink lips.

It's odd to know what someone else's lips feel like, but I still have the memory of his mouth on mine all those months ago. I try to refocus my thoughts, but then I'm thinking of a different pair of lips. Brown, full, smiling in the sunlight.

"So what do you think?" Lucas says.

Talia vanishes from my thoughts. "I'm sorry, what?"

His brows turn inward and lips hook down. "I said I think we should go to prom together."

I hear him and know it would be foolish to ask him to repeat himself again, but my brain isn't sure he spoke correctly. How is it possible to imagine something so many times but be unable to recognize it as it happens right in front of you?

"I—" I start, but he interrupts me.

"I know it's kind of last minute, but I know you don't have a date. I don't have one either. If we hadn't ended things last spring, we'd be going together anyways." He cocks his head, and I fight the urge to remind him that the end of our relationship was not a mutual decision. "I figured, why not, you know?"

His grin is so relaxed, so easygoing. I know Mom would beam with pride at the visual of him standing behind me, gripping my waist in our backyard while Dad snaps photos. I know what Lindsay would say to me if she were here right now.

And I know what I would've said a year ago, a few months ago, even just a few weeks ago, to this chance at a perfect high school moment with a perfectly cute boy.

But somehow, when "No" leaves my freshly glossed lips, I'm not surprised.

Lucas clearly is though, his eyes shooting wide open and mouth fumbling for words. For once, I'm not the one flustered in our conversation. Even when we dated, I was always struck silent by my sheer inability to understand that I was really there, really dating a boy as pretty and funny as him. How many times did I let a joke or comment go unsaid because I feared he wouldn't like it? Wouldn't get it? If I asked, would he even know what type of flowers I garden, or did he forget I was responsible for the backdrop of most of our make-out sessions? How many times have I felt like myself around Lucas? Have I ever?

And because I can't help myself, not really, the next question pops into my head just as smoothly, like it's been there all along:

How many times have I felt like myself with Talia?

"What? Did you want some fancy promposal shit? Because the team has been super busy finishing out the season, so—"

"No, it's not—I mean, I did want that, but that's not . . ." I'm fumbling again. "I just . . . I don't think we should go together."

"I don't understand. You don't have a date."

"I do, actually," I say, eliciting another shocked expression from the boy whose curls and eyes and smile still make my insides feel like melted butter. But my brain is in charge right now, not my heart or gut or ovaries.

"Who?" he asks incredulously. "Cho? Nasar?" I realize

for the first time how annoying it is that he only ever refers to boys by their last names.

"I'm going with Talia Sanchez," I say without thinking. He laughs.

"You're turning me down to go to prom with your friend? You can still hang out with her; all I'm asking for is a few pictures and a dance or two." He looks around, like he can't quite believe this is happening, confirming that this was never about getting back together. It was just about prom.

"I'm sorry, Lucas," I say, unsure of how sorry I truly am. I know when Sammie said not to be apologetic about my heart, he didn't mean it this way. But his words drive me to stand up and hand back Lucas's dandelion.

"Whatever. Hope you have fun," he says, but I'm already walking away. Head held high, I strut to the girls' restroom instead of the lunch table.

I take one look at myself in the mirror, reminded of this morning, before rushing into the closest bathroom stall and spending the rest of lunch with my head between my knees, thoughts and heartbeat racing.

❀ ❀ ❀

"Oh thank God," Agatha says as she exhales. The first thing I did when I met up with her and Linds at our lockers after school was spill the beans. "I don't know what I would've done if you'd actually gotten back together with Lucas."

"You would've been forced to be nice to him for once?" Lindsay offers. I notice she hasn't commented directly about my rejection. "At least you're not the only one who turned someone down today."

"What?" I ask, slamming my locker shut harder than I mean to. "Who asked you?"

"Not me," she says, darting her eyes toward Agatha.

"Ags?" I ask, confusion surely written all over my face.

Agatha shrugs but doesn't look at me. "Georgie Yuen asked me at lunch. It's no big deal."

"No big deal?" I ask, incredulous. I had a major crush on Georgie in middle school but got over it when he couldn't stop making jokes during the puberty presentation in health class. He grew up rather handsome though. "What did he say? What did *you* say?"

She shuts her locker, finally looking at me. "He asked me on our way to the table. I said no, because I hardly talk to the guy outside of calculus. And because his idea of a fashion statement is orange boat shoes." She shudders, but it feels forced. Like she's hiding something. "It's nothing, O, seriously. Honestly, it's so nothing that I was going to save y'all the time it would take to repeat the meaningless story and keep the list of people who know to just Lindsay."

"There is nothing *just* about me, thank you very much," Lindsay says, breaking the awkward tension as the boys walk over with Talia.

"You realize that statement has a double meaning, right?" Sammie teases, clearly having overheard the last bit of our conversation but hopefully no more than that. Agatha seems dead set on keeping this Georgie thing under lock.

Sammie flicks a strand of Lindsay's hair out of her face. She sticks her tongue out at him, but doesn't engage in their usual bickering, so he turns to me. "So what did dear old Snooze-cus want with Hamlet's favorite girl?"

"He asked me to go to prom with him. I said no," I say plainly, head down to zip up my backpack while Sammie starts a slow clap.

"Someone pinch me," he laughs, turning to Wesley with a teasing grin. Zaq reaches over and pinches him instead. Sammie hisses in pain.

"Why'd you say no?" Wesley asks. Lindsay shoots him a look.

I glance at Talia quickly, but look away before I can read her expression. We didn't talk about this at all during government. "It didn't feel right."

"But he's so cute!" Lindsay says, weirdly cheery. "And you liked him so much last year! Remember how much you cried over your breakup last summer?"

"Don't remind me," Sammie says.

"Do you want her to cry over him more?" Wesley asks with a slight edge to his voice, eliciting an awkward silence from the entire group. He and Lindsay stare at each other, leaving the rest of us watching their unspoken argument.

"I just don't want to see her miserable when we're all dancing and having fun with our dates," Lindsay says, leaning slightly into Sammie like a threat.

"Uh, Earth to Linds, technically no one here has a date yet," Agatha says. "At least, as far as I've heard." She does a slow once-over of the group.

"You've heard correct," Wesley mumbles, but we all hear him.

Lindsay stiffens. "Sammie, can you give me a ride home?"

"Sure, but I have to give O a ride home too," Sammie says, to my pleasant surprise.

"I can give her a ride," Wesley offers. If it weren't for the soft, unsure expression on his face when he says it, I would assume he was trying to make Lindsay jealous right back.

"I'll take her," Talia says finally. "It's on my way."

"Well, now that we've divvied up our Ophelia respon-sibilities, can we go?" Lindsay asks, leaving for the parking lot without waiting for Sammie's reply. He scuttles after her, shooting an apologetic glance over his shoulder before dis-appearing out of the hall.

"That was fun," Ags deadpans, but no one replies. "Zaq, I've been meaning to ask, where did you get that jacket? I saw you wearing it last week but completely forgot to mention it. It's amazing." His jacket *is* ridiculously cool, all purple denim decked out in patches and golden spikes.

"Talia helped me pick it out at a vintage clothes show back in the winter. We should check it out sometime—you'd love it," he says as they start walking away, too focused on their discussion of thrifting unicorns to notice us still lagging behind.

"Are you good?" Talia asks Wesley. He nods quickly.

Talia and I follow our friends, leaving a safe distance between us and them. I try to ask about her graphic tee with anime characters on it, about lunch, about whether she finished her English paper after dropping me off last night; all things we didn't say during our silence in gov, but she can't stop watching Agatha and Zaq, and Wesley moping alongside them.

"Are *you* good?" I ask her as we get in her car, echoing her question to Wesley. She finally shakes out of her daze.

"Yeah, sorry. A lot just happened back there in a very short amount of time." She turns the car on and starts pulling out of the lot.

"The perks of having a bigger group of friends," I joke, though there's a seed of truth to it.

"Is Lindsay always like that to you guys?" she asks me quickly, like the words have been begging her to let them out.

"Like what?"

"She used Sammie and insulted you just to get back at Wes for agreeing that going to prom with Lucas would've been a bad idea," she says, eyes forward.

"That's just Linds's way of trying to tell me she wants me to be happy."

"And would you have been happy with Lucas? I thought you wanted that classic prom experience. Cute boy, all your friends, romantic evening under the stars. Or, I guess whatever aquatic decorations we're going to get."

I laugh. "Lucas would've just complicated everything.

Plus, I couldn't abandon our nondate date pact, right?" I nudge her arm lightly, feeling bolder about bringing up my offer now that we're alone again.

She doesn't return my smile though, not immediately anyway. She turns on the radio, letting a pop song about unrequited love blast over the speakers for the remainder of the ride.

I try ignoring the gut feeling I've done something wrong by shutting down Lucas. I know Sammie, Agatha, and even Wesley are relieved. I expected Lindsay to be skeptical about my rejection, but Talia's concern is a surprise.

I know Lucas is just who my parents would expect to see me with, who I would've expected as well, once upon a time. But I have to forget about those expectations. I have to think about what *I* want *now*.

Whatever that is.

FIFTEEN

Sammie drops me off after school on Friday, an uneventful day compared to the past two weeks of utter chaos. Lucas avoided me in chemistry while Wesley and Lindsay avoided each other everywhere, leaving Sammie in an obnoxiously chipper mood. He pulls away the second I leave the car so he can go meet Linds for another movie date.

Mom is standing in the foyer when I open the front door, arms crossed and hip slightly popped. I feigned a stomachache last night to get out of dinner again and shot out of the house this morning before I could run into her or Dad.

"I picked up your prom dress from the tailor's this afternoon," she says.

"Thanks," I reply evenly. I move past her into the kitchen to grab a snack.

Dad is putting a tray of empanadas in the oven with his back turned to me. I consider going upstairs to scavenge for food in my room so I can avoid this unplanned confrontation, but Mom stops me.

"How was your day?" she asks. Despite the innocent words, I can tell she's pissed.

"Fine." I grab a granola bar from the pantry and a glass of water from the fridge. "Yours?"

"Fine."

Dad huffs a sigh and pulls off his oven mitts, slapping them onto the counter. "There is too much passive aggressiveness in this kitchen," he says, running a hand over his face as if to smooth out the wrinkles we're causing. "Either yell or don't speak, anything but esto."

"Ophelia," Mom starts, dropping her arms. "I would still like you to email Jeremiah apologizing for what you did."

"For fuck's sake," I mutter.

"Pardon?" Mom says, arms flying back onto her hips. "I don't know what has gotten into you lately."

"Because I cursed? I'd hate for you to see me at school."

"That's it," she says. "Go up to your room."

"For what? Because I won't apologize to your creepy asshole of a student?" Any residual guilt from overhearing her and Dad yesterday has dissipated. "Write it yourself if you're such a great English professor. You'd know what bullshit looks like; you complain about your students' work enough to be plenty familiar."

"Ophelia," Dad warns, but I can't stop.

"But sure, send me up to my room! God knows what good that'll do me."

"You threw a drink on my student!"

"Who was being an assss–hole!" I reply loudly, drawing out the last word.

"*Watch your language.*" She clenches her hands and exhales. "If you just tell me what happened, I'm sure we can find an appropriate resolution to all of this."

"*I* don't need a resolution, Mom," I say. "Talk to Jeremiah if you need answers. You're already used to talking to your students about me."

"Both of you need to cool off." Dad steps between us, cupping Mom's face lightly with his hand. He looks at me over his shoulder. "Go upstairs."

"Gladly," I snap, grabbing my snacks and storming to my bedroom. I slam my door shut so hard, my glass of water wobbles where I set it atop my dresser. I wait for more shouting but am met with silence.

I kick off my shoes and slip into bed, feeling exhausted.

Just tell her what he said, a small voice in me begs. *She'll understand.*

No, she won't, a louder voice inside replies. *She'll think you took what he said personally. I mean, just look at what Dad assumed. You're boy-crazy Ophelia, not some gay rights vigilante. Telling her means telling her everything. You really want to disappoint her and her dreams for you like that?*

I lean over the side of my bed, dropping my empty glass and wrapper on the floor. Huddling in my rose sheets, I drift off into a restless nap. Flashes of Mom's disappointed face, Dad half lit by streetlamps, Talia laughing on her floor, and Lucas's astonished expression float through my mind. Until, nothing.

❋ ❋ ❋

I wake up to a buzzing, at first confusing it for a headache. I fumble around in my comforter, sticky with nap-induced sweat, before digging my phone out from beneath my pillow.

"Talia?" I ask, having seen her name flash on the screen.

"Hey." She pauses. "Did I wake you?"

"No, no you're fine," I say, quickly clearing my throat and voice of its grogginess as I check the time. It's just after seven. "What's up?"

"I need your help," she says quickly, jolting me even more awake. "Sorry, that sounds super serious. I mean, this is serious but—"

"What do you need?"

"It's going to be a little dangerous," she says. I imagine Linds saying those same words, smirk on her lips and playfulness in her voice. But Talia sounds scared, a little sad even.

"But you need help?" I ask.

"Yeah," she says, and there's a pause before she adds, "yours."

"I'm in," I say.

"But you don't even—"

"I'm *in*."

"Can I pick you up in fifteen minutes?" she asks warily. I'm almost insulted after how definitively I asserted my willingness.

"See you then."

I hop out of bed and rush to my bathroom, wiping under my eyes and running a wet brush through my hair so it won't puff up as I work out the knots. I squirt some of the gardenia perfume I got for my birthday last fall on my wrists and neck. My entire body is hot and jittery.

Talia needs help and she came to me. Not Wesley, not Zaq. Not Dani or Tori or anyone else. Me.

I'm nearly out the door when I remember the reason for my early slumber and sour mood.

"¿A dónde vas?" Dad calls from the kitchen. I backtrack, stopping in the doorway. At least Mom isn't in here. Dad's heating up popcorn on the stove, and I hear *Pride and Prejudice* playing in the living room.

"Talia asked me to run to the mall with her to find lipstick to match her prom outfit," I lie quickly, hoping the details will hide my wavering tone. Sammie once told me that specificity is the key to a good lie. "She bought a burgundy shade last week, but her shoes are crimson and it's throwing the whole look off." *Okay, too much specificity.* I press my lips shut.

Dad leans against the counter on his elbows. His face says he sees right through my lie, a disappointed dip in his lips and slight squint to his eyes.

I shift from one foot to the other.

"Do you need to buy lipstick too?" he asks slowly, nodding to his wallet on the counter beside him. This feels suspiciously like a test.

"I'm good."

"You should talk to your mom. Without all the cursing, porfa."

"I will," I say. "Just not tonight."

He nods to himself, and I wonder if, for the first time, my behavior will keep me from being allowed out. I've never fought with my mom like this before, and I don't think either of them know how to deal with it. That makes three of us.

Finally, "¿Por qué me lo dijiste pero no a ella?" *Why did you tell me but won't tell her?*

I don't have an answer for him, not really, but I'm saved when headlights flicker on the street, visible through the kitchen window. "Looks like she's here," he says, standing up as he lets the question crumble away. He takes a slight step forward, like he's coming to hug me, but stops himself. "Have fun. Don't be out too late."

I smile at him sadly, apologetically, before darting out of the room and then the front door. I fly down the lawn, leaving my problems at home, focusing on what I'm running toward instead of what I'm leaving behind.

Talia unlocks the passenger door for me, greeting me with a gracious but anxious smile as she pulls away from my house. The sun is nearly set, blazing light making each strand of her curly hair glow with warmth.

"So, ¿qué está pasando?" I ask as I buckle myself in. She turns down the radio with shaking hands.

"Promise me you won't freak out," she says.

"Okay, I promise."

"We need to break into Dani's house."

"Funny, it sounded like you just said we have to break into Dani's house."

"Ophelia," she groans, making a sharp turn.

"Why don't you start by telling me what's going on?" I say. I blindly signed up for an adventure—a dangerous one—but not a crime.

"She stole something of mine, and I want it back," she replies, her grip on the wheel tightening until her knuckles look as white as Agatha's teeth. "I *need* it back."

"What did she take?"

"My abuela's brooch, the one I told you about."

"Wait, I thought you said you had no idea where that was."

"I didn't, but I asked my dad yesterday where he'd put it when he cleaned out the garage. He swore it was with my abuela's old stuff in his closet, but I practically tore his room apart and nothing. Dani and her mom came by to help him sort through old photos a few weeks ago, and now it's gone? It can't be a coincidence."

"Can't you tell your dad about it? Or her mom? They'd understand, wouldn't they?"

Talia shoots me a deadly look, softening when she notices my alarm. "Even if my dad believed me, he'd never stand up to his older sister about it. My tía thinks Dani is an angel; they'd never side with me."

"But are you even sure she took it? Why would Dani want your brooch? Doesn't she have the exact same one, just different colors?"

"Why does Dani do anything anymore?" Talia asks,

clearly more to herself than me. "My abuela loved me. She never tried to change me, ever. I know that if she had been alive when everything with Tori happened . . . I just—" Her voice breaks, and she takes a deep breath before speaking again. "I can't let Dani take this from me too."

"You have me now," I say, resting a hand atop her bare shoulder. My skin is set alight. "I'll help you."

"Really?"

"Really," I say, pulling my hand away despite every ounce of want in my body begging me to keep it there. "Let's do this."

❋ ❋ ❋

From the outside, Dani's house looks like any ordinary home, not the historical landmark for my first crime. "Okay, so I'll go in there with you and distract them while you ransack the joint?"

"'Ransack the joint?'" Talia asks, her lips curving into a smile for the first time since she picked me up.

"I've never committed a crime before, okay? I don't know the lingo."

"Good thing you're with a criminal expert," she deadpans.

"Point taken. What's the plan, then?"

Talia leans past me, taking a good look at the house. From what I can see, it doesn't look like anyone's home.

"Hold on," she says, pulling her phone from her pocket. I watch the way she chews on her bottom lip as it rings.

"Hi, Dani," Talia says in a forcefully pleasant voice. *What are you doing?* I mouth to her, but she just lifts a finger to silence me. "Are you home right now?" Her lip twitches like she's desperate to bite it again. I silently beg her not to, needing to keep my mind clear for this.

"When are you going to be back? Ah, uh . . ." Dani must be asking why Talia is so curious about her itinerary. I quickly pull at my cardigan, pointing until understanding flickers across Talia's face. "Your mom left her chaqueta at my house last week. My dad wanted me to bring it by." She lies beautifully, the words smoother than they would've sounded coming from my mouth.

"Yeah, yeah, okay. I'll drop it off tomorrow. Bye." Talia hangs up. She turns to me slowly, a smile creeping up her face. "Vamos."

I follow her out of the car, hunching as we shuffle across the dry, patchy grass leading up to the front door. Talia pauses, takes a deep breath with her fingers crossed, then lifts the welcome mat with her other hand. She straightens, a shiny golden key in her hand. "Some things never change," she sighs, her smile falling. She clears her throat, turning to unlock the door, and I hesitantly follow after her, shooting glances behind us.

The house is dark, the minimal streetlight from the open windows casting shadows across the furniture. Blankets drape over almost every surface, and open magazines are scattered around the tables.

"Let's check Dani's room first," Talia says, nodding toward the hallway.

I feel like we're in Talia's room all over again. I expected

Dani's bedroom to be elegant, if not brash. But her walls are painted a dingy yellow, one wall looking slightly darker, although I can't tell for sure with the lights still off. My fingers itch to flip the light switch, but Talia leaves it off, so I do too.

Talia is hunched over Dani's desk, sifting through drawers and stacks of paperwork. I turn to Dani's dresser, but find myself looking at the photos on her walls instead. A few of them look like family photos, likely recent ones considering Dani looks the same as she did when we saw her at Ollas Amarillas, but I can't spot Talia in any of them.

Oh.

"Over here," Talia croaks. I race to her side, where she's crouched on the floor beside Dani's desk. Her eyes are squeezed shut and face contorted in pain.

"Are you okay? Did you hit yourself?"

"No," she whimpers, finger tapping on something above us, still on the desk.

I stand up and see her hand wrapped around a small velvet box that could be black or dark blue, too difficult to tell in this lighting. A gaudy, glittery *D* sticker is stuck to the lid. Gently, I pull back Talia's fingers. She lets me, hugging them to her body once the box is free from her grip.

I cautiously pop the box open. My vision wavers as I press a finger to the gorgeous brooch within; a rose intricately crafted from curved and twisted silver, set with a vibrant blue stone in the center.

Then my finger moves to the one beside it, identical except for the gold stem and ruby stone.

"I'm so sorry, Talia."

She blows out a long breath, discreetly wiping at her eyes before standing up. She still towers over me, but I want to hold her, protect her from this.

"I didn't know for sure until now," she admits. I rest my hand on her shoulder, squeezing it for comfort. She leans into my touch, her cheek grazing my knuckles. I hear nothing but my heartbeat.

She scoops up the golden brooch, slipping it into her front jean pocket. I shut the box for her, pushing it back into the mess of paperwork. I suppose it doesn't matter if Dani knows we were here now.

"We should go," I whisper as she stares at her fingernails, lightly scratching at the bright red polish. She's always chipping it, scraping away each coat. But the next day, it's always there again.

We're back on the porch and I'm moving the mat into its original place, the scratchy fabric noisy against the brick, when I sense Talia freeze beside me.

"Talia? ¿Qué estás haciendo aquí?" an unfamiliar voice asks. I grasp for Talia's hand before thinking better of it and press it into my skirt instead as I turn around. Even if she didn't have the same bone structure as Dani, logic would've told me the woman standing before us, with her arms full of groceries, is Talia's aunt.

"Tía Eliana," Talia finally says, jolting back to life. "I called Dani and told her you left your jacket at my house last week."

"What jacket?" Eliana asks, cocking her head to the side.

"The corduroy one," Talia replies quickly, too quickly. "With the patches falling off the elbows."

"I threw out that jacket months ago," Eliana replies, eyes narrowing. Talia deflates beside me. "So I'll ask again, what were you doing in my house?" Her eyes shift to me, and my blood runs cold. "And who is this?"

"This is Ophelia."

"Another one of your little friends, como Victoria?" Eliana sets her bags down at her feet and crosses her arms.

Talia doesn't respond to that. Almost as if in a trance, she reaches into her pocket and lifts the brooch up for her aunt to see. "This is mine, and Dani took it."

"That was my mother's. It should've never touched your hands," Eliana says, completely unfazed. "She was sick and foolish when she died, wasn't seeing you clearly."

"Abuelita wanted me to have this. Dani has her own."

"Tu abuela no sabía que estabas jodiendo con otras muchachas en secreto." The words feel like a slap in the face, even though they're not directed at me. *Your grandmother didn't know you were fucking other girls in secret.*

"One kiss!" Talia cries, Eliana's words drawing something wet and miserable out of her voice. "One kiss goodbye to my best friend almost four years ago! Abuelita wouldn't have cared! My dad got over it! But you and Dani *still* treat me like some villain!"

"You and Victoria would've ruined my daughter!"

"I wasn't going to fuck my cousin!" Talia's voice is

poisonous, violent. I almost don't recognize her. "Tell your precious daughter to stay out of my stuff and you won't have to worry about my bisexuality corrupting her precious soul."

"You'll be damned for this," Eliana says, stepping forward as if to slap Talia.

Talia spits on the ground before her aunt's feet, forcing her to stop. "You think I'm headed for hell? I'll see you there."

With that, we sprint past Eliana. I throw open the passenger door as Talia flings herself into the driver's seat. Eliana catches up to us while Talia is still turning the ignition on and stares, shaking her head.

I raise a single, unpolished middle finger to the window and roll it down just enough for Eliana to hear me. "Come mierda."

And then we're off.

❋ ❋ ❋

"I can't believe that just happened," Talia says once we're a safe distance away, not that either of us expected Eliana to follow. We stop at a red light, and Talia pulls the brooch out from her pocket, twirling it between her matching fingers, aglow with ruby light. "We did it."

I know we're feeling exhilarated and empowered, but I have to say it. "I'm so sorry about what Eliana said."

Talia shrugs, for once looking like she actually doesn't care what some of her family thinks about her. "I can't change her mind. She thinks I'm a sinner, so I acted like one. At least now I've earned my damnation."

I grin, drunk on teenage rebellion. "You were pretty badass."

"What about you with your 'come mierda'?" she laughs, pitching up her voice as she mimics me. "How long have you been waiting to say that to someone?"

"Seventeen and a half years, give or take." Cursing hits different in Spanish.

She doubles over in laughter. She's barely looking as the light turns green and we race down the empty streets. I don't know how there are so few cars out on a Friday night, but I don't question it. Maybe everyone got the memo that Ophelia Rojas and Talia Sanchez were set loose tonight, breaking into houses and cursing out homophobic aunts.

We scream at the top of our lungs to the electro pop music Talia starts blaring through the radio. As we zoom past the streets I've known my entire life, I wonder if I'll ever feel better than I do in this moment. I've never felt so alive, never felt so free.

I blink and we're pulling up to my house. I beg Talia to drive around the block, again, too delirious and ecstatic to worry about how my hands are tugging on her shoulders, but she teasingly pries me off.

"I've got to get home before Eliana calls my dad and tells him what happened," she says, eyes falling and tone sobering. She turns down the music until only a vibrating thump remains. "She's probably already called him, but I should do some damage control before he can stew too long in it."

"How bad do you think it's going to be?" I ask, biting my lip. Her eyes drift up to mine, staying clear of my mouth.

"Can't be worse than when Tori and I kissed. He'll get over it." She leans back into her seat, covering her face with her hands. "Who would've thought that tiny kiss would've fucked me over like this."

I pause. "Was it worth it?"

She pulls her hands off her face. "What?"

"Kissing Tori," I say. "Was it worth it?"

She watches me, seconds turning to hours. My palms bead with sweat in my lap, but I refuse to wipe them on my legs, fearing any movement will break the moment.

"I won't change who I am for them." Her voice is so soft, nearly a whisper, but her conviction is unwavering. "I hid how I felt about Tori for so long. But when she kissed me, I knew it wasn't wrong. I knew *I* wasn't wrong. That was worth every ounce of my family's disappointment, because from then on I knew I didn't deserve it."

I don't think; I can't possibly think right now. My thoughts, my brain, wouldn't let me do any of this otherwise.

Because I'm not the girl who breaks into houses and steals already stolen family heirlooms. I'm not the girl who throws a drink on a boy at a college party. I'm not the girl who fights with her mom and avoids her for days afterward.

I'm not the girl who likes girls.

But in this moment, *that girl that I am* doesn't matter. Because right now I am this girl.

And I lean over and kiss Talia.

I finally let my damp hands move, digging them into the fabric of my skirt like a lifeline. The cloth is soft, but not as soft as Talia's lips against my own. I experience sensory overload, the press of the seat against my bare legs, the front seat divider digging into my side, Talia's minty but warm scent, her hair tickling my cheek, the wetness of her mouth mingling with mine until differentiating where I begin and she ends is impossible. It all sears into my memory so intensely it practically burns. I burn.

After a second and forever have passed, I tilt my face the way I used to with Lucas, the way I've seen every boy/girl couple do in this moment.

And then Talia pulls away.

She pulls away.

She pulls away and drops back into her seat, scooting as far away from me as possible against the car door.

"I'm—I thought you . . ." All the moisture from my mouth evaporates, words quickly following suit. I don't know what to say or even how I would say it if I could think of anything, and the silence around us is so palpable, thick like a curtain of humidity but worse, so much worse, and my hands itch to reach out and peel it away, make one of us say something, anything. My desperation climbs up my body until my lips finally find purchase. "I thought you were bisexual."

"I am," she replies, still so far away in such a small space. The car grows with each ticking moment.

But still, a small sigh of relief leaves me. I'm not wrong; this isn't wrong.

"But I'm not—I'm—I have a boyfriend."

I was wrong enough.

"Wh—what? Who?" I ask, because what else is there to say. My mind torpedoes through a list of Talia's known male associates, only two people. I mentally skip over Wesley with ease. But I freeze on the small smiles, jealous looks, and loaded gazes I've seen her share with the next boy. All the paintings in her room, signed with a Z.

"Zaq," I say before she can reply. "You're dating Zaq." She nods slowly, but I don't register the confirmation. I don't even register my suggestion. "How long?"

She grimaces, like my confusion hits her harder than it's hitting me. "We've only been together for a few weeks." Her lips quiver, and she looks torn between crying and suppressing a smile. "When Wesley and Lindsay starting hanging out more, he and I grew closer. It started out as nothing, but one thing led to another and . . ." She trails off, possibly realizing how cliché she sounds, possibly realizing that I don't actually want to know. "We didn't tell Wes because we didn't want him to feel like a third wheel, but then we joined your group and things . . . changed. We planned to tell him just before prom."

"Because Zaq is your date," I say. Another nod.

"You said you didn't have a date for prom," I whisper, looking down at my hands. They're as dry as my lips are now, no sheen to memorialize what I felt only, what, minutes? seconds? ago. My heart rate is softer than the buzzing radio. I silently beg my body for a reaction.

She winces. "I never said that."

My eyes drift to Sammie's house. A few lights are on. Sammie is probably still awake, his sisters and parents too. I don't bother thinking about my parents; I can't right now. But I do wonder at the back of my mind, how it is that the rest of the world, the one just beside me, could keep trudging along while I sit here fracturing.

I kissed a girl. I kissed *the* girl. And she has a boyfriend.

"I said no to Lucas." I pause. "For you."

Something like a sob escapes Talia's lips. A sound so tragic should have me feeling remorseful, but instead I'm internally heaving, desperate to empty myself of anything else that could hurt her.

"I'm sorry," she whispers. Her dark eyes shimmer in the light from the streetlamps seeping in through the window. "But I didn't ask you to do that. I didn't know what to say when you asked me to be your date. I didn't—I thought you just meant as friends."

"Does your family know?" I ask. "About Zaq?"

"No," she confesses, exhaling with the topic change. "If they knew I had a boyfriend, they'd think I'm 'cured.' Like I'm straight now."

"So I'm the first person you've told," I say, part question, part statement. Talia nods again. "Okay."

I open the passenger door but can't even shut it before Talia springs out of the car and races to my side, leaving her door open with the keys still in the ignition.

"I'm so sorry," she repeats, louder and more frantic than before. "I had no idea you were—"

"That I'm what?" I interrupt, crossing my arms. Like Mom, like Eliana.

Talia freezes, shaking her head subtly and blinking wildly. "Oh. Well, I mean are you bi or pan or . . . ?"

"We aren't the same," I insist, an awful heat coiling around my chest, begging to be freed with whatever horrible words I can throw at Talia. "I'm not Tori. You and I are not you and Tori."

She takes a long breath, in and out. "I can come inside. We can talk about this. I've been here before, and I can help you. Nothing has to change between us."

"Nothing has to change?" I feel slapped.

"Let me help you." She reaches out for my hand, but I jump away before she can touch me, scared of what it'll do to me.

"I don't need you" is all I say before leaving Talia, the ruby-nailed girl, the shy government girl, the girl who kissed a girl and liked it but didn't like kissing me, alone and half crying on my front lawn.

The house is still when I get inside. My parents are asleep, all the doors locked and lights turned off. I pass their room without hesitation, the blue glow of their television sliding on and off my face like water.

I go into my bathroom and run a bath for the first time in years, watching the tub fill. I strip off my clothes, my skirt feeling stiff and abrasive against my dry hands. I slip under the water and scream at the top of my lungs.

SIXTEEN

I don't have words for what I feel. I wish I did, but I think I left them all on the lawn last night.

When I wake up, the sun shines through the gap in my gauzy curtains, the hum and scent of the coffee maker downstairs trickle in from beneath my door, and my mouth is dry and rough. I watch and listen and smell and taste, but feelings have left me.

I think of myself, nearly a year ago, crying in this very spot over Lucas. Crying over the way I'd never run my fingers through his hair or part his lips with my own or press my head against his chest ever again.

But right now, I only think of never making Talia laugh again. I think of never watching the fracturing sunlight bounce off her car window to catch on her nose ring and sparkling nails. Never again seeing her without instantly feeling like I've been punched in the gut.

How many times has Zaq earned the exact smile I've

treasured so privately? Has he ever seen the way her lips creep open and split her face into something so bright and brilliant and pure that I ache now just remembering it?

Lucas was nothing compared to this. None of those boys ever were. Hell, even giving up whatever small crush I had on Sammie as a kid, a silent promise I'd made to myself to protect my closest and oldest friendship, didn't leave me this hollow and unfeeling. I gave and took away my affections so often, I think my heart has always half belonged to the world and half belonged to me. But I would've given her the whole thing, had she asked me to.

And now I know she never will.

"Ophelia?" Dad calls outside the door, almost too quietly to be heard over my thoughts.

I take a deep breath like I'm going to answer him, but instead I hold it and wait. My lungs ache as I watch his shadow under the door disappear down the hall.

I release my breath into my duvet. The rumpled roses are unrecognizable at this angle, this close. I press a finger down to smooth out the design, but the fabric refuses to flatten, bubbling up to counteract wherever I apply pressure.

Turning over onto my back, my eyes scan my bare ceiling. I wait for something to hit me, something to draw tears from my eyes. I want to scream, to cry and yell like I did last night. But maybe I left more than my words on the lawn; maybe I really did give Talia my whole heart. And maybe we both left it out to rot.

Boys left me with a broken heart. But at least they left me with something.

I don't close the curtains. I don't cover my ears or plug my nose. I don't open my mouth to let any of this out. I do what I should've done in the first place, back at that party when one look at one girl ruined my simple, predictable heart.

I don't feel anything. Not this time. Not ever again.

SEVENTEEN

The first thing Sammie says when I get in the car Monday morning is, "Damn, you look like shit."

I plaster on an expression that feels more bared-teeth than start-of-the-day-smile. "Gee, thanks."

He's not wrong. My hair was so knotted when I woke up that I lazily threw it into a bun to avoid dealing with it. My skin broke out, so I lacquered my face with an old bottle of foundation since my newer one ran out. But I've gotten slighter tanner as summer approaches, so the thick coat doesn't match my skin and gives me a ghostly pallor.

It wouldn't be so bad if I hadn't also run out of clean laundry, forced to wear the bright orange babydoll dress decorated with cartoonish daisies that I'd thrifted with Agatha months ago. I forgot to ask her to tailor it, so it swallows me whole, completing my Toddler Who Got In Her Mother's Makeup aesthetic.

"So," Sammie starts, pulling down the street and

adjusting the air-conditioning. The spring heat has come back with a vengeance, and I wave the hem of my dress up and down on my legs while I wait for the cool air to kick in. "What were you doing all weekend?"

"Homework," I reply noncommittally, watching cars zoom by us.

"We didn't have anything due today."

"It was for chemistry."

"But you and Wesley finished all your chem work last week when he gave you a ride home." The air-conditioning finally blasts me, goose bumps erupting down my bare legs.

"It was extra-credit work, Sherlock. What did you do this weekend?"

"Waited for my best friend to reply to my messages," he says, batting his eyelashes at me. "Especially the ones concerning a certain screaming match I heard Friday night."

"So no progress with Lindsay, huh?" I bite back.

Sammie sighs, running a free hand over his curls. They look damp, like he just hopped out of the shower. "I think I'm just gonna go for it. No flowers or posters bullshit. Just me and her. Linds has never been one for all that romantic crap anyways, so being straightforward is my best bet."

I make a noncommittal hum.

"Unless you've got a better idea," he says, turning into the student parking lot. I don't reply, too busy watching some couple kiss by the main gate. The boy tucks a strand of the girl's hair behind her ear before their lips meet again. Students rush by them, groups big and small, but they remain stock-still in their PDA. No one walking by even gives them a second glance.

I force my eyes away in time to see Sammie driving straight toward the empty parking space beside a familiar white truck. Talia is leaning against the back bumper, chewing on one of her ruby red nails while scrolling through her phone in her other hand.

Her hair is also up in a bun, but where mine looks like a rat's nest, hers looks flawless, signature curls spilling out around her face. I curse the universe for the way the sun, still rising in the early morning, illuminates her. It's like someone dictates the sun to place itself exactly where it will best flatter her at all times. It's getting sickeningly annoying.

"Why don't you park over there?" I suggest, nodding toward an empty space in the neighboring row.

"Because there's a space right next to Talia's car?" Sammie replies, eyeing me sideways.

"But that spot has shade from the trees so your car won't be all hot and gross after school," I reply frantically as we crawl toward Talia. She's yet to look up from her phone and we're still stuck behind another car, but my heart begins to pound as we get closer.

"Bold of you to assume a parking spot can keep my car from getting hot and gross," Sammie laughs. My hands tingle in my lap, desperate to jerk the wheel out of his grasp.

The universe must be watching me though, trying to

make up for that damn sunlight, because the car in front of us steals the space beside Talia.

"Damn it," Sammie mutters, turning to park elsewhere. But it's too late. Talia looks up as we pass by, her eyes meeting mine for a solitary second. Her lips part slightly, as do mine, but I look away.

We park, and I hop out immediately, zigzagging between the cars before Sammie can even shut off his engine. Talia doesn't chase after me as I skip my locker and rush to the bathroom to hide until the bell rings, and I can't decide if I'm disappointed or relieved.

I pray for an uneventfully quiet homeroom. Instead, Quan Vu bursts in with a dozen sunflowers and a WILL YOU BE MY SUNSHINE AT PROM? poster to ask Andrea Chávez to be his date. Plus, Sammie keeps nagging me about ditching him until I mutter an excuse about needing to change my pad, banking on his infuriating but reliable aversion to menstruation. The second the bell rings, I shoot out of class with the hope of walking to chemistry without Wesley.

But apparently today is the day all my peers with long legs test my patience, because Wesley skyrockets around the corner before I can even make it out of the hall.

"What happened between you and Talia?"

"Excuse me?" I reply, letting the door leading out of the hall shut behind me.

But he barrels through it with ease. "I overheard her and Zaq talking when they were at my house yesterday," he says quietly, the guilt from eavesdropping apparent in his voice. "She seemed upset about a fight between the two of you."

"Frankly, I don't think that's any of your business," I snap, spinning around to face him. I don't let myself think about the fact that Talia told Zaq what happened.

"Well, Zaq suggested taking you to talk to someone from the center, so I thought maybe—"

"The center?" I ask, and he covers his mouth momentarily.

"I didn't—uh," he stutters before closing his eyes and taking a deep breath. "Are you homophobic or something?"

"What?" I step back, a chill rushing over me. "I—why would you ask that?"

Wesley squirms with regret. He guides me away from the chaos of students exiting the building behind us. "I just thought, based on what she said, or I guess what I heard, maybe that she told you that . . . uh . . . that she's not . . . um . . ."

"That she's bisexual?" I ask, and he nods, seemingly relieved I already know and he wasn't accidentally outing one of his closest friends. "She did tell me."

"And then she kissed you?"

Damn it.

"We're going to be late for chem." I try to move past him, but he lifts one of his huge arms, stopping me dead in my tracks. I could push past him—despite his strength I know he'd let me—but I'm exhausted. So I relent.

"She should've asked for consent, I know," he starts, and

I cover my eyes—this is so painful. "But if you're really this upset with her over a kiss, maybe we should talk about wh—"

"She didn't kiss me," I interrupt. Wesley cocks his head to the side and furrows his thick brows.

"But she mentioned an out of nowhere k—"

"*I* kissed *her.*"

"Oh" is all he says.

And that's when the first tear falls.

❀ ❀ ❀

After ten minutes of storytelling between embarrassing sobs, I finish catching Wesley up on everything.

We're sitting on the ground outside the sciences building, backs pressed against the rough stucco walls. My dress is getting dirty, dimming the obnoxiously bright color. Which feels fitting, all things considered.

"Wow," he says, and I nod because I can't think of anything to say. "She's mentioned Tori and Dani before, but I didn't realize how bad things were with her aunt."

I feel guilty for sharing what happened with Eliana, but once I started talking, I couldn't stop. Besides, he needed all the details from Friday to understand why things ended the way they did. Or at least that's what I tell myself.

"So Talia and Zaq are really dating?" He doesn't look up, picking at the skin around his thumb.

"That's your second takeaway?" I ask, borderline offended as I wipe my mascara tears away. If things go on like this, I seriously need to invest in something more waterproof.

He shrinks in on himself. "Well, what do you want me to say?"

I'm taken aback by his obliviousness. "You just don't seem very surprised."

"About you?" he asks, and I nod. "Well, I didn't know you weren't straight, but for me, that's not that surprising."

"I never said I wasn't straight," I say, and he gives me an unconvinced glance I opt to ignore. "Wait, what do you mean 'for me'?"

Wesley looks giddy but nervous. He sits up, clearing his throat, before smiling shakily at me. "Ophelia . . ."

"Wesley?" I reply, confused.

"I am not heterosexual."

I laugh without meaning to, the moment too silent and serious. "What?"

"That look on your face?" He waves a finger at me with a slight smirk, and I quickly smooth my features into a neutral expression. "Is that what you wanted me to look like when you told me about kissing Talia?"

"Sorry." A blush creeps up my face. "But you and Lindsay . . ."

"What about us?" he interrupts, his tone slightly sharp.

"Well, you clearly like girls."

"Clearly." He smiles, enjoying this more than I'd expect him to. "But you don't have to be het for that. I'm asexual."

"Asexual," I repeat, and he nods proudly, beaming. "You've never mentioned that before." My mind races to remember what exactly being asexual means.

"You never asked," he replies. Anyone else would be smug right now, especially after my sob story, but Wesley's counterpoint is genuine. I never did ask. "Did Talia ever tell you how she, Zaq, and I met?"

"Something about mutual interests?"

"I asked her not to tell you guys the full truth if you asked. Zaq too." He takes a deep breath, looking less energized than before, returning to shaky uncertainty. "I came out to my parents as ace right before we moved here. They didn't really know what it meant and had all these questions about grandkids and marriage or if I was somehow broken. They weren't angry or disappointed, but they were confused. So we found a youth center nearby for LGBTQIAP+ teens and their parents."

"And that's where you met Zaq and Talia?" I ask, tapping my nails against the concrete ground.

"Exactly. That's actually where we went last week when I lied about us studying. Talia and Zaq were the first people I met there, and the only other kids who went to this school, so I stuck with them. They knew about me being ace from the start, and they were never weird about it because we were all there for roughly the same reason."

I hesitate, taking everything in. "Can I ask about Zaq?"

"Ask about . . . oh, you mean his sexuality?" I nod. "Zaq is openly pansexual."

"I've never heard him mention that."

"Again, you never really asked," he says, definitely smug this time. But his expression quickly sobers. "Honestly, I asked Talia and Zaq not to tell any of you about my sexuality when they started sitting with us at lunch, which meant not talking about how we met."

"You asked them to stay closeted for you?" I ask, and he winces. I trace a crack in the ground while I wait for his response.

"No, I would never do that," he says, pausing to take another deep breath. "But I think they avoided bringing it up to you guys because they didn't want to pressure me into saying anything. It's selfish, I know, but sometimes it's hard to be around people who are so out and proud when you're still mostly closeted. They inspire me, especially with everything surrounding Talia's family, but I'm still jealous of how unapologetically they live. The few old friends I told about being asexual thought I just hadn't met the right person yet or that I had a bad experience that made me sex-repulsed." He sighs. "It's hard to explain to people sometimes, exhausting more than anything else. So I keep it to myself, or at least I planned to."

"Well, at least you only like girls," I try, searching for a positive. "That probably makes things easier for you as far as telling people."

"First of all, it's still rough telling people I'm ace." He picks up a bit of loose concrete and rubs it between his fingers. "But you're also not the only one disappointed to find out about Talia and Zaq."

"You like Talia too?" I ask, then immediately realize my mistake. "Oh. *Oh.*"

He looks up from the rock and nods, a sad smile playing on his lips.

"But what about Lindsay?"

"What about her?" he asks, stretching out his long legs in front of us. I lean over and check his watch, noticing the period is almost over.

"You like Zaq *and* Lindsay?"

"You've never liked more than one person at once?" he rebuts, already knowing the answer.

"Touché," I groan, flopping back against the wall.

"I probably should've formally introduced myself as biromantically asexual, but I'm still figuring out the biromantic part," he confesses, and I feel a surge of companionship flicker in my chest where the angry fire previously burned.

"I feel like I'm still figuring out all my parts," I admit quietly.

The bell rings, ending first period. We stand; my legs are stiff. I look up from adjusting my dress to see him staring down at me.

"Is this the part where you tell me it gets better?"

"This is the part where I tell you that you already know it will." His tone is solemn, but not pitying.

I roll my eyes.

"I'm serious," he says. "I know what you're going through."

"I'm not *going through* anything."

Wesley frowns. "Come to the art studio at lunch if you want to keep avoiding Talia," he says, surprisingly changing the subject. "I know Zaq already agreed to show Agatha some vintage plus-size fashion magazines he brought today, and Talia rarely comes into the studio unless Zaq and I are both working."

I nod, grateful. I doubt he'd be working today if it wasn't clear I needed an escape. Before he can turn away and head to his next class though, I have to ask.

"Your parents, are they cool about you being biromantic and asexual?"

He smiles, that proud beam returning to his face. It hurts, and for a second I get what he meant about struggling to be around Talia's and Zaq's openness. "Mom's got an ace pride flag on her office wall, and my dad has bought me at least ten graphic T-shirts with asexual puns on them. They just placed orders for some bi stuff after I talked to them about my questioning."

I try to imagine Mom with a pride flag and Dad gifting me punny shirts. But I don't know what flag would represent me, if I even deserve any of them. I can't imagine what I don't know, and maybe that's been the real problem, for all of us, this whole time.

EIGHTEEN

Even when I took a drawing elective freshman year, I never spent much time in the art studio. I stubbornly didn't see the point in spending more time than necessary in a place dedicated to an activity I lacked any and all skill in. But after narrowly missing Agatha and Linds at our lockers, I headed straight for the studio to meet Wesley for lunch.

"What're you working on?" I ask as I sit on the stool beside him, pretending like I don't feel a little weird being in here.

He slides the paper on his desk toward me hesitantly, staring at my face as I take in his gorgeous drawing.

It's a collection of doodles, all depicting different scenes of him and Lindsay, eating next to each other at the lunch bench, laughing in his car, playing video games, and even leaning into each other while stargazing. The entire thing is drawn in black and white, leaving Lindsay's vibrant orange hair the only color on the page. From what I've seen, it's different than his other work, but just as incredible.

"It's beautiful, Wes," I sigh. The drawing isn't for me, but I feel flattered on Lindsay's behalf.

His cheeks burn red as he slides the drawing into a black folder and sticks it in his backpack. "I was going to show it to her on Thursday if she still hasn't said anything to Sammie or me about prom."

"Look at you taking a stand to get the girl."

He shrugs, lowering his head, but looks pleased. "I'm surprised you aren't discouraging me. Considering Sammie is your best friend."

"True," I concede, pulling out my bag of cheese crackers. Not talking to Mom means packing my own subpar lunch. "But I'm tired of all the prom date drama."

"Really?" He pulls out a tiny bottle of yogurt. "But you and Agatha love this stuff."

"Loved," I correct, stuffing a handful of crackers in my mouth and trying to talk around the crumbs. I can't believe our bet was only a few weeks ago. It feels like a lifetime has passed since then. "Like seriously, it's just a dance. Who even cares?"

"Uh, you do."

"Not anymore," I say. "I haven't even started making the corsages or boutonnieres; I don't know how I'm doing my hair; I haven't planned my makeup or picked what sandals I'm wearing. We never looked into renting a limo or booking a hotel for a mini after-party. It's like none of it even matters anymore."

"So you've just . . . given up on prom?"

I shrug. "I guess."

"Then why did it hurt so much to know Talia was going with Zaq and not you?" He finishes off the last of his yogurt but pulls out another before I can even blink.

"I just wish she would've told me," I insist, then crush a mouthful of crackers between my teeth hard enough to earn a nasty glare from the girl drawing a few stations away.

"And if she would've told you she was dating Zaq before-hand, you wouldn't have yelled at her and cried to me?" He cocks his eyebrow.

"I don't like your drawing anymore."

"You're only proving my point," he laughs.

"So what if I got upset about it? That's not who I am." I toss the remaining crackers back into my backpack. My appetite has vanished.

"If you mean someone who gets upset over your expec-tations letting you down, I feel like that's exactly who you are." He pauses, fiddling with the remaining foil on the rim of his yogurt bottle. "If you mean queer, then . . ."

My stomach drops. "What did you just say?"

"Queer," he repeats. "As in not-straight. Not 'the default,' whatever the heck that means."

"Isn't that word . . . controversial?" I ask, my mind flash-ing to Jeremiah, my hand instinctively fidgeting for a drink.

"For some," he says, and to his merit, he doesn't react to

my disgusted expression. "But for others, it's reclaimed. Not everyone likes it, and that's totally their right, but it makes me feel good. Talia and Zaq use it too, even if it isn't the main word any of us identify with."

"Oh." It's weird to see the word in two different lights—insult and comfort.

I turn away from Wesley, letting my eyes scan the artwork plastered around the studio. Half the space is filled by high desks like the one we're sitting at, two stools per station, while the remaining area is split into desktops and empty easels. Up against the back wall, above the computers, my eyes are drawn to a large surrealist painting of a girl, her face comprised of triangles painted various shades of brown. The big Z in the corner confirms for me who painted it. I look for Wesley's work, but it's hard to tell what's his, given his diverse style.

"Okay." Wesley stands and claps. "What classes do you have for the rest of the day?"

"Government next," I reply, dreading sitting behind Talia for an hour after this morning. "Then math, then English."

"Anything due in those classes?" He starts packing up his bag and checks his watch, pursing his lips at the time.

"No? I think we're going to keep reviewing for AP testing, but that's it." At this point, any other tests feel useless. Most of us have picked our colleges or made plans for gap years or alternate career paths, so what's the point of wringing us dry with more exams?

"Okay, good," he says, zipping up his backpack. His smile

is bright but has a mischievous glint that I've never seen, nor would expect to see, on his face before. "We're going to ditch."

"Oh," I reply, standing. "Wait, what?"

❀ ❀ ❀

"Are you sure this is a good idea?" I ask Wesley as he casually walks toward the student parking lot, where the gates are wide open. I can't stop glancing around, expecting someone to stop us. Getting away with ditching chemistry felt like sheer luck, but this is definitely pushing it.

"Trust me, I've never been caught before," he says as he unlocks his car and motions for me to get in. I can't believe I've gone here for nearly four years and had no idea how easily I could just leave or skip class. Not that, admittedly, I ever would have had the nerve to try. But still, what kind of security is this?

"Student athletes usually leave around this time for games," he explains as we buckle in. "But they hardly ever have someone checking for passes. I thought they would've cracked down on security by now." He pulls out of the lot with ease, no guards in sight. "But I guess not."

Wesley's words catch up to me, and I face him, my mouth agape. "Wait, you've ditched before?"

His lips twitch upward. "Junior year was shitty when I first transferred. I had a free period after lunch and used to ditch about once a week for the first two months until my parents caught on. They made me switch my classes around to discourage me from doing it anymore, and counselors started keeping an eye on my attendance."

"Okay, so just to summarize: You're not straight, you ditch school, and you curse?" I say, and his mouth transforms into a full smile. "Geez, you think you know a guy."

"The things you learn about someone when you don't just passively sit across from them at lunch," he laughs, and, surprisingly, I do too.

The car drives as smoothly as I remember from when he dropped me off last week, and he's eerily confident behind the wheel for someone who usually seems so nervous.

"Where are we even going?" I ask, fighting the temptation to prop my feet up on the dashboard. *One rebellious act at a time, Ophelia.*

"I thought we could just drive and talk until school ends."

"Boo," I moan. "What's the fun in that?"

"The fun is getting to open up about everything you've kept bottled up for the past several weeks," he says with forced enthusiasm. "We can't ditch every day until graduation, as much as I'd frankly love to avoid Sammie's teasing."

I groan loudly, lying back against the leather seat. "Talking about my feelings never got me anywhere. I'm taking a new approach."

"Which involves you ignoring your parents and best friends?"

"Precisely."

"Looks like it's working out for you." He eyes my hair and dress unsubtly.

If he were anyone else, I'd flip him off right now. "It was only one kiss."

"And how many people have you kissed otherwise?"

"Only Lucas," I admit, still looking down and away.

Wesley doesn't reply to that, letting my words speak for themselves. But I can't tolerate the quiet, so I decide to speak up.

"Can I ask you something?" He nods without moving his eyes off the road. "What does being asexual actually mean? I thought I knew the basics, but you seem to have crushes on multiple people and are clearly open to dating and pursuing them, so . . ."

"So where does asexuality come into play?" he finishes for me, and I nod. He considers for a moment, tilting his head. "I feel versions of love, like liking and crushing and even love itself, but I don't feel the lust. When I look at Lindsay, I don't feel the urge to push her against a wall and make out with her like I imagine Sammie does." He grimaces. "But I do want to date her, and don't mind the idea of kissing her. I don't know, it's hard to put into words sometimes. It's a spectrum and different for everyone, like most things. Basically, I don't want or need sex the way most people seem to."

I let his words sink in as I brush aside a strand of hair that escaped my bun. "So when you asked if Lindsay was hoping to have sex after prom . . ."

"Yeah," he says, finishing my thought again. "One day, maybe I'll be open to trying, especially because I do want kids eventually." He blushes profusely, but still speaks as if talking about sex with me is no big deal. "But I don't think I'd enjoy it that much. I'm not that disgusted by it—some ace people are, and some aren't—but it definitely isn't appealing to me."

"You should tell Linds about it," I say. "I think she would understand."

"Pot, meet kettle, much?" he says.

"Leave the metaphors to the child of the English professor, please."

He laughs. "Fine, okay. Forget about the kiss. I know it's scary to talk about sexuality—like I said, my old friends didn't exactly support me the way I'd wanted—but why are you, specifically, scared of it?"

"They know me," I say without thinking. "My parents and Sammie and Agatha and Lindsay. I garden, I wear floral prints and eat papas rellenas and like boys. I like boys—all the time, obsessively. That's who I am; that's who they know me to be.

"So what happens when I can't tend to my garden in the fall when I'm away at school? I'll be studying botany, but I won't be out there every Sunday morning, fertilizing and pruning and watering. What happens when I find a cute dress or skirt or top that doesn't have a trace of flowers? Or what about if I find a new favorite food? My friends will be different. My clothes, routine, diet, surroundings . . . everything will be different in a few months. Agatha will be in SoCal, and Linds will be halfway across the country. I won't eat dinner with my parents every night or wake up in the same room I have my whole life. And I'll have Sammie, but what's to say he won't ditch me again like he did in middle school? Then what'll I have, who will I be? This is the one thing that I can control, the one thing that doesn't have to change."

"Liking boys?" he asks, taking a turn sharply but safely. "Liking Talia doesn't take that away. You don't have to pick one gender if your heart feels something for more than one. And you definitely don't owe it to anyone, least of all yourself, to hide the way you feel just because it would change things."

"But that means I lied to them. All those times I said I was straight and liked boys and couldn't imagine kissing a girl, I lied." I tug at the hem of my dress, suddenly feeling the need to rip something. The lack of control feels dizzying, like the most painful kind of relief. Like stepping barefoot off icy concrete and onto carpet, feeling the heat tingle back into your body.

"It wasn't a lie if it's what you thought was the truth. And, okay, let's say it was a lie. Who cares?" We've pulled into a random parking lot, but I'm too focused on his words to stop and look around. "You don't owe anyone consistency. We're graduating, Ophelia. Things are going to change, no matter what. Hiding from how you feel isn't going to stop that."

"That advice is a bit ironic given that we're hiding from school and all our friends right now."

He laughs and digs around in his backpack. "Oh, we're

definitely hiding from our friends, but we're not hiding from school." He pulls out calculus homework. I groan, but pull out my government notes too.

And as we settle into our work, I realize that this moment in itself is a change. A new friendship, an honest conversation, a rebellious act—minus doing our homework.

It doesn't do much to alleviate my stress, but it does feel kind of nice.

* * *

Wesley drops me off hours later. The skin around my eyes is puffy, even though we dropped the emotional talk and spent the remainder of the afternoon studying and watching DIY corsage videos on my phone.

I get home before Sammie does, but I've got half a dozen texts from him and Agatha asking where I've been all day, which I delete as I unlock the front door.

"Mija," Dad says as I shut the door behind me. He's shuffling through the mail but stops to kiss me on my forehead. "Baby's breath is in the fridge."

Sexualities and kisses aside, I have corsages and boutonnieres to make. It's ironic that the only thing that'll give me a semblance of normalcy centers on the exact event I'd like to ignore right now. But prom is only a few days away, and if I don't get disowned by everyone I love for one reason or another by then, I'll certainly be hated for not pulling through on my promise to provide the floral accessories. Especially if they follow Zaq's lead and actually pay me.

I head outside with the fresh baby's breath and a bag of supplies that've been shoved in the back of my closet since homecoming. To the playlist of the afternoon birds and emerging crickets, I eye roses from around the yard.

I've neglected this. The browning white blooms, the bruises in yellow petals, the dry leaves adorning every bush. They stick out like sore thumbs in what was once a prized garden. Photographing this feels embarrassing, and preemptive humiliation warms my cheeks like a shameful fever.

"I'm sorry," I whisper to a Lady X bush, one of my newer plants. When I bought it on a whim over the summer, the lavender shade reminded me of the sunsets that signal the start of autumn, my birth season. The plant's leaves are now riddled with holes from caterpillars, the petals dried around the edges. I've never granted myself my own rose, but I realize that if I had to, I would choose this one. I know the least about it, have no idea what the discovery year is or what the technical strong suits are. I couldn't describe the scent with the same certainty I could a golden Voodoo or rusty Caribbean. But maybe that's why it's more me than any of these other roses are.

Because maybe I don't know myself with the same certainty I've always claimed.

NINETEEN

The next morning, my luck in avoiding Talia runs out. She's waiting at my locker, picking at her nail polish.

"Hey," she says softly.

"Hi," I reply, inputting my locker combination with more attention than necessary.

"How are you?"

I take a deep breath and try to force a smile, but it just reminds me of our day at the photography studio. "Great!"

"That's good," she breathes, nodding to herself. "That's really good." Heavy silence. Her earthy, minty scent invades my senses as she leans closer. "So, have you talked to anyone about Friday night?"

I step back and close my locker but refuse to look at her. "What's there to talk about? What happened was meaningless, right?" I force out a laugh, but it comes out like a cough.

She blinks once, twice. "'Meaningless'? Ophelia, you kissed me."

"Shhh!" I immediately cover her mouth with my hand, pulling it away almost as quickly. Her lips felt just as soft against my palm as they did against my mouth. "Believe me, I know. It was ridiculous and weird, and you know what? I've already forgotten about it." My smile returns as I mentally bat away everything Wesley said to me yesterday. "Poof, gone from my memory!"

"But—" she starts, but I cut her off when I spot a familiar mop of blond curls walking in the opposite direction behind her.

"Lucas!" I shout. Talia and Lucas both spin around to face each other. He looks between the two of us before approaching, a slight swagger to his walk.

"Hey," he says, nodding to me and smiling at Talia, though I doubt they've ever spoken.

"Did you end up finding another date for prom?" I ask.

"No," he says slowly, confusion plastered on his beautifully carved face.

"I'd like to go with you. If you still want to."

"What are you doing?" Talia hisses to me, under her breath, but I ignore her.

"Seriously?" Lucas asks, looking both offended and pleased at once.

"I think it would be fun," I say, shrugging like I couldn't care either way. But I do care; I need this.

"Yeah." Lucas's complicated expression eases into a relaxed grin. "Yeah, I'm down to go together."

"Perfect. You can pick me up at my house on Saturday, two hours before the dance," I say. "Don't worry about a corsage; I'll be making my own. But try to find a lavender tie if you can."

"Lavender?" he scoffs, and my stomach clenches.

"Or whatever. We don't need to match."

"Sounds good." He smiles, looking me up and down briefly, without shame or discretion. "I'll text you."

"See you in chemistry," I reply, and wave as he exits the building, more swagger in his step than before. I watch him go, trying to ignore Talia's face out of the corner of my eye. But without meaning to, I shift my focus, and her disappointment hits me hard.

"What was that about?" she asks, hands on her hips.

"I decided going with him would be fun after all."

"You said it didn't seem right to go with him."

"And now it does," I say. "I always dreamed of going to prom with a cute boy, and now I can. Things are going exactly the way they should."

"The way they 'should'?"

I look around for Lindsay's hair and Agatha's undoubtedly bright outfit; any beacon of refuge. I don't know how they're going to take the news of me going with Lucas after all, but I'll cross that bridge when I get there.

"Ophelia," Talia says gently, pulling on my shoulder until I turn around.

How is it that even in awful hallway lighting, she still manages to glow like this? Her pupils are wide, taking up most of her already dark irises, and I want, more than anything else, to taste her mouth again.

"I don't know why you care so much," I say. "You've got Zaq now; you don't need me."

"I always had Zaq," she says like a swift kick to my gut. "This whole time we were friends, I had Zaq." I fight the urge to vomit. "And regardless, you're not replaceable. You're one of my best friends now."

"No, I'm the girl who fooled herself into thinking—" I cut myself off.

"Into thinking what?" Talia coaxes me, resting her hand gently on my forearm. I look at where her skin touches mine, and instead of calming down, I see red.

Every moment between us becomes strikingly clear. Her unzipping my dress and helping me when I lost my balance hiking and following me inside Wes's house and coming to me for help with Dani. Lindsay's party. Everything I feared romanticizing, every sign I read so horrifically wrong. The rose-tinted glass shatters.

I shake myself loose of her touch. "Nothing. Just typical Ophelia bullshit."

"Like going to prom with Lucas?" She looks behind me.

"Wait, you're going to prom with Lucas now?" I follow her gaze to see Wesley, looking disappointedly down at me. "I was going to ask you to be my date . . ."

"*What?*" Talia and I say at the same time. Given that she

knows nothing about Wesley's and my ditch-day bonding session yesterday, she's probably even more confused than I am.

"I was thinking about it last night. I don't know; it makes sense. Sammie can take Lindsay, and"—he pauses to look at Talia for a second, something unspoken about her and Zaq lingering in the air—"and you won't have to go alone. Everyone wins." He shrugs but doesn't look me in the eye.

"Okay, let's unpack this." I tick off on my fingers, "One: Everyone wouldn't win because Agatha would still be going solo, I'd be going with a pity date, and you'd be going with me instead of Lindsay. Which brings me to point two: You've been in love with her for months and already drew that lovely illustration, so I'm not letting you throw away your chance to finally be with her just so the guy who's mocked you nearly every day since you transferred to this school can date her."

"You know you're talking about your best friend, right?" he interjects, and Talia laughs, reminding me we have an audience.

"I have more than one, it's fine. Point is, I don't need you missing out on your high school fantasy on my conscience. And, again, I already agreed to go with Lucas." I look down at my hands. "I think that's point number three."

"Which is still a bad idea," Talia says, stepping closer to me again.

"I'm done talking about this," I finally snap at her. "Who I do or don't date is none of your concern. I've done a perfectly fine job failing at love for the past seventeen years on my own, thank you very much."

"He doesn't deserve you, and you know it," she says before quietly adding, "Don't go with him just to prove a point." She walks away, shaking her head. I swallow the burst of anger and let it simmer in my stomach before turning back to Wesley.

He lifts a brow at me. "Did she really deserve that?"

"I don't have the energy for a moral dilemma right now. Let's just focus on the positive: You got out of taking me to prom!"

He smiles at the ground, visibly relieved, which I try not to be offended by. Until a familiar shadow falls over us.

"What?" a voice behind me says, calm and full of rage all at once.

I turn around slowly to see Lindsay and Agatha standing side by side, books in their hands and shock on their faces. *Shit.*

"Oh hey, guys! Love the butterfly clips, Ags," I say, pointing to the twin pink plastic butterflies pinning back sections of her Afro.

"Did you just say Wesley got out of being your date?" Lindsay asks. I have to force my eyes to meet hers. Her normally soft green irises are seething, the white around them turning pink.

"No! Oh no, no, you misheard all that." I wave vaguely at Wesley. "I'm going with Lucas."

"You're *what*?" Ags asks.

"But you just said—and I thought we were—" Lindsay

starts, facing Wesley, but her voice trails off as Sammie comes over.

His long, easy steps show he has no idea what he's walking into. "O, you can start walking your ass to school if you're going to keep ditching me in the parking lot."

"You thought we were what?" Wes asks Lindsay, ignoring Sammie. Pride surges through me as he straightens under her angry gaze.

Sammie looks between the two of them, cocking his head to Agatha as if to ask her what's going on. But she stays frozen, watching the awkward confrontation unfold. My Ags, queen of gossip and drama, looking at the mess I caused with nothing but sad confusion in her eyes.

"Just—what is going on here, Ophelia?" Lindsay turns to me, abandoning her face-off with Wesley. Her pale, freckled face is flushed with anger. I take a hesitant step backward, nearly onto Wesley's foot.

"Nothing! Nothing is going on. I'm going to prom with Lucas! Woo!" My empty cheers land flatly. I scramble. "And you! You're going with . . ." *Yikes. Wrong direction, abort mission.*

"You're going where with whomst?" Sammie butts in, but Lindsay and I both ignore him.

"Weird you two both magically disappeared after lunch yesterday," she says, eyes narrowed and flashing between me and Wesley. "Even weirder that now it sounds an awful lot like you're turning him down as a prom date. Care to explain?"

"Wait." Sammie finally pushes his way between all of us,

leaving Ags alone on the outskirts. "So there *is* something going on between you two? I knew it!"

"You knew something was going on between them?" Lindsay demands.

Sammie waves her off. "You got so pissed at me for just *asking* about you two."

"That's *not* why I was pissed," I insist, but neither he nor Lindsay is listening anymore.

"I'm not shocked you have a thing for Wes given your history, but you could've at least talked to me about it instead of going after him behind my back," Lindsay spits out.

I can't help it. I laugh. "*My* history? God, hypocrite much? And I'm sure you would've been *totally* cool with me liking Wesley."

"So you admit you have a thing for him?" Lindsay asks. Her face is turning as red as her hair.

"No!" I laugh more, bitterly now. "I don't have a *thing* for Wes." She flinches at my use of his nickname.

"We should go," Wes says gently. "Everyone should cool off." He reaches out for me, but I pull away because while he means well, his playing my knight in shining armor right now will only make things worse.

"No, I want to know why my friends seem to think all my problems have to be centered around boys," I say, crossing my arms. "And why they think I can't be friends with a guy without being in love with him. And why I can't have, like, three days of being moody without it being the end of the fucking world."

"I don't think you want to do this," Wesley mumbles, stepping toward me again. Maybe I don't, but it feels too good to stop.

"We don't think that," Sammie says, voice more tender. "You and I are friends, and no one thinks we're secretly in love with each other."

Lindsay doesn't soften though. "I'm just saying, Ophelia, you could've saved us all a lot of time and drama if you would've just talked to me."

"So I could make your decision between Wes and Sammie easier for you? Take some of that responsibility off your perfect little shoulders?" I'm exhausted and infuriated all at once, every moment of jealousy I've ever felt for Lindsay pouring out, the anger over Talia supporting the flood. "*You* could've saved them plenty of time and drama by telling them what you told me and Ags, that you have no interest in them past graduation."

She straightens instantly. "Fuck you."

"Maybe we should just drop this," Wesley tries, looking around for someone to agree. But Lindsay is still staring at me, taking deep, controlled breaths, like they're the only thing stopping her from mauling me. Agatha can't stop shaking her head at both of us.

"I think you've done enough, big guy," Sammie says to Wes.

"Okay, you know what? Fuck you too," Wesley says, hands immediately flying to clamp over his mouth. Sammie takes a quick step forward, but out of nowhere, Zaq jumps in and stands between the boys. I knew we were missing someone.

With a hand on each of their chests for equal measure, he asks, "Is there a problem here?" But his eyes are trained on Sammie when he says it.

"Not anymore," Lindsay nearly whispers, looking at Wesley. My heart squeezes, and I want to apologize a million times over for getting him wrapped up in all of this so quickly. How did it even go this far? The vindictiveness that flooded me only seconds ago is gone, and all I see now is a friend group broken months before we were meant to fall apart.

All because I dared to change the way things were.

"You know, I finally figured you out," Lindsay says.

I exhale. "Please enlighten me."

"You're not a hopeless romantic. You're just desperate. You act like you're better than everyone else because you pretend to be some cheesy optimist while the rest of us are just—"

"Disillusioned?" I offer.

She rolls her eyes. "And nothing ever happens in your life, so you're obsessed with everyone else's."

"You've got me there," I deadpan. The worst part is, I think she's right.

She may as well be standing on a stage, waving with her prom queen crown atop her head already with the confidence she's exuding. It's a front, of course. I've always known it was. I just didn't think our friendship was too.

"See you in fucking homeroom," she says, storming away.

Agatha and Sammie head in the same direction. I can't tell if they're following after her or just going to class, but neither turns around to spare me another look.

"Anyone want to fill me in here?" Zaq asks, looking between me and Wesley.

I fight the temptation to tell him to fuck off too.

❊ ❊ ❊

Homeroom goes . . . well, honestly not as terribly as it could have. Sammie pettily scoots his chair over to Agatha and Lindsay's desk, burying his head in one of his encyclopedias. It's like he completely missed my—admittedly pretty inappropriate and treacherous—exposure of Lindsay's lack of interest in a romantic future with him, and is icing me out instead of letting that news settle.

At least that's what I tell myself.

On the bright side, Talia just barely missed the big fight, so the only yelling of mine she witnessed today was directed at her. I guess that's not actually very bright. On the substantially dingier side, Wesley's also in a mood after everything that went down. I gauge this from the way he silently walks me to chemistry and doesn't complain or even grimace when Lucas asks to be my partner again.

I work in silence as Lucas tells me about how soccer season has been going, how many teams recruited him back in the fall, and what kind of guy he hopes he doesn't end up with as a roommate for training in the summer. When that topic veers toward not wanting a gay roommate, "Not because I've really got anything against that shit, it'd just be weird, you know?" I say nothing. I clench my fist, pressing my nails deep into my palm, until he changes the subject.

I zone out, thinking about how Zaq hasn't once looked at me with the same anger that Lindsay did earlier, even after knowing I kissed Talia. I expected him to be stand-offish at best and outright accuse me of trying to steal his girlfriend at worst. But out of everyone in our group, he seems to dislike me the least right now, even offering me a sympathetic smile during homeroom and when we pass each other in the halls.

I wonder if he knows I'd do anything to be him. To get to kiss Talia without wondering if it really is just a kiss, without having to talk myself into believing it. He gets to take her home to his parents without preparing a speech beforehand. He gets to love her without confusion or doubt.

I get why they've kept it all a secret. It's actually astonishing I didn't let their relationship slip while airing Lindsay's dirty laundry. Though I'm grateful I didn't, I still hate him a bit for it all.

But then I think about Talia's family, how countless people would say they aren't really pansexual or bisexual for being in a "straight" relationship together. I think about how Zaq is Black and Talia is a Black Latina and how they'll always deal with intolerant bullshit regardless of who they're dating.

And then I just feel worse about everything altogether.

So much so that I decide tuning back into Lucas's new

rant about the superiority of strapped shin guards over strapless ones, even if they're childish, as he puts it, is miraculously less painful than my internal pity party.

* * *

I spend the rest of the day avoiding everyone, taking my lunch to the library and going to the nurse's office afterward during government, claiming my food gave me a stomachache. The school nurse sees right through me, like they always do, but she still gives me a glass of ginger ale and lets me rest on one of the beds in the back.

By the time school is over, I feel as though I've aged ten years, which honestly would be a less depressing explanation for losing my closest friends. I head for the parking lot, pulling out my phone to call Dad and beg for a ride home when a hand plucks it from my grip.

"Come on," Agatha says. I follow her to her car. It's a newer model, immaculately clean. She throws my phone at me once we're inside.

She zooms through a yellow light without blinking and barely buckles her seat belt a block later. She's always been an awful driver.

"Spill," she finally says. "Whatever bullshit is going on that's making you freak out on Linds and Talia and avoid Sammie and ditch school with Wesley, I want to hear it. Now."

"You know about Talia?"

"You two were glued at the hip for the past two weeks,

and suddenly you're skipping lunch and she looks ready to burst into tears every time someone so much as mentions your name? Somehow I managed to put two and two together," she sighs, picking at one of her butterfly clips.

I ignore the implication that they've been talking about me when I'm not around. "Nothing is going on."

"Okay, sure." She rolls her eyes so far back I wonder how they don't get stuck. "So suddenly you're someone who spills your friend's secrets and skips class and crawls back to Lucas, of all the losers you've drooled over? That's the story you're going with? What you did to Linds, calling her out on Wesley and Sammie, after everything? That was a dick move of you, O. You know you're my best friend, and I'll shoot the shit with you any day of the week. But lie to me again about how nothing is going on with you, please."

I don't know what to say. "Things got messy with Talia," I admit, leaving out every important detail. I fiddle with my hands in my lap. "It threw me off, and Lindsay was being a bitch; even you can admit that."

"Lindsay is always a bitch," she says. "But she's *our* bitch. The same way Sammie's annoying teasing and hair ruffling that he knows not to try with me makes him our bitch. And Wesley's quiet mouth and awkward commentary makes him our bitch. And your roses and crushes and gossip and sarcasm make you mine." She sighs and taps her sharp acrylics against the steering wheel as we zoom down a nearly empty street. "But when that shit gets too much for you,

you tell her to cut it out. You don't chew her out in front of everyone."

"She could've done the same with me," I retort.

She glares at me out of the corner of her eye. "What she said was messed up, no doubt about it. But this is about more than Lindsay being jealous and catty, and you and I both know it." Her phone lights up with a text from Sammie. "I told him I was giving you a ride home," she says, nodding to her phone. "So don't get pissed at him over that too. He was going to wait for you.

"I believe you, by the way, that nothing is going on between you and Wesley. But if he's the one helping you deal with this shit, I sincerely hope he starts doing a better job." She pats my hand twice. "As for whatever you're doing with Lucas . . ."

"Why is everyone giving me so much crap for Lucas?" I snatch my hand back.

"You said no to him originally," she says, tilting her head. "What changed?"

I did, I want to say. *Regression is compensation.* But I say nothing instead.

Ags sighs. "Prom is prom, babe. You've always had the right idea about it, in your hopelessly romantic little heart. But the dresses and corsages and dates and yes, even the goddamn theme, are not the end of the world. It's *one* night. We've got weeks of school and an entire life beyond that to worry about too."

I pause. "Can I ask you something?"

"Given that you avoided all my questions? Yeah, yeah, I guess you can."

"Why didn't you run for prom queen? Why go through all the effort convincing Lindsay to run and helping her campaign instead of running yourself?"

She cackles, wiping an invisible tear from the corner of her eye. "That's on your mind right now? O, I don't want a pointless title. Lindsay, bless her, drunkenly admitted it was always a dream of hers back at that party she had before the year started."

"What? When?"

"After everyone left," she says, pulling onto my street. "I mean, you were there. It was literally just us three. You were all spaced out though."

Spaced out about Talia, about her kissing a girl and liking it. About me wondering, I suppose I can admit now, if maybe I could kiss a girl and like it too.

"Wait, but if Lindsay has always wanted it, why'd she fight you over it so much?"

Ags cocks her brow. "Did she really fight that much?" I make a noise of agreement. "Linds likes to play it cool, I get it. But look, for her? Prom queen is *it*. It will define her senior year. It will define *her*. That's not a bad thing; it's good to have hopes and dreams and all that sparkly rainbow-feelings shit you love and that she'll never admit she does too. I was annoyed about the theme and our grad song for aesthetic purposes, but I've got my eyes set on New York and Milan, not prom queen. And honestly? The campaign was good practice for dealing with diva models as a designer and shoot director one day." She fluffs out her hair. "But I'm playing the long game with my successes. Looking at all those other people accepted into FIDM with similar designs as me made me realize that I needed to switch things up and challenge myself." She hands me her phone, open to a collage of various dress sketches. They're unlike anything she's ever created before—all sharp edges and deep jewel tones. "I even got inspiration for a new line from all the campaign chaos."

It takes me a second, but when I see the crowns on the models and recognize the color schemes, it hits me. "You designed prom queen dresses based on classic fairy-tale princesses?"

"The ridiculous prom theme and all of Sammie's jokes about Lindsay looking like Ariel did one good thing, at least." She laughs and puts her phone away again. "Even if it's going to be scary as hell in the fall, I've got this. Who I am in high school isn't my endgame. I don't want to be defined right now, especially not by a plastic tiara that'll probably have fucking seahorses on it."

I laugh and feel something loosen. It's not bitter, not angry or self-deprecating or forced. It's genuine laughter, because holy hell, I really, honest to God, hope that fucking prom queen crown will have seahorses on it.

"I don't think I want to be defined right now either," I admit suddenly. "Is that okay?"

She places a hand on my knee. It doesn't give me

butterflies, not totally, but it doesn't feel like nothing either. I decide that's okay. "Whatever you want, O. But please, try to get at least *some* of your shit together."

"Thanks, Ags," I laugh once more before exiting her car, and then watch her nearly hit all of Sammie's trash cans as she drives away.

❋ ❋ ❋

"Glad you're feeling better," Dad says as he closes the back door behind him. I'm knee-deep in damp dirt, tugging at mushrooms that started to sprout around my Olympiad roses.

"Me too," I reply, tossing the spongy fungi into a small bucket for fertilizer. I wipe my sweaty forehead with my upper arm, careful to keep the muddy gloves away from my face.

I expect, or rather hope, that Dad will go back inside and leave me to make up for Sunday's lack of gardening. But instead he strides over to stand behind me, taking a long sip of Materva.

"Samuel came over on Saturday. Él me dijo que you weren't answering his texts," he says casually.

"Hmm?"

"He said something about you and Talia fighting." Dad looks down at his soda, reading the nutritional facts, or at least pretending to.

"We talked about it this morning. We're all good now," I lie, turning back to my bucket. Sammie may have been desperate to hear from me a few days ago, but I doubt he wants anything to do with me now.

"Ophelia."

"Hmm?"

"What about you and Talia?"

"What about us?"

"Was Samuel right? Were you two fighting? Weren't you *just* fighting with him?" He pauses. "And Mom?"

I huff out a frustrated breath and spin around, catching myself before I yell. "Dad, I have a lot of work to get done out here. I don't really have time to discuss my social life."

"You always made time before," he counters, setting his soda on the grass and taking a seat. I pause to watch the Materva wobble.

"We had an . . . argument. It doesn't matter." Dad frowns. I push aside dangling stems of Midas Touch and step around the bush. "We weren't that close anyways, so it's whatever."

"You've been spending an awful lot of time together." He picks at the grass with one hand, tapping against his Materva with the other.

"We studied for some tests, and she gave me a ride when Sammie was too busy trying to court Lindsay." I tug a dead bloom off a bush harder than necessary. "I'd hardly call that 'an awful lot of time.'"

"And what about Samuel and Mom?"

"Dad," I moan.

"Have I ever told you about the first girl I ever loved?" he asks out of nowhere. Despite wanting him to leave me alone moments before, I soften and shake my head. Dad doesn't talk much about growing up. I lean against the garden gate and listen. "Paola Dominguez," he sighs. "Gorgeous girl, Mexican and Cuban. I swore on my life I was going to marry her."

"I thought you didn't date anyone before Mom." Mom used to tease Dad about being his first and only girlfriend since she'd dated around so much as a teenager. She dropped the joke once I hit my teens, probably realizing before I did that I would be following in my father's footsteps dating-wise.

He laughs. "I didn't. I tried to tell Paola how I felt, pero era un cobarde. The night before we graduated though, I showed up at her house. I told her I'd loved her for years and wanted to be with her even if it would be long-distance."

"What did she say?"

"She turned me down. At graduation I saw her kissing this girl from another school she used to bring around to parties. It was a big scandal—huge. And I'll tell you, mija, between you and me, I felt like el mayor tonto and cried like a baby until your abuelo knocked some sense into me. He told me, 'La vida de esa chica no se trata de ti,'" *That girl's life isn't about you.* "And he was right."

I swallow. "Why are you telling me this?"

He tilts his head. I feel like I'm watching myself, distorted slightly by age and gender. The look in his eyes is so painfully familiar that I have to look away, picking at a chip of white wood threatening to break off the fence.

"At the time, it felt like the end of the world. We'd been good friends; we were some of the only Latinos in our white-bread school. We dealt with enough assholes already. The guts it took for her to kiss her girl like that in front of everyone?" He whistles. "I didn't see it then, but she was brave, braver than I've ever been. Then I met your mom a few years later, and it was everything I'd ever felt for Paola and more." He nods to himself and moves to sit up. "I won't be as harsh as my dad was with me, but whatever is going on with your friends, even if it isn't anything at all, like you say, just know it'll pass. You'll see in a few months when you start college, mija, that the world is much bigger than it feels in high school."

He gets up to head back inside, but at the last minute, turns around and places the Materva on the ground outside the door. "Don't tell your mom I was cursing."

I leave my garden and grab the soda as soon as he closes the back door, sipping on the fizzy brown cola as I walk toward the Olympiads. They're one of my newer accomplishments, since the roses bloom in smaller clusters than most other types I grow. I had to adjust my routine to accommodate their more individualistic style of growth, but they've been worth the effort.

I remove my gloves and rub the pad of my thumb over a rubbery petal. The color is a sharp red, bright as blood, like I pricked my finger on a thorn and stained the clean, white petals of an Honor rose. They don't smell as strong as my other roses, but I still lean in to inhale their scent and feel a sense of clarity when I open my eyes. This close my vision swarms with red, sparkling in the sunlight.

Like Talia's nails. Like that damn brooch.

If I hadn't gone with her that night and gotten so caught up in what it meant to be the one she turned to for help, I wouldn't be here. I wouldn't have ruined our friendship, or set off the chain of events that led to me ruining almost all my other ones too.

But I did. All because of a red rose brooch.

Before I can think better of it, I lean over the gate and dump the Materva across the Olympiads and their roots. I practically feel the bubbles boil against the flowers, corrupting their growth.

Regret grips my chest. They could be dead in days, all my hard work down the drain.

Or they could withstand this, the love and nurturing I've consistently given in the past strengthening them enough to prevail beyond the damage of today.

TWENTY

Lindsay doesn't come to school today, a bold decision for someone in the final three days of her prom queen campaign. Agatha doesn't bring up her absence, instead passively commenting on Danica's newly dyed neon green hair when she picks me up for school. Sammie doesn't speak to me in homeroom, and I work with Lucas again in chemistry, grimacing when he tells me he couldn't find a lavender tie, so he'll be wearing a red one he already owns instead.

So things are going about as swimmingly as expected.

I get Lindsay being mad at me. I'm not too keen on her at the moment either. But Wes and Sammie pulling the silent treatment because I had to be the bearer of bad news seems a tad unfair. Shoot the messenger, fine, but at least talk to her.

I pointedly ignore the hypocrisy of my annoyance considering I muted all of Talia's incoming texts last night. But the last thing I need right now is her and her pity. If the fact that she didn't show up at my locker again is any indication, she finally got that message.

After all that, while Wesley's not the *last* person I expect to see waiting for me in the library, where I plan to hide away again during lunch, he's definitely in the bottom five. I chastise myself for assuming he's there for me, but when he looks up and notices me hovering in the doorway, clutching my lunch bag, he moves aside his stack of comics to make room for me at his table.

I walk past shelves of classics, the smell reminding me of my mom's office. "Not hiding out in the art room with Zaq?" I ask as I sit across from him.

"He offered," he says sheepishly. "But I had a feeling you'd come here again." I smile awkwardly, unsure about this change of heart. "I'm not mad at you."

"How about Lindsay?" I ask, trying to mask my relief.

"Oh, she's definitely mad at you."

I roll my eyes. "I know *that*. But how are you feeling about her?"

He shrugs, his gray sweater swallowing his neck. "I can't really be mad at her for not wanting to date me, can I?" I feel a surge of guilt, and it must show, because Wesley instantly cringes. "I'm so sorry, I didn't mean you and Ta—"

"It's fine."

We sit in silence. I peel an orange while Wes flips through a comic book and eats trail mix out of a sandwich baggie, a sort of sad expression on his face.

I decide to ask him something I've never let myself question before, my previous loyalty to Lindsay keeping it brimming beneath the surface of my thoughts until now. "Why do you like Lindsay?"

He doesn't seem surprised by this, but if he wasn't frowning before, he definitely is now. "Does now really seem like a good time to ask me that?"

I almost flinch. In Wes's world, that was basically him telling me to fuck off. Though I guess I did witness him literally tell Sammie that yesterday. "I'm sorry. But I've always understood Sammie and Lindsay. They're both flirts and a little promiscuous and like being the center of attention." Wes gives me a look that says talking about Sammie and Lindsay's great chemistry isn't helping. "But you're not like that."

He scrunches his face. "Thanks?"

"I just mean that whenever we're all together, you seem content to just be there with us. I see that now. Honestly? I used to think you hated me and Agatha because you never jumped into our conversations the way Sammie and Lindsay did."

"You thought I hated you because I didn't interrupt you?"

I press against my temples. "I'm saying this all wrong. I'm trying to compliment you, I swear. You're just . . . a good person, that's all. So I don't really get it."

"Because Lindsay and Sammie aren't good people?"

My stomach drops. "No! That's not what—"

"Why are *you* friends with Sammie and Lindsay?"

My head falls into my hands. "This was supposed to be about you."

"It'll come back around, I promise."

"We always talk about me. Why can't we psychoanalyze you for once?"

Someone shushes us, and we both cower for a second.

"Why are you friends with them," he insists, less question and more reminder.

I take a moment to consider it. Why am I friends with them? Sammie and I grew up together. He's been a part of my life forever. Even when we grew apart for a few years, he was always there—across the unbridged space between our windows.

But how much of my friendship with Sammie has been occupied by his drama with Lindsay lately? It feels like every conversation we've had for the past few weeks has been about him and her.

"He makes me happy," I say finally. "Sammie knows how to make me laugh like no one else does. He knows how to turn an insult about me into a compliment with only a handful of words." I lean back in my chair but keep my voice soft. "And he's reliable, even when he isn't. If I ever needed someone to help me hide a body, I know Agatha is the one I *should* call. But I'd call Sammie, every time."

Wes scoots his chair closer to the table. "And Lindsay?"

"Lindsay was a part of the package deal," I say with a shrug. It's an honest response, one of the most truthful things I've said in weeks. "Lindsay was friends with Agatha, and I wanted to be friends with Agatha. So she came with." I never really thought about it. I mean, I knew I always had been and always would be closer to Sammie and Agatha than to Lindsay. But it's not like we weren't friends too. We had classes together and decorated each other's lockers for our birthdays and did our makeup for school dances cramped in the same bathrooms. But how much of that was because it was more convenient to be friends than not?

"She's . . ." I'm about to say *kind*, but I second-guess it. Then *funny*, but she's more sarcastic than humorous. She's smart, but that's not why we're friends. Neither is her being pretty or charismatic or popular. They're the words that come to mind when I think of her, but they have nothing to do with us, together.

"I like her because she has drive," Wesley says, finally fulfilling my wish by interrupting me. "She likes training during track season and likes the challenge of tutoring struggling students. I think she even likes running for prom queen. Because she's focused and disciplined, but also knows how to have fun." He pauses, smiling to himself. "She's not the sweetest girl in the room, I know. But she'll say hi to everyone in it. It's like . . . it's like she never runs out of space inside. She always has room for new goals and hobbies and friends. She welcomed me into your guys' group, after all. She's so full, but she always has room for more." He smiles sadly. "After a certain point, I think I knew she didn't want to commit to Sammie or me. It's been over a year of this. And I understand it, from her point of view. We're young and graduating, and not everyone is a romantic about this time in our lives." I scoff. "She has the world at her fingertips. I don't blame her for not wanting to settle."

"She wouldn't be settling," I tell him, then, maybe against my better judgment, I reach across the table and give his folded hands a squeeze. "I think she's scared. Like you said, she's always had room for more. If she loved you or Sammie back without reservation, she'd be full. That would be enough for her, I think."

He looks down at his hands, opening and closing his mouth a few times. Finally, he glances up. "Ophelia, do you think romantic love is all you need to have a full life?"

I flinch.

"I'm sad that Lindsay doesn't see a future with me, obviously. Because being around her, when it's just the two of us, makes me happy. Whether she's complimenting my art or listening to me rant about a new comic or helping me cook dinner with my parents . . . she makes me happy. But if all I get with her is high school, I'm okay with that."

"How? How can you feel all of that with her and still be okay?"

"Because I have a whole life outside of her," he says gently. "I have friends, family, goals, and a future that, yeah, of course I'd hoped she'd be a part of. But I'll survive it if she isn't." Now it's his turn to reach out and squeeze my hands. "You will too."

I don't ask him who he is referring to.

❀ ❀ ❀

I'm working on notes for our Socratic seminar in English tomorrow, sprawled out on the floor with my curtains shut tight, when Mom lightly knocks on my door.

"Dad's doing a load of laundry, if you need anything washed," she says, tone impartial. But her eyes light up when she sees my notes. "What's all this?"

"We're finishing up our unit on literary theory." My throat dries at the memory of me and Talia working on our unit papers together. Was that really only a week ago? How long has it been since Mom and I had a normal conversation? Time flies when you're having an identity crisis.

"One of my favorite undergraduate classes was on literary theory and criticisms," she sighs, leaning against the door and tucking a lock of thin hair behind her ear. "Barthes was always my favorite."

I perk up. "Really?"

She nods excitedly, the first real smile she's shown me in what feels like forever emerging on her face. "Oh yeah, I ate up his work as an undergrad. 'The lover's fatal identity is precisely: *I am the one who waits*'?" She clutches her chest and sighs. "That one really got me."

"Me too."

Her knees crack as she lowers herself to the floor across from me. "Roland Barthes believed that what we truly want is our own desire—"

"Yeah, the cake and the idea of the cake," I interrupt, then catch myself. I don't want to waste this amicable moment. "What's your take on the lover part though?"

"In his work *A Lover's Discourse*, he claimed that"—her eyes get hazy as she looks off—"'The lover's fatal identity is precisely this: I am the one who waits.'"

"What does it mean?" I ask softly, so softly I worry Mom hasn't heard me. She doesn't react immediately, but when she finally looks at me, she seems content.

"It means those who love are always waiting. Waiting to be seen, waiting to be understood. Waiting to be loved back." She sighs. "'The lover is the one who waits.'"

I swallow, my saliva thick and heavy. "Did he think the lover would ever find another lover? You know, someone just like them? That one day their waiting would end?"

She smiles sadly, tight-lipped and closemouthed. "I don't think so."

"Oh."

She stands, knees cracking on the way up too, before adjusting the blue cotton cardigan Dad gave her for Christmas years ago. Somehow it still looks vibrant and new, despite the years of washing. "I think you can see why I ate up those words during my youth."

I lean back, propping myself up on my palms. "You don't believe it anymore?"

She pauses, fingers grazing my prom dress where it's still hanging on the back of my door. "I believe he believed it. I believe I believed it. And I still believe it's absolutely beautiful. But I don't think the truest love is deemed so because it's the most painful. Waiting for someone to love you back seems beautiful in a miserable way when you're young. No offense." She smiles. "But a life spent waiting is not a life spent loving. It's a life spent wasting away on the promise of something you're not guaranteed."

My words are tough to get out amid the sound of my heart pounding in my ears. "I can see why you have such a high score on Rate My Professors."

Mom laughs hard, harder than I've seen her laugh in a long time. "Thanks."

I go back to studying, losing myself in the theories and analysis of everything from love to loss to perspective to humanity. And I get it, I really get it. Not the theories—God knows I'm a lost cause right now when it comes to anything existential. But I get why Mom loves this; I get why she wants *me* to love it.

And, I guess, I get why I do.

TWENTY-ONE

I groan and rub at the kink in my neck. My phone is ringing way too loudly for my liking. I fumble for it for so long, I nearly miss the call. I answer and press it against my ear without checking the caller ID.

"Hello?" I say groggily, rubbing my eyes as they adjust to my pitch-black room. I must have passed out while studying, sometime after showering, because my notes surround me in bed.

"Finally! Ugh, I know it's late, bu—"

"Get to the point, Ags," I mumble, recognizing her voice. I check the time—three in the morning.

"I was *getting* to it," she replies sharply. "Did you see the Insta post?" The seriousness of her tone, switching so quickly, jolts me awake.

"What post?" I ask, putting her on speakerphone so I can check Instagram, my own anxiety working faster than her storytelling abilities.

"Wesley and Lindsay are going to prom together," she says. "He asked her tonight, showed up at her house with flowers and this cheesy drawing and—well, you'll see it all in the post."

I mouth several choice words in relief. I don't know what I was expecting, but it wasn't this. "Was the bet really this urgent? I'll give you your money tomorrow."

"My money? Wha—no, O, I'm not calling about our fucking bet."

"Then why are you calling?" I sigh, flopping back into my pillows.

"Because Sammie is freaking out! Are you kidding me right now? Is whatever you're dealing with really so serious that you forgot about your best friend?" she yells. "He called me like fifteen minutes ago half sobbing, muttering complete nonsense. I tried to calm him down, but he hung up on me and said he was going to go to your house since he figured you'd listen to him." I can't see her, but I can guarantee she's rolling her eyes. "I called you, like, ten times before you picked up."

I check my notifications, and sure enough, I have eleven missed calls from Agatha. Good on her for not exaggerating.

Before I can reply, I hear something downstairs.

I spring out of bed, nearly tripping on my comforter, and fly down the stairs with my phone still in hand, Agatha shouting my name over the speaker.

Sammie bursts through the front door with the exact grace one would expect of a heartbroken teenage boy. He tries to jam his key, that *goddamn* extra key that my parents just *had* to give him, into his pocket, but his hand misses and the key hits the hardwood floor with a sharp ping.

"What are you doing here?" I whisper-yell as I pocket the key and my phone. I drag him to the living room and push him onto the sofa.

"Did you see it?" he croaks, eyes red.

"No, I haven't seen the post yet. But it's three A.M., and you have to be quiet." I curse myself for not walking him home when he was still upright. He flops over, wetting the cushions with his sweaty face and hair.

"I thought about going to her house tonight," he moans, ignoring me as I try to hand him the tissue box we keep on the coffee table. He swats my hand away. "But she wasn't replying to my texts and she didn't come to school, so I thought she might be cranky if I just showed up, you know? Plus, I'd wake up her sisters and her mom, and so I told myself tomorrow was fine, tomorrow could still work." He clenches his fist and raises his voice. "But then fucking Wesley—"

"Sammie, you really have to keep it down," I say again, looking toward the stairs. "My mom and I are barely talking again, and I'm running out of leniency here."

"You and your mom weren't talking?"

"I will tell you all about it tomorrow on the way to school, when you've had time to think and calm down."

"Calm down? Are you kidding me?" he yells. I give up. "First of all, I'm not going to school tomorrow! Not to see that, that *guy* with his nice car and fancy sweaters and pretty face be with *my* girl." He gets up and starts sloppily pacing the room. "I *loved* her! And *this*? This is the thanks I get for *years* of yearning and—and wanting and *trying*? I get to watch this *fucking guy* take away the girl I love *and* my best friend? Fuck no . . . *Fuck* no."

"Sammie . . ." I sigh. "I'm sorry, but Wes didn't do anything wrong here."

"Oh, of course he's *Wes* now."

I ignore that. "You knew it would come down to one of you. You can't be pissed that he stepped up before you did. I love you, Sammie, but you missed your shot." I hope my honesty will ground him, but instead his eyes widen, startlingly big.

"Who are you?" I open my mouth to answer, but he stops me before I get the chance. "No, seriously. Who are you? You of all people are going to try to tell me to just— just get over this? Little Miss Romantic, Little Miss Cried Over Lucas For Months? You sob over guys you barely even know! I loved her for *years*. But I get it, *Wes* and O are BFFs now, so fuck the rest of us, right?"

I swallow the burning feeling in my throat. "You're hurt right now. I'm giving you the chance to stop."

"It only took him a few months to steal Linds away from me. With the rate you fall for guys, I bet you won't even know my name by the end of the week."

"Samuel Yadid Nasar."

He storms up to me, sloppily pushing damp curls out of his face. "She was *mine,* and he took her away."

I don't shove him, don't knock him away like my anger begs me to. But I do explode.

"Lindsay was *never* yours! And breaking fucking news: She liked you too! For years! But you never did anything about it. You sat around making googly eyes across a lunch table and threw food at her and played with her hair, but you weren't brave enough to be honest for once in your life about how you really felt, so don't you dare come to me expecting pity over this!" My voice is dangerously loud, but my mind is buzzing with years of being overlooked, being teased for my foolish crushing heart by two people who didn't have the gall to step up and confess their truth either. I learned the hard way that I wasn't and never would be enough for the people I fell for, but at least I had the guts to admit it.

He throws his head back, laughing once—sharp and bitter. "This is rich relationship advice coming from you. When was the last time you were actually honest about your feelings with anyone but your parents or me or Ags? Huh? You think you're better than us because you can fess up about love when there aren't any consequences? You've never taken a risk in your life! You couldn't even go away to college without me! Face it, O, you're a coward."

"You know what, asshole? You're right! You're so fucking right! In fact, I kissed Talia, who will never love me back, by the way, and I'm such a goddamn coward that I kept my mouth shut about it this whole time! How's that for bravery? How's that for being fucking honest?"

"What?" His voice softens so quickly that my words are still echoing.

"You think I don't know about consequences, Sammie? You think I don't know what it's like to feel your heart burning a hole straight through your chest because you know if you open your mouth, if you let yourself admit the truth even for a second, that everything will change? I *know* what that feels like. I will never forget what this fucking feels like."

The satisfaction of seeing the confusion in his eyes as the realization settles that he didn't—doesn't—have me all figured out is so visceral, so satisfying, that it takes me a second to notice he's no longer looking at me. He's looking behind me.

I turn my head slowly, catching my reflection in the mirror above the sofa. In the fuzzy darkness, I swear my reflection winks at me, of all things. Like Mirror Ophelia is saying, "Well, what did you expect?" The words I kept hidden inside for so long, finally free. But the relief from Sammie's reaction a second ago is absent. I'm still panting, but cold dread floods my entire body. My joints beg me to drop to the ground. But I complete my rotation and face my parents where they stand in their pajamas in the doorway.

Mom clears her throat. "Samuel. I think it's time for you to go home." She extends a hand, which Sammie hesitantly accepts. She drags him from the room, the image reminding me of when we were kids and she'd chaperone our class field trips, dragging us from exhibit to exhibit with maternal certainty of where we needed to go next. I crave that certainty now.

Sammie stops at the front door. His eyes are sadder than I've ever seen them before. "Ophelia . . . ," he starts. "I—"

"Let's go, Sammie," Mom says, softer now, coaxing him out of the house.

Dad and I stand there, listening to me pant, as I try to process what just happened.

They didn't hear; they couldn't have. And even if they did, surely they assume they misheard me.

Dad places a hand on my shoulder, the warmth of his palm scattering my thoughts. "¿Quieres hablar? *Should* we talk?"

My hands are shaking so much, I feel my skin vibrating. "I . . . um . . . Sammie just showed up and I didn't know what to do and he was so upset and—" I'm cut short when Mom comes back.

"We will talk about this in the morning," she says, brushing past Dad and me on the way to the stairs. I watch her leave, the way I both did and didn't expect her to. The way I hoped she wouldn't. I look at Dad.

"She's just tired," he says.

"I am too." I choke back a sob. My eyes are glistening, and I'm ready to open up, let it all out, when I hear a beep come from my pocket.

No. No, not her too.

I pull my phone out and check my call log. My call with Agatha ended less than a minute ago. I never hung up the phone. I never took her off speaker.

"Ophelia?" Dad asks.

I go back to my room. I don't sleep all night.

TWENTY-TWO

My alarm's been going off for twenty minutes, but I haven't moved. Mostly because the second I do, I know I have to face the real world. But also because the mind-numbing blaring almost manages to block out all thoughts of last night. Of what last night means for today, for tomorrow, for prom and graduation and the rest of my life.

If the sunlight pouring in from the crack between my curtains is any indication, it's far too bright and sunny out. I hear shuffling outside my door and imagine Dad pacing the hall, building up the courage to say something to me. I wonder if he and Mom argued over this too.

"Ophelia?" Dad raps twice on the door. "Necesitas levantarte."

"I'm awake!" I reply. "Don't come in. I'm changing."

"Bueno," he says, but I don't hear him leave. "I'll give you a ride today. I already told Samuel."

Great, Sammie stopped by already. "Okay!" I wait until

his footsteps fade down the hall to dig around in my bed for my phone and finally turn off my alarm.

I open Instagram. Might as well see what this damned Wes and Lindsay post is all about. I'm prepared to be annoyed by it, but a smile naturally tugs at my face when I pull up Linds's profile and see the photo of them. She's in pajamas, hair in a bun and the glasses she never wears in public perched on her nose. She's gripping a bouquet of lilies (inferior to roses, but still sweet) and Wes's drawing. As happy as she looks, her smile is nothing compared to Wesley's, his cheeks stretched so wide his face looks ready to burst.

I get a little choked up at the image, despite everything that's going on. Or maybe because of everything that's going on. Because at the end of the day, I think Wes and I are more alike than I wanted to admit. Sure, he's a lot quieter, gentler, and altogether *better* than I think I am, but we're both waiters. We wait for love, wait for the people we love to see us the way we see them. And in the face of waiting for one of the most popular and loved girls in school, who already had a funny, kind, loud, and attractive boy with his sights set on her, Wesley went for it.

He stopped waiting for change and made it happen himself.

I get out of bed, rushing to wash my face and brush my hair. The bags under my eyes will just have to be my accessory for the day. Dad knocks again, warning that we should leave soon, so I slip into an old pair of jeans with roses stitched on the back pockets and a plain white tank top.

"¿Lista?" Dad asks as I enter the kitchen. I grab a banana off the counter and not-so-subtly check for Mom. "She left already to pick up groceries," he says, reading my mind.

I plug my earbuds into my phone when we get inside the car, but Dad places a gentle hand over mine as I fumble to unravel the cords. "We should talk." My stomach turns, but I nod. "¿Recuerdas algo de tu abuelo?" he asks suddenly.

I shake my head, confused at the subject change. Abuelo died when I was a baby; all I remember about him are stories.

He presses his lips together as he drives. I wonder if that's the end of it. But he sighs and turns to look at me quickly, allowing me to notice the tears welling in his eyes. I'm too stunned to speak.

"Después que falleció mi padre, mi madre me dio sus cartas y documentos personales. Ella me dijo que necesitaba leerlos para comprender las cosas que él no podía compartir conmigo cuando estaba vivo. En los documentos, encontré un poema para mi padre de un hombre en Santa Clara, la ciudad donde creció. El poema era romántico. No leí todo porque . . . porque no era asunto mío. Pero entendí la intención de mi madre."

My brain rushes to catch up with his words, his Spanish faster than I'm used to. But when their meaning hits me, I'm left even more confused. *After my father's death, my mother gave me his letters and personal papers. She told me I needed to read them to understand things he couldn't share with me when he was alive. In the papers, I found a poem for my father from a man from Santa Clara, the city he grew up in. The poem was romantic.*

I didn't read it all because . . . because it wasn't my business. But I understood my mom's intention.

"I don't understand," I say. "Not the Spanish, I understood that, but . . . what are you saying?"

"My father, tu abuelo, was loved by another man. And from what I read, I think he loved him back. I didn't read any of the other letters, and I never asked my mother about them or who that man was. And I don't know why he never told me, why my mother wanted me to know after he passed, or what happened between him and that man.

"I heard you last night. I'm not going to ask any questions. I want to show you the same respect I showed my father. But I needed you to know this, to know about your grandfather. Not even your mom knows, but I felt like you needed to."

"Why didn't you ever tell me? Why haven't you told Mom?"

He runs a hand over his face. "En mi familia, I was taught not to talk about these things. It's how my amigos grew up too. We all knew someone like that, un tío who had a male "roommate" or primo who never brought una novia around but always wore that look of being in love." We pull up to the drop-off, and I see Wesley waiting at the front gate. The car behind us honks as I hesitate to get out. Dad still won't look at me.

"Did you mind? When you found the letters about your dad? Or when that girl turned you down because she had a girlfriend?"

"I'd be lying if I said I didn't mind at first. I just didn't understand," he says, and my stomach sinks. As a single tear slides down my cheek and onto my lips, Dad places his hand atop mine. "But I loved my father. I loved Paola. And I love you. None of that changed, mija. *I* did."

I kiss him on the cheek before getting out of the car, whispering, "Gracias."

Wesley shoots me a tentative smile as I approach him, stuffing his phone in his pocket.

"So I came out last night," I say plainly, and his smile drops instantly.

"What?" He takes a step forward, placing a careful hand on my bent elbow. If Lindsay could see us now . . .

"Oh yeah, congrats on the promposal," I say as genuinely as I can muster, my thoughts reminding me.

"Are you okay?"

"I'm—can we not go to school today?" I ask, and he frowns. "I know, I know. We're graduating soon, and AP testing is around the corner, and . . . look, this'll be the last time. I promise."

He bites his lip, considering, but we both already know what his answer will be. "Got anywhere in mind?"

❋ ❋ ❋

The LGBTQIAP+ center is smaller than I imagined it would be. But sitting in the parking lot, staring at it through Wesley's spotless windshield, it feels massive.

I explained what happened last night on the ride over.

We've been waiting here for a few minutes now, not entirely on my accord, but because Wes has to double-check who is running the front desk today. Not-Straight Emergency or not, I'm a minor who legally should be in school right now. He finally gets a text that seems to please him, and we head inside wordlessly.

He opens the door for me, and the first thing I notice is the wall of family photos. Dozens of sloppily cropped photos are pasted up. Families of all colors and ages make up the collage, and I find myself searching for Talia's without realizing it.

"Wait here," Wes says, nodding to the small collection of plastic chairs surrounding a weathered coffee table and bright blue rug that looks like the newest thing in here. I take a seat and watch him head farther down the hall to the help desk. I can't see him from here, but his voice echoes.

"You really want me to lose my job. That's it, right?" a feminine voice hisses. I assume she's who he was texting.

"One time, Addy, come on. I covered for you when you showed up hungover."

"That was over a year ago, and don't pretend like you were doing me any favors. You were too chickenshit to tattle on an employee."

"You were a volunteer," he corrects, but I can hear the smirk. "You weren't being paid."

"Well, now I am, so you can go get your ass back to school." I hear the finality in her tone and take Wesley's silence as surrender. I stand up, prepared to head back to the car and find somewhere else to kill a few hours, when Wesley speaks.

"My friend is with me. She needs help."

A beat of nothing. "What kind of help?" the girl, Addy, asks.

"The kind we've all needed before," he says. After a beat of silence and a sigh, I hear the jingle of keys and Wesley's sneakers against the floor as he comes back to the waiting room.

"I want to show you something," he says, dangling the keys.

He leads me down the opposite hallway, and I'm admittedly disappointed I don't get to meet Addy. I'm so distracted by this thought, I run into Wesley's back when he stops suddenly.

He doesn't say anything as he unlocks a plain blue door in front of us, opening it for me to enter before him. I step inside and gasp. The family photo collage was nothing compared to this.

The room is small, but the ceilings are high and the walls are packed with string lights that Wesley turns on with a switch by the door. Beneath the lights are rectangles of vibrant fabric. It takes me a moment to recognize them for what they are: flags.

Pride flags.

My awe must show on my face because Wesley says, "I felt the same way the first time I saw it. They've replaced the flags since then, wanted to freshen up the colors and include more, but still. It takes my breath away like it's the first time, every time." He plops into an orange beanbag on the floor. "It's usually saved for small-group therapy, but it's free for lounging when no one is using it."

"It's beautiful," I say, taking the yellow beanbag beside him. He leans over and points to a flag opposite the door.

"That's for asexuality." Black, gray, white, then purple stripes.

I look around for one I can recognize. I spot the familiar rainbow one, but it has stripes of black and brown I've never seen before. I ask Wes about it.

"The black and brown stripes represent queer people of color. Just because we're a community doesn't mean everyone's experiences are the same, especially when race and ethnicity come into play. I'm glad this place acknowledges that."

"Sounds like you've learned a lot here."

He smiles. "I've definitely spent my fair share of time here. Not much lately, but it's still the reason I want to minor in queer studies in college."

"You should," I say, and his smile deepens. My eyes freeze on another flag behind him, this one pink, purple, and blue. "That's for bisexuality, right?"

He nods, watching my face. He looks away for a second to point to another flag, this one pink, yellow, and blue. "That's for pansexuality." He's looking at me again.

"I should be feeling something, shouldn't I? That's why

you're staring? There should be a sign or fluttering that means I've found a label that gets me."

"There's no *shoulds* or *shouldn't*s here," he says. I roll my eyes. "You don't have to label yourself as anything until you're ready. Or ever, if you don't want to." He waits, fidgeting with a button on his shirt. "Was that why you wanted to come? To put a label on *only one kiss*?" If I hadn't already rolled my eyes, I would now.

"I came to see if this felt right."

"And?"

"And . . ." I run a hand over my face. "And, okay, what if it really was just a kiss?" I'm grateful Wesley doesn't sigh and throw his beanbag at me for regressing, even if he has every right to. So I keep going. "I've never felt this way toward a girl before, ever, not a little crush or moment of attraction or flash of heat . . . nothing. What makes Talia so special? What is it about her that made my heart make an exception?"

"Don't hate me," he starts, which instantly makes me want to, at least a little bit. "But are you sure that's true, about not feeling anything for any other girl?"

I think of Lindsay in her dress at Wes's for the photo shoot. I think of Agatha reapplying lip gloss. I think of Dani in her tight leather. I swallow. "I don't know."

"You knew Talia liked girls before you knew you liked her; maybe that has something to do with it too."

"Like she . . . unlocked this?"

He presses his lips together to hide a smile. "I wouldn't use those words, but maybe you hadn't considered it until you had an option, for lack of a better word. But it's okay if you just plain don't know. Or even if Talia really is the only girl you ever have or will like."

"But is that enough?" I ask without thinking.

"Enough for what?"

I hesitate, anticipating his disappointment. "To label this as anything more than an outlier. To be allowed to use any of this." I wave around at all the flags, dozens of rectangles of striped fabric with labels that escape me. But I know the power of language. If Mom's profession and Dad's bilingualism have taught me anything, it's that words *mean* something.

"I love my heritage, but I don't speak Korean," he says suddenly. "Not well, at least. And my parents and I don't regularly celebrate Chuseok like most of my extended family still does or Korean New Year for all three days."

"Okay," I reply, confused but attentive.

"Does that mean I'm not Asian 'enough'?"

"Of course not," I say automatically. I recognize the frustration in his eyes when he asks this. This isn't just a rhetorical question for my benefit. This is an admission to a struggle I know all too well.

And I know a small part of him, a little voice in his head, was worried I'd say yes. The same little voice that I hear when I can't understand something Dad says in Spanish right away and I watch him, slightly tired, stop and repeat himself in English. I feel it when I can't handle the extra spices he adds to his sopas or in the ají for empanadas from Ollas Amarillas. I feel it in the way my name is spelled with a *ph* instead of an *f,* Spanish not sliding over it as easily as *Miguel* or *Rojas.* The way diaspora colors my relationship to Cuba and the legacy of my blood.

And when Mom celebrates Saint Patrick's Day or cheers for Ireland in an international competition, I never know if it's my place to stand there beside her. If my skin and last name and distance from her heritage mean they aren't mine to touch.

Half of my blood and heritage is one thing, half is another, and more often than not, it leaves me feeling less like a whole person with a complete, unique makeup, and more like two halves of a girl who is never enough.

I guess I've always struggled with the expectations set for me.

"Liking one girl and countless boys doesn't make you less queer than if it were half and half. Or if you liked countless girls and a couple of nonbinary people, or people of all kinds of genders in any assortment of percentages," Wesley says. He leans toward me and takes my hands, the sincerity in his eyes so intense I don't worry about how clammy my palms are or whether or not it means anything that a cute boy is holding my hands in a dark room, alone. Because yes, he's a boy, and yes, he's here and kind and cute and wonderful, but I don't like him. It shouldn't mean the world to me to realize this, but it does.

"Being queer is hard enough. Don't lock yourself out of all of this just because you're scared you won't fit in the keyhole, without even trying."

"Metaphors, again?" I joke, my eyes wet. But as quickly as the laughter comes to us, it subsides. "How do I talk to them? Sammie and Agatha and my parents?"

"However you want to," he says, rubbing his thumb across the back of my hand.

"I just feel like, especially after these past few weeks, that everyone thinks they know me completely, but *I* don't even know me completely. If anything, what happened with Talia is proof of that. I know kissing and liking Talia shouldn't change who I am to them, or to myself, but it *does*. And maybe they'd say 'Oh, this doesn't change anything!' or 'You're still the same Ophelia we know and love!' but it does, and I'm not the same. And they can't possibly understand that. It's not just that I'm scared they'll hate me for this; I'm scared they won't even see it."

"People confuse acceptance with erasure," he says with the weight of understanding that only someone else who has battled this same internal conflict possibly could. I think of Dad saying he loved his father and Paola and me and wonder if sexualities outside of "straight" are just qualifiers for that kind of love.

"I don't want to risk everything if this isn't real," I whisper. "But I also don't want to pretend like this doesn't change things for me. Because it does."

"I know," he says. "Your sexuality doesn't define you,

but it is a part of you." His words are tight, voice breaking ever so slightly. I squeeze his hand gently, an understanding passing between us. "But questioning who you are? It's a risk we all take. It's *your* risk to take if you want to. No one else gets to decide this for you; it's your life."

I don't reply, the single tear trickling down my cheek saying what my voice can't. So Wesley turns to the walls instead, using his free hand to point out more flags for me as I nod silently along.

He uses words and labels I recognize, and defines the ones I don't. Gay, lesbian, bisexual, transgender, pansexual, asexual, demisexual, polysexual, genderqueer, nonbinary, aromantic, grayromantic, demiromantic, and on and on.

Even if none of them click for me, if none sound like my experience wrapped up in a convenient label, I know they do for other kids out there. Kids who may have sat exactly where I am now and realized who they were for the first time. Today, that's enough for me.

I'm nearly drifting off to sleep from the comforting hum of Wesley labeling the flags for the second time around, taking an endearing amount of pride in his ability to recognize them as quickly as he does, when I feel my phone buzz in my pocket.

"Shit," I say, awake in an instant. I answer the call against my rebellious desires, too scared to let it go to voice mail. "Hi, Mom."

"Do you want to tell me why the school just called to say you were absent for the second time this week? I had to listen to some snotty secretary tell me my daughter was probably ditching after I said your father dropped you off this morning."

Foolishly, I avoid the question. "I'm okay. Can you come pick me up?" I say, voice quivering. She asks me to send her my location and hangs up.

I take one last look around as Wes gets up to leave.

He returns his keys to the mysterious Addy while I wait outside, joining me right as Mom's car skids into the parking lot. With a final wave and tight smile, I silently thank him for what he's done for me. I'll thank him better later, but for now I focus on walking toward Mom without running away again.

Maybe none of those flags or words are me. Maybe one day they will be. But maybe I don't need them as armor to have this conversation. Maybe all I need is the thing I lost more than my confidence in knowing myself: my honesty.

TWENTY-THREE

Mom is scarily quiet as I get in the car. At first, I think she's taking me back to school, but we drive straight past it, as well as home. I start wondering if she's just driving off her anger, waiting for her steam to run out, but then she pulls into the parking lot of Ollas Amarillas and gets out, slamming the door behind her after saying, "Stay here."

I wait for ten minutes. When she comes out, she tosses a paper bag at me and pushes back her seat. I recognize the smell immediately but peek inside to be sure it isn't my mind playing tricks on me. Sure enough, half a dozen papas rellenas are steaming inside, two of them already smushed.

"I don't understand," I say, closing the bag. It feels like a trap.

"That makes two of us," she sighs, fussing with the hair around her temple. "Why were you at a gay youth center with Wesley?" She motions for me to pass her the bag and tears into a papa before I can reply.

"You don't seem mad," I risk, pulling out a papa. I bite into it and let the hot carne burn the roof of my mouth.

"I was mad. No, actually, I've been mad. I had a rough term, was worried about the department letting me go because of the specificity of my experience. But I made it through. And on the night my colleagues and I are celebrating the relief of making it another term closer to tenure, my typically lovely, obedient, and polite daughter dumps her drink onto one of my best students. And then she refuses to apologize or even explain herself to me. She tells her father though, specifically asking him to keep her reasons from me. She shuts me off; he shuts me out. We no longer joke together about her crushes or her friends' drama." She takes another bite. "You know, my other friends with kids always tell me they're jealous of how comfortable you are with me and your father. And after the way most of my family reacted to me marrying Miguel and having you, I treasured that relationship." She dips her head, shielding her eyes with her free hand. "As a parent, all you want is to do right by your kids. I always thought your father and I did right by you. But now you're having screaming matches with your best friend in the middle of the night and ditching school and . . . kissing girls? And you're about to move away and go be an adult, and I have no idea how to talk to you about it."

She's crying now, looking unbelievably young, and I'm so consumed by shock, I don't react. I swallow the last of my papa, the mound of crusted mashed potatoes sliding roughly down my throat as I watch my mother weep into her pale hands.

"It's not an explanation, or an excuse, I know. But what you heard last night . . . it's not unrelated to what happened with Jeremiah.

"He made homophobic comments." My chest loosens. "He was talking about that *Hamlet* adaptation where Hamlet and Ophelia are lesbians, and he . . . he said things he shouldn't have."

She furrows her brows. "So you dumped your drink on him?"

A laugh breaks free from my lips. "I did. And I didn't want you to know that what he said made me that upset, because I didn't want you to know that I took it personally."

She nods and bites her lip. "So, um . . . so, you're a lesbian?"

"No, I still like boys," I say with a smile. "But I think I can like girls too. Probably any gender. I don't know if gender even matters anymore."

"But why wouldn't you tell me this?"

"I didn't want you to see me differently. I don't know how to be anyone besides that lovely, obedient, polite daughter you mentioned," I admit, whisper-quiet. "I don't know how to not live up to that."

"You don't clean your room, have never cooked a real meal for yourself, and you snap back at us way more than we should allow." Mom laughs and looks up. Tears blur my vision. "You're really not as perfect as I'm giving you credit for."

She's joking now, but I ignore the temptation to let the serious moment pass. "I don't tell you everything, Mom," I confess, and she nods sadly, like she realized this long ago but is only now accepting it. "I try to, but it's hard." I want to say that she doesn't want to hear that Sammie gets intense whenever he's sad. That Lindsay had a pregnancy scare last year after a one-night stand with a boy from another school, and that I was more worried about what it meant that she told Agatha weeks before she told me than I was about the actual pregnancy. That I'm absolutely scared shitless about going to college and growing up and not having the same little life I've always had. But instead, I say, "I don't want to be your *boy-crazy* Ophelia anymore."

She flinches, and I feel it, deep within my own chest, like her heart and mine are still connected in some maternal, fetal way. I watch in horror as my deepest fear comes true, that this'll be the thing we can't come back from. That one day we will be just like her and most of her cousins and aunts and uncles, passive and shallow in their love for one another, as if they never shared a family tree at all. Just like Talia and Dani.

But she recovers in a second, and when she smiles, quivering mouth and pink eyes, she looks resolute more than disappointed. "Have I ever told you that I was torn between naming you Ophelia or Juliet?" she asks, somewhat wistfully.

I nod. She mentioned it on a near daily basis when I was in the third grade and a boy named Romeo transferred to our school. *You two could've been so cute,* she cooed. It was the one time she rallied for a boy more than she now does for Sammie. It was also the one time I didn't tell her about a crush I had on a boy, like even then I dreaded being too similar to her expectations.

"Did I ever tell you why I chose Ophelia though?"

"No," I admit, surprised I never asked. "I always figured you wanted something more unique. Or that Dad vetoed Juliet." Dad never wanted to watch adaptations of *Romeo and Juliet*, claiming it was too tragic for him. The irony of him still loving *Hamlet* isn't lost on me.

She laughs. "No, he always knew it was my dream to name a child after one of them. Juliet and Ophelia were always my favorite because they are two of the most quickly dismissed among people who refuse to dig past the surface narrative. Juliet is remembered as a foolish teenage girl who threw away her life for a boy she hardly knew, and Ophelia is remembered more for her virginity and inability to accept Hamlet's rejection than anything else."

"Great legacies you left me."

"But that's not who those girls were," she corrects firmly. "Romeo was just as much a hopeless romantic as Juliet, and they gave their lives to show the world that true love mattered more than senseless hatred. Juliet cared enough about her family to die so they could live brighter, wiser lives. I respected her as a character for being more mature than most give her credit for."

"Then why'd you pick Ophelia?" I ask, dusting my hands

against my jeans. She narrows her eyes at the crumbs I'm spreading in the car, but keeps going.

"Ophelia was all those things too. But she also wore her heart on her sleeve. She wasn't 'mad' in her final scene; she was grieving without shame. She was begging for someone to hear her desperation beneath the offered flowers." She exhales shakily and takes my hands, not unlike the way Wesley had, gently, like she fears I'll pull away if she's too firm. "When you fell in love with gardening and roses, I took it as a sign that I made the right choice on your name. And I never wanted to be like Juliet's or Ophelia's parents and get in the way of your happiness, so I tried to encourage your crushes and romantic tendencies. I never meant for you to follow in Ophelia's footsteps by struggling so much with love you felt you had to hide. I didn't mean for her suffering to become your legacy too."

"Mom—" I whisper.

"I love you, Ophelia. You could ditch school every day and dump punch on my boss and I'd still love you." She takes another unstable breath, steadying herself with the exhale. "But please don't do those things, because I'd *really* like for you to graduate and not get me fired." We share a teary laugh. "I won't lie—I don't understand it all. This stuff about your . . . sexuality? But I'm willing to be the student for once. Because I love you whether you love Romeos or Juliets or both or neither or live out the rest of your days with Dad and me and your garden. No matter what changes or who you do or don't love, *I* will always love *you*. That is the legacy I want for you, not to be the girl who loves too much, but to be the girl who is loved more than enough."

"Thank you," I say, a little frozen. She kisses the back of each of my hands and cups my face for a second before reaching into the bag and pulling out two more papas, handing me one.

"Now, why don't you tell me all about you and Talia?"

❊ ❊ ❊

In the end, Mom didn't let me off scot-free for ditching. Turns out identity crises don't actually excuse you from your educational obligations. I'll be helping clean her office all next weekend and doing extra chores around the house, including learning how to make papas rellenas with her as a surprise for Dad's upcoming birthday.

As for this weekend, however, I still have prom. And quite a few explanations and apologies to give before then. Luckily for me, Agatha and Sammie are sitting on my front porch when I get home, laughing about something on Sammie's phone.

They sit up as Mom and I pull into the driveway. She shoots Sammie a loaded glance as she unlocks the door and heads inside without me.

"Hey," I say.

"Hey," Ags says. She nudges Sammie, who mumbles a greeting as well, looking more embarrassed than mad. She lifts the bag in her hands. "I brought you some ribbons for the corsages and boutonnieres."

"Thanks," I reply, shifting my weight. "So . . . last night," I start as Agatha scoots away from Sammie and pats the space between them. Her thick, neon green plastic rings smack against the porch bricks.

Sammie clears his throat as I sit between them. "Your mom told mine about my, uh, well, about what happened last night. My parents sat me down, full intervention-style this morning. They were embarrassed on my behalf for showing up here like that so late, but mostly they were disappointed I didn't come to them first. Honestly, I'm surprised they're still letting me go to prom at all, but they've never bought into the sunken-cost thing, and my suit was pretty expensive." He ducks his head, rubbing at his neck. "They want me to start seeing someone. Like a counselor, therapist, whatever." His voice quiets. "I think it might be good for me." He leans back on his palms, stretching his legs down the steps. "Just thought I should let you know."

I lean into him. "I'm proud of you."

Agatha pats his knee. "Me too."

"Whatever." He ducks his head, but I catch his small smile. "But, uh, you and Talia, huh?" he says, ruining the tender moment. I groan into my hands, hanging my head.

"Ignore him," Agatha says, and I feel her arm reach over me again to slap Sammie. I lift my head and tuck my hands beneath my legs, bouncing them with nervous energy. "You don't have to tell us anything if you don't want to." My eyes stay trained on the ground, watching an ant scamper around a broken leaf by my feet.

I could leave it. Save this conversation for another day, for another Ophelia who will maybe know how to explain everything that's happened over the past few weeks better than I currently do. But here they are, my best friends, so ready to let me hide my heart away again. And I don't think I want to anymore.

"I liked Talia, a lot. I probably still do. But I kissed her and messed everything up." I suppose part of me still expects the ground to split open and swallow me whole, for their faces to swell with disgust, betrayal, and anger. But it doesn't. But they don't.

"So you're . . . ?" Sammie wafts his hand, waiting for me to finish, his expression unreadable.

"I don't know." I shrug, honest. "Maybe I'm bisexual or pansexual. Maybe I'm queer." The word still feels a bit sour on my tongue, but there's something thrilling about it too. Like it's a dare just to say it this way, adoptive instead of vicious. I hope Jeremiah is spilling punch on himself somewhere. "All I know," I start, taking a deep breath, "is that I'm probably—no, *definitely*—not straight."

"So you *did* have a secret crush," he says, a sly grin slipping over his face. Agatha and I groan loudly before all three of us burst into a fit of laughter. It's unexpected, but I welcome it. I think I should do that more often.

When we finally settle, Ags tucks a strand of hair out of my face and pouts at me. "So this is what's been bugging you out lately? Why didn't you just talk to us?"

"I was scared," I whimper, feeling my lower lip quiver.

Sammie wraps his arm around me, grasping for Agatha's hand over my shoulder.

"But you know we don't care about that stuff," Ags says.

"Yeah, half the fun of being your friend is making fun of your crushes. If you like girls too now, that's like double the material to work with," Sammie adds, both helpfully and unhelpfully.

I sob and laugh at the same time, something broken and beautiful croaking out of me. "I didn't know if you'd care." I turn to Ags. "If this would change our sleepovers and us sharing makeup and you calling me 'babe.'" I turn to Sammie. "If this would just be some big joke or fetish for you." I look down. "It's been hard and messy and scary. I want you guys to care about it and what it changes for me, but without it changing *us*."

"Of course we care, O." I can't tell who says it, my ears buzzing with the sound of my own snot and tears leaking out of my face. For a few minutes, we sit like that, my best friends holding me together and letting me pour it all out.

I don't feel relief, not exactly. There isn't a massive weight lifted off my chest. Because I realize this is something I'll have to do for the rest of my life, correct the assumption my heart belongs to boys, and boys alone.

I'll never stop coming out.

And yeah, that really sucks. But in this moment, it doesn't suck as much as it could. It kind of feels like the first big dip of a roller coaster, all nausea and fear and excitement and knowledge of more dips to come. I've never thought of myself as a fan of adrenaline rushes, but I also never thought of myself as a fan of kissing girls. Things change.

I curl around the realization that I've now come out to my dad, mom, and two best friends, all in one day. I know I've got a lifetime of these moments to go, but somehow, crushed between Agatha and Sammie, I'm not as scared as I was, even just yesterday. Because if I could make it through these ones, I can make it through them all.

I wipe my nose as Agatha's phone goes off. She checks her screen and rolls her eyes, groaning.

"Georgie, again?" Sammie asks. Ags nods. I guess she let that cat out of the bag.

"You know, I still don't get why you said no to him," Sammie says. "I mean, I know you were playing the long game in the hopes of snagging me as a date, but the odds weren't exactly in your favor for a while."

"I will hurt you," Agatha says, clawing her hand. Her aggression melts into a faraway look as she rests her screen against her knee, Georgie's dozens of unanswered texts lighting up her skin.

"You good?" I ask.

"Need me to beat him up for you?" Sammie offers.

"I wasn't going to say anything, but since you already shared . . ."

"Are you finally going to tell us your middle name?" Sammie springs up.

"No, Samuel, I most certainly am not."

"Come on! We're going to hear it at graduation. You

can't pay off the announcer like you did in middle school. They're having teachers call out the names."

"Then you can wait a few more weeks."

"Ignore him," I say, stealing her line from earlier. I face Agatha with my whole body, a hard feat given how packed we are on the steps. "Go on."

"Well," she says, and for the first time in forever, Agatha Jones looks less than confident in what she's about to say. "I'm not sure how to put it, but here goes. I don't really like people."

Sammie drops back down. "Relatable."

"Sammie, shut up," I scold.

"Sorry." He winces, then pokes Agatha's knee. "What do you mean?"

"It's like . . . I don't *like* like people. As in, romantically. I've been attracted to people, mostly guys, but I've seen a girl or two who . . . well, whatever. Point is, I don't want to date any of them. I used to think maybe I just didn't like boys and was a lesbian, but I don't feel anything romantic for girls either. I just don't like anyone that way." She shifts uncomfortably on the porch, picking at the black sequins decorating her skirt. "I wasn't going to say anything to y'all because I didn't know if that was even a thing. Especially with how much y'all *do* like people romantically."

I think of Wesley earlier, his quick recitation of labels and terms I'm still new to. I'm no expert, but it brings me joy to get to tell Agatha she might want to search up the word *aromantic* later tonight.

"I had a sexy dream about Zaq last week," Sammie says out of absolutely nowhere after Agatha finishes typing the note to herself.

"*What?*" Ags and I say at the same time, not even taking a moment to appreciate our synchronization.

"He's a good-looking guy!" Sammie defends, raising his hands. "What? You can kiss Talia, but I can't *accidentally* consider the possibilities with Zaq? What kind of double standards . . ."

"Sammie," I start, joy cracking my lips into a growing smile. "Are you not straight?"

"Whoa, let's not get ahead of ourselves," he says, then shrugs. "I'll look into it and report back."

"Did you two . . . did you two just *hijack* my coming out? Both of you?" I look back and forth between the two of them, my mouth gaping and smiling at the same time.

"Not our fault you opened up the dialogue," Sammie says, picking a scab on his knuckle. "Heh, I might actually have a decent time with the whole therapy thing."

"We didn't hijack it; we're meeting you halfway," Ags says, then adds, "You're not the only one still figuring it all out, babe. We're at the start of our lives, not the end."

"I love you guys," I say, and collapse back into their arms.

TWENTY-FOUR

Turns out Lindsay caught a cold that's been going around and, according to Zaq, so has Talia, hence both their absences over the past few days, including today. It's for the best, considering my unresolved drama with both of them. But weirdly, I'm not as scared as I should be for the fate of our friend group.

Especially because I have something far scarier to do.

Agatha leaves me at our lockers in the morning, noticing Lucas before I do. As expected, he doesn't acknowledge me until I chase after him, tugging on his arm in a way that once would've sparked nerves in my stomach. Now I'm nervous for an entirely different reason.

"Oh hey." He looks over his shoulder at his friends, other boys from the soccer team, and nods them onward before turning back to me. I feel them watching us, even hear trickles of their teasing, but I have to shut it out or I'll freeze up.

"I can't go to prom with you," I say, ripping off the bandage. I expect anger, maybe even a little concealed hurt, but Lucas just chuckles and pats me on the shoulder twice, harder than he probably means to.

But then I watch the realization hit him. "Wait, are you serious?"

"I'm so sorry," I say, and mean it. He may be shallower than the roots of my roses, but he doesn't deserve the whirlwind I've put him through regarding prom. If I were another girl, at another point in my life, I'd probably still go with him. We'd laugh and dance, maybe even kiss a bit if the lighting was right and the music swelled at the perfect moment, just like in my fantasies. Maybe, if I were really different, none of it would mean anything at all.

But I'm not that girl, I'm me. And prom still means something to me, enough that I'm not willing to throw it away on him. He was my first boyfriend, my first kiss, my first real heartbreak, but I can't let Lucas be the prom date I remember for the rest of my life. Maybe it's melodramatic to think so, but I've reclaimed my clichés, and I'm not letting them go for anyone.

"You're kidding me," he exhales, laughing again, not with me and not quite at me, but almost *through* me. "First you say no, then you ask *me*, and now you're backing out again? What happened to the girl who acted like life was some chick flick?"

"I just think I'd have more fun going with my friends."

"Unbelievable," he mutters, roughing up his hair. Distantly, I try to find the girl who would've killed for this.

He's so pretty. And he wants me. And Talia doesn't. And now I *know* I'm being melodramatic, but maybe no one else ever will. Even if I can love any gender, if that's who I really am, there's still a chance I'll never find someone who makes me feel as special as Talia did the night we stole her brooch back.

Honestly, when Talia told me about Zaq, it wasn't just about the girl who made me realize I wasn't straight being unavailable. It was feeling like I'd kidded myself into thinking I had a chance. Into thinking that someone met me and saw something worth loving, for once.

I deserve, one day, to find that again. And to know, no matter their gender, that I'm not settling. Even if that means being alone and unsure for longer than I thought I'd be.

I know I'm being unfair to Lucas, but I also know that this is such a shock to him because I've always been predictable. I am a romantic. But I don't feel hopeless anymore.

Like Ags said, it's the start. Not the end.

Lucas storms off, leaving me still flipping through my own thoughts as he mutters some choice words I probably, at least a little bit, deserve. But boy is he lucky I don't have any punch.

✻ ✻ ✻

Sammie's driving us home, looking a little dejected after overhearing Wes tells Ags he's going to drive over to

Lindsay's house to check up on her. Since he's already in a mood, I decide now's as good a time as ever to ride my wave of honesty.

"So, we talked about what I said the other night about Talia. But we never really talked about what you said about me." I turn down the radio and tuck my chin against my chest. Sammie stops tapping his long fingers on the dashboard and looks at me. I take a deep breath. "You called me a coward. You threw all my insecurities about love and rejection into my face to make yourself feel better. And I know you were upset, but is that really how you see me?"

Sammie pulls over. He kills the engine and stares at his hand, frozen on his keys in the ignition. "I've liked Lindsay since I was thirteen. I watched her date guy after guy, watched myself date girl after girl, and let every opportunity I had to tell her how I felt slip through my fingers. And then Wesley came along. And I want to hate him; I mean, I kind of do, but he had the guts to do what I couldn't, that bastard." He chuckles to himself and rubs his face. "Sorry, this isn't about me and Lindsay. I've just always seen the way you let yourself feel things. Maybe you don't always shoot your shot, but you don't front about wanting to. So when you and Wesley got all chummy, and then he stepped up and went for Linds, I guess I kinda hated you for a minute too. Because I couldn't put my feelings for Lindsay over my fear of being honest with her about how much I cared.

"I was an ass about it, to you, to Linds, and especially to fucking Wesley." He looks up, tilting his head and smiling a little. "I'm so sorry, O. I made my shit your shit. I'm sorry that I said and did stuff in the past that made you feel like you couldn't talk to me about Talia. And I'm sorry I called you a coward. You're not, and you never have been."

"Thank you," I reply, leaning over to ruffle his hair a little. "You finally managed to give a good apology."

He laughs as he turns the car back on and pulls into the street again. "Yeah, well, let's hope I stop doing shit that requires me to apologize."

"Unlikely. But I, for one, still have a few rounds of apologies to get through before graduation."

"Better get to it, then, Rojas."

"Sammie?"

"Yeah?"

"I'm sorry for not telling you the truth about what was going on with me."

He brakes suddenly, and I thank God we're at the end of an empty street or he probably would've gotten us killed just for dramatic effect. "No," he says firmly, staring me down. "You don't apologize for that. Apologize for calling me Samuel when you really want to call me an asshole, or apologize for forgetting at least twice a year that I don't eat meat that isn't halal while still scolding your mom for forgetting. But don't apologize for not coming out before you were ready."

"Okay," I say, biting back a smile. "But can I apologize for what I'm going to say next?"

He continues driving. "Depends."

"You've still got another stop to make on your apology tour."

"Don't worry—I'll apologize to your parents for breaking in and screaming at their daughter."

"No, that's not—okay, yeah, actually, you probably should do that. But I meant Wesley."

If we weren't pulling up to our houses already, I'm sure he'd slam the brakes again. "Oh, come on." He throws back his head. "Can't I just be extra nice to him until graduation and call it a year? I'll even sign his yearbook and everything."

I reach over and pat him on the knee. "Not gonna cut it, buddy," I say patronizingly, and he flips me off, the way I hoped he would. "So, what happens now with you and Linds?"

"Ugh, I don't even know. I mean, I'm still heartbroken or whatever. And it could be hindsight or just some defense-mechanism shit, but besides flirting, I don't know if what Linds and I had was ever even real, especially since we've never even sat down and talked about it. I've seen her with Wesley, and I think it's more than just chemistry with them." He gags. "I guess what I'm trying to say is there's something kinda relieving about all this bullshit being over, even if I'm sad. I don't know what that means for the two of us as friends, but for me, I think it means freedom to see what else is out there. College is all about exploration, right?"

"Cheers to that."

We say farewell, joking about having nothing big planned

for the weekend, but just as I'm opening my front door, Sammie shouts my name from his porch.

"What?" I shout back.

"You didn't have to, but I'm really glad you told us!" he yells. He waves and goes inside, but I'm frozen with such overwhelming relief, the kind I missed yesterday, that I nearly collapse right there.

I don't though, because I still have a long list of things to do before tomorrow, the first of which being all those damn corsages and boutonnieres I agreed to make.

❋ ❋ ❋

"Uh, I'm pretty sure I'm doing this wrong," Wes warns, looping ribbon intensely in his lap. I accidentally prick my finger on a thorn and immediately pop it into my mouth. "You don't look much better off though."

We're sitting on a blanket in my backyard, surrounded by bundles of baby's breath, ribbons of every possible color from Ags, and clippings of various roses. I texted Wesley to see how Linds was doing once I got home and casually mentioned I needed an artist's help. I could've asked Sammie— this didn't *really* require an artist—but after everything, it felt right to ask Wes.

"That's fine, but if you mess up Agatha's corsage, know my death is on your hands," I say. "Actually, same goes for your date's." He blushes.

My time crunch made it easier to decide on everyone's final roses, especially because it didn't give me the chance to mourn having to choose roses that weren't "their" roses. For Linds, and subsequently Wes, I picked out three Honor roses, the classic white perfectly fitting for a prom queen and her date. For Ags I picked Keepsakes, the vibrant blend of pale and bright pink perfectly accenting her planned makeup and glittery gown. Ags will probably hate me for it, but I chose a Tequila Sunrise for Sammie instead of making his boutonniere match her corsage. And I manage to find three tiny, and absolutely perfect, Lady X roses for myself.

I neglected most of my roses. But to my shock, and no one else's, my garden didn't go to complete and utter shit just because I took a few weeks off from my usual routine. I wasn't able to see it when I was down in the dumps, but it's really not that bad. Maybe it could've looked nicer by now, the Honors a little brighter, the Midas Touches less sparse, the Keepsakes a bit fuller, but they'll do. So will I.

I don't know what Zaq is going to wear, but I assume as Talia's date he'll somewhat match her color scheme, so I set aside Olympiads for them both. Despite my questioning-my-straightness-induced breakdown, those damn Olympiads just wouldn't die.

I gather the three blooms I clipped off earlier and trim their stems horizontally with just enough room to bind them together with floral wire. Stabbing Talia on top of everything else doesn't seem like a great idea, so I double up on the floral tape until all the sharp edges are covered and repeat both steps with some of the filler flowers. I twist more floral wire around the bundles to attach them to a faux diamond band and manipulate one of the expertly crafted bows Wesley's made and ta-da: corsage!

Only three more to go, then on to the boutonnieres.

"Ugh," I moan into my hands. "Remind me, again, why I agreed to do this?"

"You didn't agree," he says, tossing me the silver ribbon meant for Lindsay. I still don't know what her dress looks like, but Wes said he was told to wear a silver tie. Interesting choice for his navy suit, but not my concern. "You volunteered."

"Even worse," I complain, and he laughs. "Do not let me volunteer to make graduation leis. Straight Me really didn't take into consideration how much work this would be."

Wesley glances up from where he's tying together sparkling white ribbon, the bow for my corsage. "Straight You, huh?"

I shrug, feigning casual. It probably would've been more convincing if Wesley hadn't seen me cry enough that I could've watered my garden with my tears twice over in the past few days. "It feels weird, but there's no point denying it anymore. I don't have a label for it, but I'm okay existing in the gray space. Not-Straight Me can take her time."

He hands me my bow. "Any predictions for tomorrow?" he says, getting to work on the hot pink ribbon for Ags.

"I'm guessing you and Linds will look adorable during your first dance together after she wins prom queen," I say, and enjoy watching his blush return. "Agatha and Sammie will be the best dancers, no doubt. Talia and Zaq will be the best dressed," I add, and mean it, even if it stings. "And I'll be the best friend I haven't been lately."

He frowns at me. "You're seventeen. You're allowed to be a not-so-great person every once in a while."

"I know, but I still have to apologize. Unfortunately, not being straight doesn't give me a free pass to be an asshole." I sigh. "Pass me the next bundle." He hands me the Tequila Sunrises. "Speaking of apologies though, I hear Sammie has one coming your way tomorrow."

"Oh yeah?" Wesley says, and with a dangerous flash in his eyes, turns around to face the wall dividing Sammie's and my yards. "Is that true, Sammie?" he shouts.

I don't see his mop of curls over the wall, but it's impossible to miss the hushed, "*Shit*," as Sammie runs from his hiding spot back to his house.

Wesley and I fall atop each other, laughter burning my lungs and my eyes watering so badly that I wonder, after this week is done, if I'll have any tears left in me.

TWENTY-FIVE

My favorite quote from *Hamlet*, because you need one when you're named Ophelia, has always been, "Doubt thou the stars are fire; Doubt that the sun doth move; Doubt truth to be a liar; But never doubt I love." In the context of the play as a whole, it seems silly to focus on such a romantic quote, knowing Ophelia and Hamlet's love is doomed. But in a tragic play in which the character I'm named after dies by suicide, heartbroken and alone, I've tried to look on the bright side and remember happier times.

But when I pulled out my nicer makeup for prom this morning, I found the old copy of *Hamlet* that Mom gave me for my thirteenth birthday wedged among the palettes in my dresser. I had a few hours to spare before getting ready, so I decided to flip through and read my old annotations, remembering that I'd highlighted every single one of Ophelia's lines, because of course I did. I stopped on act 4, scene 5,

Ophelia's mad scene, and amid her convoluted meltdown, noticed the line "Lord we know what we are, but know not what we may be."

I'd read it before, obviously, but never paid it much attention. And I'm not sure why.

Or, maybe I do know. I've spent most of my life telling myself I know who I am—a lifeboat of identity in the turbulent waves of growing up. A hopeless romantic, a rose gardener, a chismosa, a girl who falls for every boy who looks her way. I forgot that there are parts of me I've yet to discover, versions of me I've yet to become.

I'm tempted to say I have a new favorite quote, but it feels wrong to abandon my old favorite, to give up on the sliver of true romance buried beneath all the tragedy. I could try, with the power vested in me as the modern-day Ophelia, to propose my own mashed-together quote and boldly rewrite Shakespeare. But instead, I'll give myself this:

I may doubt the truths of the world, but never again will I doubt whether or not the person that I am, or may be, is loved or worthy of love. I know myself, and I don't. Both can be true.

I am not Ophelia: daughter of Polonius, sister of Laertes, lover of Hamlet.

I am Ophelia Rojas: daughter of Miguel and Stella, best friend of Sammie and Agatha, aspirational lover to many, many boys and one girl.

And I am so much more, just waiting to be discovered.

For now though, I'm just a girl who needs to get ready for prom.

❁ ❁ ❁

I never knew I could look like this.

Facing my mirror, still wearing the daisy-print pajamas I saved for the occasion, I can't quite believe those are my eyes staring back at me. I watched a couple of eye shadow tutorials this morning, having a decent enough grasp of makeup to think I'd be capable of handling the task myself. But the silver glitter on the inner corner of my eyes, the blended gray in the creases, and the way my lashes fan out, thicker than usual with the extra coats of mascara, have me convinced I'm a magician.

I finally tear myself away from my reflection, only because everyone will be here soon and I can't let Sammie catch me making kissy faces at myself or he'll never let me live it down.

Mom did my hair earlier according to Agatha's suggestion, curling the ends on a low-heat setting so my waves would be more pronounced but wouldn't look unnatural or like the curled ribbons on a birthday present (Ags's words, not mine).

And yeah, when I woke up, my chest was heavy with the uncomfortable realization that I did come out to a bunch of people this week. The high of it was finally wearing off and turning to anxiety, worsening as I remembered I'm facing Talia and Lindsay today.

The little voices, the ones that always made me imagine the worst of my family and friends, have returned to taunt me, to tell me I made a mistake by being honest. They tell me I'm a fraud and a liar and never should've opened my mouth.

But unlike weeks, maybe even just days, ago, I don't let these voices faze me. I know what they are: an accumulation of every questionable joke made by Sammie, every hateful comment made by people like Jeremiah, every expectation of Mom's, every assumption of Dad's, every judgment of Lindsay's, everything that made me so scared to admit how I felt about Talia.

So, frankly, those voices can go fuck themselves.

I unbutton my pajama top and drop my shorts, unearthing my dress carefully from my garment bag. I shimmy into the fabric, pulling the shoulders over my arms and zipping up the back as high as I can at this angle.

It's lilac, adorned with tiny pearl-centered tulle flowers all across the skirt and a thick ribbon belt to give my boxy frame some shape. Mom said the V-neckline complements my collarbones, which is a nice way of saying it shows off my nonexistent boobs. I always imagined myself in something pink, light and rosy, or white with those massive, almost cartoonish, watercolor flowers across the skirt, but this dress just spoke to me. I felt a bit like a fairy princess the first time I tried it on, like the type of girl who'd never be lacking in suitors.

"Mom!" I shout as I adjust the neckline in the mirror and puff out some of the tulle flowers. "Can you come zip me up?"

Almost immediately, she knocks on my door. "Come in!" I lean into my reflection and wipe away some smudged lip gloss. But when I turn around to show Mom the big reveal, I'm the one left surprised.

"Your mom let me in," Talia says. She looks scared, but I can't dwell on my guilt because I'm too busy trying to catch my breath.

Her hair is slicked back against her scalp, gathered in a thick ponytail at the base of her neck that her curls explode out of. Her lips are painted crimson, the same color as the suit I heard Dani bitch so much about. I can see now why she hated it so much. Wearing it, Talia may just be the most beautiful thing I've ever seen.

It takes all my willpower to look away from where the black top beneath her suit hugs her every curve and dip. But not before I notice the brooch pinned to her jacket's lapel. The ruby rose looks stunning, tying the outfit together in a way that makes it impossible to imagine her without it.

"Hi," I say, voice small.

"Hi," she replies, smiling softly. "I hope it's okay I came up here. I wanted to talk to you before everyone else came." Her voice is scratchier than usual, lingering effects of her cold, I assume. It makes it harder to focus on her words.

"You look beautiful," I say without thinking.

She either doesn't notice my eyes beginning to water and hands beginning to shake or pretends not to for both our sakes. "Thank you. You do too."

"Is Zaq downstairs?" I ask, immediately regretting the way my voice catches.

"He's meeting me here," she says, clearly hesitant, rocking back and forth on her feet in my doorway. "Our parents wanted to take photos of us together, so we figured it would be easier this way."

I swallow. "Both your parents?"

She nods, a bigger smile creeping across her beautiful, bloody lips. I want to reach out and touch them, see if my fingers will come away stained. I fight the temptation, but not the thought.

"I told my dad about Zaq and me yesterday," she says, still standing awkwardly across the room. I wouldn't be surprised if Mom and Dad were down the hall eavesdropping. "I was tired of hiding it from him and knew if he reacted poorly, at least I'd only have to deal with it until I left for school. But he actually took it really well, and it even got us talking more candidly about everything surrounding my sexuality and Dani and Eliana. He's going to try to be there for me more." Her grin tears at my heart. "Zaq told his parents too, but they already had their suspicions. And we told Wesley together this morning, but it seems he already heard about it from a little birdy."

I flush guiltily. "In my defense, he's a much bigger gossip than we've ever given him credit for."

The tension in her shoulders melts as she shakes with a laugh. "Fair enough. We probably should've told him ourselves weeks ago, but—"

"But it wasn't anyone's business." I touch the undone zipper at my back. "Do you mind?" I ask, turning so she can see it. She shuts the door behind her and steps forward. Her cold hands and long nails graze my back. I watch her in the mirror, her tongue sticking out as she focuses. "Talia, I'm sorry."

"Like I said, we should've told him our—"

"No," I cut her off. She meets my eyes in the mirror, hands stilling behind me. "Not for telling Wes, although I am sorry about that." I take a deep breath, and then quickly exhale so I don't make her task more difficult. "I'm sorry I shut you out for not liking me back and for having a boyfriend, and that I made that night with Eliana all about my problems. I threw away our whole friendship after I kissed you. I'm also sorry about kissing you without asking; being a girl doesn't make it okay. I was wrong for it, all of it. I'm just so sorry." By the time I finish, I'm shaking and Talia's hands have gone from my back to my chest, hugging me from behind. She shushes me softly, coaxing me out of my tears before I ruin my makeup.

"Thank you," she says, letting go. I face her, composing myself and brushing away the remaining tears. "I could've told you about Zaq sooner. I spent so long convincing myself it would be okay to date a girl, no matter what my family said, that I think I felt guilty for dating a boy."

"You don't owe me an explanation. Your sexuality is about your attraction, not who you're dating at any given moment," I say, doing my best Wesley impersonation. "I shouldn't have made mine all about you."

"I'm sorry I couldn't be that person for you. I've always been bad at telling when people like me, and it's even harder with girls. I was just so excited about having a girl best friend again. I think it kept me from seeing things the way you were," she says, the words pinching my heart. "I'm just so sorry."

I feel myself unravel inside, a puddle of a person gathered in the hands of the girl she finally let herself love, even if the timing and feelings were off.

"You don't have to apologize. Not at all." I step back a little because proximity is still too difficult with the wound of rejection this tender. She looks so beautiful, smells so lovely. And I cannot touch her. "I'm going to work on me for a bit. I think I'll be okay."

"So no more crushes?" Talia teases, and I half laugh, half sob. She moves to finish zipping me up, hands working much faster now that we've cleared the air.

"Who knows? I am Ophelia, after all," I reply, smiling despite my wet cheeks. I'll really need to rush to touch up my makeup now.

Maybe it's not about whether my crushes work out in the end. Maybe it never was. Maybe it's about letting myself have them. Letting myself feel love and lust and heartbreak, my own version of magnificent misery in the process, and never changing my heart for anyone's benefit but my own. I don't mind being the lover, the one who waits, but I won't hesitate to love myself with all I've got in the meantime.

"I suppose your dating pool is a bit bigger now, no?" she says, and I feel my smile grow wider.

"The perks of being queer," I reply, a sense of freedom blooming in my chest. My puddle-heart solidifies just a nudge.

"The perks of being queer," she repeats, looking freer and more solid herself.

Talia leaves me to touch up my makeup and goes to help arrange snacks for the parents in the backyard. Slipping my feet into my silver sandals and tossing my phone and portable charger into my pearlescent clutch, I head downstairs.

But I freeze, because at the bottom of the stairs is a scattered pile of pink rose petals in a shade I don't recognize.

I pick one up and turn it over in my hands. They aren't even real flower petals.

My eyes follow them down the foyer and toward the living room, feet following soon after. When I walk in, I spot Sammie dumping a bowl of the fake petals onto the carpet while Agatha kicks them around, spreading them across the room.

"What are you guys doing?"

They both spin around at the same time, looking dazed and beautiful all at once. Agatha's hair looks longer and fuller, floating magnificently around her head. Her eyelashes must be lined with tiny rhinestones because they scatter light as she blinks; a slit in her white glittered dress rides up her thigh as she straightens. Sammie is completely still beside her, his sleek, entirely black suit glistening like his greased-back hair.

"Shit," Agatha says, eyes flitting to Sammie. "I told you that we should've asked Talia to distract her when she went up there."

"Well, I thought their definitely unrelated problems would occupy her for more than five minutes," Sammie says, putting down the empty bowl. "Sue me."

Confused, I watch Ags grab an envelope as well as our corsages off the coffee table as Sammie reaches behind the sofa.

"You weren't supposed to get those yet," I whine as I take a step forward.

Agatha swats my hand away with the envelope. "We paid for them; they're ours to take."

"You what?" I take and open the envelope. It's full of cash. "What is this?"

"We all pooled our money to pay you for your hard work, although I hear Wesley deserves a cut. And I gave myself a discount for providing the ribbons."

"I—thank you. I don't know what to say."

"Hold that silence," Sammie says as he finally frees whatever he crammed between the sofa and the wall. He sways a basket of fake flowers in one hand, flipping a poster around in the other. "Ta-da!"

Agatha sighs. "Samuel, it's upside down."

"Oh." Sammie looks down and awkwardly adjusts the poster one-handed. "There. Ta-da!"

Written in block letters filled with the same glitter covering Agatha's dress is a message that takes me three tries to read. And even then, my spinning thoughts don't fully grasp it: HAMLET MAY HAVE BEEN A TRAGEDY, BUT OPHELIA DESERVED A COMEDY.

Sammie clears his throat and hums a high note. "White his shroud as the mountain snow . . . mhm . . . with sweet flowers which be—something? Uh, to the grave did not . . . mmm . . . true-love showers!" he sings horribly, with absolutely no rhythm, in a high-pitched voice. He turns to Agatha and shimmies. "Take it away, Ags."

She sighs, then sings, "To-morrow is Saint Valentine's day, all in the morning bedtime, and I a maid at your . . . window?" She grimaces. "We didn't exactly have time to memorize the words."

"Do either of you want to tell me what's going on? And why you're quoting Ophelia's mad scene at me . . . badly."

"We're asking you to prom," Agatha says.

"Yay!" Sammie adds, shaking the poster. I watch glitter trickle onto the carpet.

Warmth spreads across my body. "Both of you?"

"Both of us," Sammie says, setting the poster down. He and Agatha slide my pale purple corsage onto my wrist, the ribbon sparkling like Agatha's dress.

"You like boys," Ags says, and hands me her corsage.

"And you like girls," Sammie says, waving a hand at Agatha. "Er—I guess one girl. So far. But she wasn't exactly available, as you know."

"Please shut up," Ags groans. She twirls her hand around, and it takes me a second to realize she's waiting for me to put it on her. Still stunned, I slide the vibrant rose onto her wrist.

"I know we don't have all the genders covered," Sammie says. "Or I guess I should say 'any' gender. It's a spectrum, so there isn't, like, a limit, right?"

"The point is," Agatha starts, as she moves to pin Sammie's boutonniere to his lapel, "we know that maybe this isn't how you dreamed your promposal going. But if we could give you more sexuality-accommodating options, it's the least we thought we could do."

"I mean, we're no Talia and Lucas, but I think we clean up pretty nicely, don't you, Ags?"

"I concur. So, what do you say, Ophelia?"

"Would you like to go to prom with us?" Sammie finishes.

I look at the ground, covered in fraying pink petals, and then to the poster leaning against the table. Sammie and Ags watch my face, earnestly smiling as they give me a moment to process, and it's then that I understand what Wesley meant when he said his life would be complete even if Lindsay didn't love him.

One day I'll be loved the way Mom loves Dad and Wes loves Linds and Talia probably loves Zaq. But I'm loved already, right here, right now. Loved even if I change, even if I'm not the same Ophelia I've always been. Loved by people who are willing to try memorizing a song from a Shakespearean play the night before their senior prom in the simple hope that it'll make me smile, make my not-so-foolish dreams come true. It's more than enough, and here, right in front of my watering eyes, is undeniable evidence that I am too.

I press my glossed lips tightly together and nod jerkily, tears blurring my vision.

"No, no, no," Ags says, immediately engulfing me in a hug. "No ruining your pretty makeup."

Sammie comes up behind her and pulls both of us in with his long arms. "Ophelia, I swear if you make me start crying I will take these Dollar Mart flowers back to the store immediately."

I choke on laughter as we pull apart, careful not to smear my fresh layer of foundation onto their outfits. "Thank you. Thank you for this."

They both shrug, but they know what they've done, and so do I.

"Oh, look at you," Mom says, stepping into the room with Talia and Zaq behind her. Her eyes well and spill over with tears just as mine dry, hands clutched in front of her heart. "You look beautiful, mija."

"Thank you." I smile and motion behind me. "Did you know about all this?"

She tilts her head. "I may have been asked permission to allow a certain pair of teens to wreck my living room with the world's least accurate adaptation of Ophelia's mad scene."

"I resent that—we killed it," Sammie says, squeezing my shoulder before leaving Mom and me alone in the foyer. The rest of my friends drift to the backyard with him.

"Your father is going to have a field day with this if he catches me crying so early. I told him he'd cave first." She envelops me in an embrace, my chin sitting on her shoulder despite our near-identical height. "My sweet, loving Ophelia."

Loving, not *boy-crazy*. I'll take it.

"By the way, am I supposed to hate Talia?" she asks as she pulls away. "Is that my motherly obligation?"

I laugh. "No, Mom. You don't have to hate her; we're good."

"Thank God." She presses a hand to her chest. "She's such a sweetheart."

My stomach clenches. "Yeah, she really is."

My eyes stay dry even when Dad comes in to see what's taking us so long and gets emotional, teasing Mom for breaking before he even had the chance to see me.

The doorbell rings, and we're forced to disband. I'm wiping under my dry eyes as I pull open the door. Lindsay is adjusting Wesley's bow tie, so I have a moment to brace myself before she faces me.

She turns, looking almost surprised to see me here, at my own house. "Hi," she says.

"Hey." I take in their outfits. Linds's dress is deep navy, slightly darker than Wesley's suit, and it brings out the lighter hues in her eyes and hair. The subtle nod to oceanic colors isn't lost on me. It's also mermaid cut, because of course it is. They both look fantastic, her hair pushed to one side so it spills over her shoulder in waves, Wes's glued in place by a shiny layer of hair spray. He fills out his suit, fabric bulging at the arms, and stands proudly, like for once he knows how good he looks.

Sammie calls my name, and I watch Lindsay's eyes soften and lips droop as he walks up behind me.

"You guys look great," Wesley says, the uncomfortable air in the foyer tangible. He pulls me into a tight hug, then gives Sammie what I can only describe as possibly the world's most uncomfortable handshake.

"You guys too," Sammie says, clearing his throat and looking at Lindsay for one second, but no longer. "I hear I owe you an apology, Wesley." He shoves his hands in his pant pockets, letting the words settle.

"We can talk outside," Wes says, his eye twitch betraying his confidence. Sammie nods, and they leave Lindsay still standing on the porch, fiddling with the delicate silver choker around her neck.

We're both quiet for a minute before she speaks. "Are we dishing out apologies already? I thought we'd at least have to suffer through awkward small talk first."

"It's going to be a long night. Agatha probably would've written it up on an itinerary if she wasn't so busy making sure her lipstick perfectly matched her shoes. But we can talk about the weather, if you'd like," I joke. Lindsay steps inside and pulls me into a hug.

My first instinct is to push her away. Because even if we're joking around, I'm not sure if I really forgive her for everything. But I guess if Talia could forgive me, show me and my broken-heart-induced jerkiness some empathy, maybe I could try with Lindsay.

I'm not a fool. I know that in a few months, once we're

both graduated and states apart, Linds and I probably won't really be friends anymore. It's one of the many truths I've been hiding from all year, something I didn't want to face because it meant another thing would be changing.

But that's months away. Things will start changing no matter what happens tonight or tomorrow or the day after. So I choose to hug her back.

"I'm scared I'm going to lose tonight," she whimpers into my hair, sounding the most vulnerable I've heard her in all our years of friendship.

"You won't," I assure her. "And even if you do, Ags will burn the place down before anyone else gets a chance to wear that tiara."

Her laughter vibrates against me. Once she lets me go, she runs her fingers over her hair, despite every strand still being perfectly in place. "I snapped at you, for basically no reason."

"Not for nothing, but I was kinda a bitch too," I admit.

"I was a bigger one." She laughs, ever the competitor. "You and Sammie have just always been so tight. You got to see the parts of him he'd never show me, the parts that weren't all Casanova and innuendos. You're even going to college together. But with Wesley, I got to be that person. I got to see his art, see how funny he was, meet his family . . ." She looks up at the ceiling, blinking rapidly. "It's so embarrassing and selfish and *ugh*. But when I realized he was showing you some of that person too, it hurt. And I'm really sorry I took it out on you instead of just, like, actually talking to him about it."

"I'm sorry too, for telling Wes and Sammie what you told Ags and me," I say. "I've also had a lot going on in the insecure-romance department."

At that, she raises her brows. "Maybe we could talk about it? Sometime this week, you know, when it isn't the biggest night of our lives." She rolls her eyes as she says it, like she didn't just whimper over potentially losing the title of prom queen. I don't call her out on it though, at least not now.

"I'd like that," I say, and as we join hands, I think maybe I am a little bit of a fool. Maybe I have hope for our friend-ship, for change to come and make us better for it.

We meet our friends in the backyard. Lindsay's mom and Wesley's parents must've come around through the back, because Miss Hawk is chatting with Mom over the cheese platters while Mr. and Mrs. Cho are fussing over Wesley's hair. Linds beckons Wesley over to the table where Mom put the rest of the corsages and boutonnieres, recruiting Talia for help.

"Lilac suits you," Zaq says as he sidles up to me. "Thanks for the roses," he adds, shimmying his chest to draw atten-tion to the jiggling Olympiad on his lapel.

"Thanks for asking everyone to pay me. You didn't have to do that."

He bows his head. "One artist to another, it was my moral obligation."

No one has ever referred to my gardening as art before. Despite hating him a bit over the past week, I actually like Zaq. In another life, I could've *really* liked him. "I would've given you a Midas Touch if I wasn't trying to coordinate the colors," I admit, nodding to the yellow buds on the other side of the yard. He looks at them appraisingly. "By the way, I'm sorry for kissing your girlfriend."

He chuckles, shaking his head. "You didn't know we were together. I can't really hold it against you. Plus, I get it. She's a keeper." I think he's being an ass for a second, egging me on. But I watch him watch Talia adjust a bobby pin in Linds's hair, and I know this isn't a taunt; it's solidarity.

"So I take it this is you two officially coming out as a couple?"

He smiles bashfully, running a hand over his close-cropped hair. "Yeah. Yeah, I guess it is."

I recognize the look in his eyes, not quite hunger but something deeper. Longing, love, profound admiration. I'm sure he'd find the same things in my eyes when I look at Talia too, and instead of swallowing that sting of realization, I embrace it. Running from these feelings did me no good. I don't cling to the idea that I have a romantic future with Talia anymore, a future I'm still mourning the loss of, but I shouldn't have to pretend I never wanted one.

I didn't ask her earlier about that night back in September in Linds's basement. I know I could've, could've at least let Talia know where this all began for me, the way it maybe began for her all those years ago at orientation. But standing beside her no-longer-secret boyfriend, I feel confident that it doesn't matter *how* my feelings for Talia bloomed, what matters is that they did. And even if—*when*—they fade away, I will still be a girl who liked a girl the same way Zaq is a boy who liked a girl. The same way we can also love boys or anyone else. I like Zaq a little more knowing that he gets it, my love for Talia. My sexuality.

"Think I'll be seeing you around the center?" he says, springing me from my thoughts.

"You know, you just might."

"I'd like that," he says, brushing a hand against my elbow. "I'm sure she would too."

He joins Talia and their parents. I watch him, not thinking of the lingering touch of a boy's hand, nor the way he wraps that same hand around Talia's waist. Instead, I think of how happy I am for them.

I think back to how I imagined prom for years and compare that image to the one unfolding before me. My eyes don't settle on Talia too long, the memory of her lips beginning to fade, but she and Zaq are cheesing hard, their parents snapping photos wildly. Zaq's mom is whistling, and Talia's dad is wiping a tear from his eye.

Standing on the other side of the yard where the yellowy, almost white, Garden Party roses dangle over the garden gate, Wesley hesitantly places his hands high on Lindsay's waist before she giggles and guides his hands lower. Lindsay's mom rolls her eyes but snaps the shot regardless, and Mrs. Cho is too busy trying to wipe away her and Mr. Cho's tears to catch the candid.

Suddenly, Ags and Sammie race over and grab my hands, pulling me to the Honor roses. We position ourselves so

Sammie's arms are around my waist and mine are around Agatha's. Mrs. Nasar asks Sammie to stop slouching, and Mrs. Jones shouts that we look amazing. Once they get enough shots of us together, we split apart and take a few in pairs, some individual shots, and then selfies on our own phones, which all the parents badger us to send to them immediately.

Everyone gathers for a group shot, the parents screaming for us to look at *their* phone as if we can look at all of them at once, all of us laughing more than posing, knowing we'll ruin the shots but not caring, not really. It's good practice for the real thing: graduation.

When we split into height order and Talia cups her hands around my stomach, I feel my heartbeat spike, then settle. She's just a girl, *the* girl, sure, but not my girl. So I take the moment for what it is, one moment, not *the* moment, even if it's damn close to the one I pictured all those weeks ago.

As we split off into cars, Agatha and I with Sammie, and Zaq, Talia, and Linds with Wes, I realize the rest of the night doesn't matter. What matters is that we're here, we made it.

Agatha was right. Prom was never about the dresses or the dates or the ridiculous theme. It was about celebrating, through all those little details, the feeling that *holy shit, we actually survived high school.*

Well, almost survived it.

But tonight, we'll forget about the fights and confusion and pressure of senior year, of the new countdown to graduation. For the next couple of hours, it's not that I'll forget about my sexuality, I'll forget to worry about it. I'll slow dance with Agatha, with Sammie, maybe even Wesley if Linds lets me borrow him for a song or two. We'll all dance together, in a messy jumble of limbs and hair and fabric we paid way too much for. We will cheer when Linds wins prom queen, wipe away tears when she gets that silly plastic crown she always secretly wanted. We will pat Agatha on the shoulder as she lifts the end of a limp cellophane streamer with disgust, and stop her from flipping the punch bowl when she sees the plastic fish sunk at the bottom.

We will hide our shoes in the bushes outside the gym when our feet get tired and let our hair fall from curls and clips when the night is late enough that no one having a good time is expected to look as good as they did when they showed up anyway.

We will act like teenagers who have been told our entire lives that tonight *means* something. Because it doesn't. Because it does.

But first, as we pull away from my house, waving goodbye to our misty-eyed parents, I turn around in Sammie's front seat and nudge Agatha with my closed fist.

I open my hand, revealing a wad of crumbled one-dollar bills I stole from the envelope she gave me earlier. "I think I owe you five bucks."

EPILOGUE

"Do you really think they'll confiscate our phones during the ceremony if they catch us using them?" I ask Wes as I buckle my seat belt. "Or do you think it's just a rumor they let spread so no one will try to take a selfie as they cross the stage?"

We stayed after school for a few hours to help the senior council move chairs onto the football field for graduation, which is now only two days away. Turns out they organize graduation as well as prom, and Ags decided to offer up her supreme planning skills, as well as our group as volunteers. Linds had a banquet for the track team, but Zaq, Talia, and Sammie are still helping Agatha with the sound system. Wes and I have to drop off some poster designs at the youth center before it closes, so we dipped early.

I figured other kids, ones just starting to work out their sexualities or ones who've always known who they are but never had a place where they felt like they could show it, could use the center. It worked for me at least, having someone like Wesley and the counselors I've spoken to alongside Mom and Dad for the past few weeks.

If the center and our school approve, the posters Wes and Zaq helped me design will decorate the halls next year, advertising the center so those kids will have a place to turn to. We'll be long gone by then, but maybe this'll be the legacy Wes and I can leave behind.

A PLACE WHERE YOU CAN BLOOM, the posters say, bordered in roses painted various pride-flag colors. I'm proud of them. I'm feeling more of that these days—pride.

Wesley finally replies, "I don't know about the phone thing. Maybe Agatha can ask Evan if he knows." He rolls his eyes. Agatha spent half the afternoon dodging the affections of Evan Matthews, now that he's truly given up his vindictiveness over his ex, Danica.

Agatha's been trying to embrace her aromanticism though, even stopping by the center a few times since prom along with Sammie and Lindsay. So I did my part to distract Evan. Ags and I had enough gossip stored up over the years that it wasn't hard for me to keep him busy, but I got so carried away that by the end, I was almost sharing that I once kissed a girl and liked it. Not that that's much of a secret for me anymore.

I'm not the only one on a path to self-improvement though. With help from therapy, Sammie's been a good sport about Wesley and Lindsay making things more official. Nothing is set in stone, but they're giving it a try, taking it slow for both their sakes, even though they'll be long-distance in the fall. Sammie even managed to compliment Wes on some of his drawings yesterday, so he's giving it a try too.

We pull into the center's parking lot. I almost asked him to let me drive today—I've been getting good since I started taking lessons—but we're in a rush to get the posters into the office mailroom before closing. Plus after everything he's done for me, I'd hate to crash his car.

Wes is heading down the long hall when he notices the front desk is empty.

"Hey, would you mind checking for Addy around back? I need her keys to grab the sweater Zaq left in the flag lounge on Saturday," he asks before skidding around the corner, uncharacteristically frantic.

"Sure thing," I reply, saluting to the empty hall and heading back outside, following the scent of paint and hum of rock music. I still haven't met the infamous Addy since she's been busy with college finals over the past few weeks, but when I spot the girl painting a mural of a rainbow on the back wall of the center, I get the feeling I've found her.

Long, sleek black hair. Skin a deep, warm brown. Angled brows that frame eyes lined with thick, black liner. I notice her in pieces before I notice her as a whole. Paint-splattered denim and a loose-fitting concert tee from a band I've never heard of but suddenly need to listen to. A pink, orange, and white lesbian pride flag pinned to her left jean pocket.

"Hi—uh, um, are you Addy?" I ask when she notices me.

"Addy Gupta, the one and only," she says, tucking the

thumb of her free hand into her front pocket. She tosses the paintbrush in her other hand into a bucket on the ground. "And you are?"

"Ophelia. Ophelia Rojas," I manage to get out as I shake her now-free hand.

"Well, Ophelia Ophelia Rojas, what can I do you for?" she asks, and cocks her head to the side, her glittering eyes scanning me in one quick sweep.

"Hi—uh, um, Wesley—"

"Needs my keys, right?" she says, rolling her eyes. "Typical."

"Yeah," I say, still trying to get my mouth to work.

"Well, let's go help the poor bastard, then." She's nearly around the building when she turns and sees me still standing before her mural. It's a messy rainbow reflecting off a puddle. The paint bleeds down the wall, sloppy and unfinished, but the reflection is sharp, precise. A vision, a promise.

"You coming?" she asks.

I watch the way her eyes crinkle as her pouty lips part into a smile, the birthmarks lining her neck stretching out. She dips her head again, placing her hands on her narrow hips, flakes of dried paint scattering off her like confetti.

I don't know when it happened and if the feeling will stay. I don't know if there will ever come a time where I'm completely and unapologetically queer. Even now, I'm still learning and unlearning, figuring out what I want for myself and my future.

But as I stand there, watching this girl who I know I will

text Agatha about the second I leave, I only have one thought circling my mind. And it has less to do with her and more to do with the way I know what this is: attraction to a girl. Attraction I'm not fighting anymore.

In this moment, and hopefully for many after, I don't miss being straight. Not one bit.

ACKNOWLEDGMENTS

Reading other people's acknowledgments has always made me incredibly emotional, so it's surreal to finally be writing my own.

Thank you to the team at Sandra Dijkstra Literary Agency, especially to my incredible agent, Thao Le, for all you've done to champion me and Ophelia. The first time you called Wesley a precious cinnamon roll, I knew you were the agent for me. Your insight, suggestions, and support have made a world of difference in my writing (Agatha and Sammie asking Ophelia to prom was all you). I couldn't ask for a better person to represent me and my words.

Thank you to Rachel Diebel, editor of my dreams. You understood this story better than I ever could have hoped for and helped shape it into something magical. I'm so grateful you believed in me and Ophelia, and gave me a million reasons to believe in you too.

Thank you to my cover designer, Aurora Parlagreco, and cover illustrator, Nicole Medina, for creating the most beautiful representation of Ophelia imaginable. Thank you to the Feiwel and Friends family at Macmillan: Jean Feiwel, Liz Szabla, Rich Deas, Holly West, Anna Roberto, Kat Brzozowski, Dawn Ryan, Erin Siu, Emily Settle, Foyinsi Adegbonmire, Avia Perez, Olivia Oleck, Gabriella Saltpeter, Lindsay Wagner, and Ilana Worrell, for working so hard to bring Ophelia's story to the world.

Thank you to my fellow authors who aided this journey: Brittany Cavallaro for giving me publishing advice and priceless feedback on an early draft of this book—while on vacation! Laura Taylor Namey for helping me with my query letter, and for offering to do so enough times to dismiss my anxiety over accepting. Sarah Hollowell for being the best agent sibling ever and always being down for an all-caps DM about publishing feelings—good and bad. Nina Moreno for perfectly capturing the heart of my book in a blurb I'd happily get tattooed across my forehead. I'll settle for it being on my cover. Courtney Summers, Leah Johnson, Mark Oshiro, and Brittany again, thank you all for the absolutely lovely blurbs. Tashie Bhuiyan, Christina Li, Zoe Hana Mikuta, and Chloe Gong for our combined Gen Z chaos and for helping me feel less like a lonely, confused baby and more like a confused baby with informed baby friends.

Thank you to BookTube and the online book community I found sanctuary in for so many years for celebrating alongside me every step of the way. I really am Blonde With A Book now, huh?

To any and every friend who has been a cheerleader for me

and this book, including but not limited to: Emily Minarik, Taylor Nakatsuka, Sierra Elmore, Fadwa, Liv, Chris Echeverri, Adriana Botley, Jake Maia Arlow, Joelle Wellington, Stacey Manos, Yitmarak, Caroline Smith, and Elisa Ragus, thank you.

Thank you to my best friends who lived with me throughout college, for giving me a home away from home and safe places to write this book in the first place. Dania Hassan, I miss gossiping in our shitty little dorm. Velma Smith and Monika Gustilo, we can drop the Schuyleur Sisters, but we're still keeping thunder, lightning, forever. Essance Jackson, Cynthia Ruiz, and Araciel Velazquez, thanks for offering to pay me for messy, early chapters of this book. We'll win Solstice one day, girls, I swear it. Band practice soon.

To Jennifer Ordoñez and Alisha Russell for being the best bubs a girl could ask for. I've had the honor of calling you friends for most of my life, and I can't wait to do so for the rest of it. To Catherine Smith for being one reason I know how to write a best friend. To Joanna Roecker for being the best prom date and for every late-night drive. I forgive you for telling your mom I write science fiction.

Thank you to my big family, full of love and support. To Grandma and Grandpa Mac for teaching me the powers of sarcasm, good storytelling, and surrounding yourself with family. To Abuela Mireya, gracias por tu apoyo, por creer en mis sueños y especialmente por tu amistad. To Claudia, Maggie, and Oliver for every inside joke that still makes me laugh years later. Thank you for every Ophelia drawing,

Clauds. To Kylee, my mini-me, for being the other half of my soul and for every time you asked me to tell you a good story.

Shout-out to my fellow Junior Mac N Rolls! To Daniel for every elaborate game of The Great Adventure in the backyard and the hours spent watching you play video games in the living room, and to Breann for every Littlest Pet Shop Christmas tree festival and marathoning session of bad CW shows, all of which kept my imagination and love of stories alive and well. The race for which one of us gets a Nobel Prize first is still on. I love y'all.

To my parents, my best friends, for believing in me when I said I wanted to become an author as a kid, and again as a young adult with a plan. My gratitude for all you've both done for me is beyond words. There is a reason I wrote a book about a girl who loves her parents this much. Dad, you taught me that my voice matters long before I started lending it to fictional characters. Mom, don't hold this against me, but there's no way your constant speculation didn't foster my love of storytelling. (Shortly before you unexpectedly passed away, I made sure you were cool with the previous line and didn't think I was making fun of you. You gave the line your full blessing but still argued that I was, in fact, making fun of you. I swore I said good things too though, so here are a few more: Thank you for gifting me this life, Mami. I promise to live it well. I'll miss you every day, but I'll see you on the other side.)

Thank you from the bottom of my heart, dear reader, for picking up this book.

And lastly, thank you to sixteen-year-old Racquel, who had the bravery to first admit to a hidden slip of paper that she wasn't straight. It wasn't easy, but I couldn't have gotten us here without you. I hope you're proud.